# Dunkard's
# HOLLOW

# Dunkard's
# HOLLOW

M.K.B. GRAHAM

Copyright ©2023 by M.K.B. Graham

Published by McKeadlit LLC

Book and cover design by Stephanie Pierce

ISBN 979-8-9895553-0-7

*All biblical quotes and references are from the King James Version.*

*Cover photo: "Southern Appalachians" by Brenda C. Bell. Used with permission. No use in any other capacity is permitted without express written permission of the author.*

Visit the author at MKBGraham.com

Who hath measured the waters in the hollow of his hand,
and meted out heaven with the span, and comprehended the
dust of the earth in a measure, and weighed the mountains
in scales, and the hills in a balance?

*Isaiah 40:12*

And the angel of the Lord called unto him out of heaven,
and said, Abraham, Abraham: and he said, "Here am I."

*Genesis 22:11*

# Preface

Those who have read my previous books, *Cairnaerie* and *Fleuringala*, can expect to have a different experience in *Dunkard's Hollow*. When I began writing this book, my goal was to write a literary novel, one that relied on character development more than plot and one that explored eternal themes. What I found as I wrote, however, is that changing my objective did not change what I am drawn to write. As with the Snow family's Cairnaerie estate and the small town of Lauderville, Virginia—and in the isolated Dunkard's Hollow readers will discover here—place is an integral part of the story. The places we live throughout the world's vast landscapes have an overwhelming influence on our lives. "Where we come from," as they say in Southwest Virginia, often makes us who we are.

Along with place, I am drawn to the certainty that change is as much a part of life as birth and death. While we often bristle at change, content to savor times that seem perfect only to be dismayed at their passing, the conflicts and interruptions that drive change are inevitable. Sometimes, however, change can bring its own kind of perfection.

As you meet Pearl and the Dunkard, Ned and Sky, and the other residents of the hollow—Ernie and Ruth Fowlkes, Estes and Parthenia Adams, Shep and Sunshine McCleary, and Miss Louisa—their lives may strike a familiar chord even if your "place" and your "change" are different. My hope is that the recognition this novel evokes will bring the story to life for readers everywhere.

Gratefully,
M.K.B. Graham

# Prologue
## 1941

The air is eerily quiet. The theater of trees along the banks of the new lake is attentive as the audience—the birds, the squirrels, the cicadas, and crickets watch in silent anticipation. Above the lake, the firmament is cloudless and expectant. A lone heron soars through the blue. Summer is leaving. Autumn is coming. Winter will come again, freezing the earth, heaving rocks from its soil, and completing cycles, only to begin new ones when another spring emerges, as it has for a thousand years. Throughout the forest, leaves begin their change into golds and crimsons, curling like tiny fists and falling away from branches, scattering. Some float on the water, tiny livened boats.

From horizon to horizon, ridge to ridge, water stretches along steep, tree-covered banks that rise abruptly out of the water. Far out across the broad expanse, a few white caps form. Calmer waters prevail in the shallows cut back through the trees, where, lapping gently, they fill deep and crooked coves.

In one cove, a tree stretches out over the water as if bowing, awkwardly tethered to the ground where saturated soil has given way, and its roots have come unhinged. Woven into one branch like a spider's web is the remnant of a shawl, worn and unraveled. Caught closer to the bank, a tattered apron swings casually on a breeze. Its ties float aimlessly just beneath the water's surface. Dangling from its pocket is a locket—the faces inside curled and sun-bleached. The locket sways back and forth until with one gust it drops and disappears beneath the blue-black water.

Nearby, a few dozen yards from the bank, a limestone chimney breaks the water's surface. The lake slaps its edges, turning the light gray stone to a dark slate, but the chimney is unmoving, anchored far below to a cold hearth that once held fire. Low on the horizon, storm clouds gather. They are dark and powerful, erasing the blue sky as they advance. Suddenly, running ahead of the clouds, lightning breaks above the lake and crackles across the face of the waters. It is rare blue lightning, the color of a summer sky. It dances across the surface on thin spry feet, shimmers across the new lake, and hangs in the air to wait for the thunder. Again and again, as the clouds roll, the sky showers the lake with pure, blue sparks in taps and an occasional cabriole. High above the water, sheltered from the storm in the branches of a poplar, a wise old owl opens an eye to survey the scene. A lonely red hawk seeking shelter sails through the charged air on the blustery wind. Rumbling behind the flashes of blue lightning, the devoted thunder follows.

# The Virginia Highlands

# Part One

## PEARL AND THE DUNKARD

*The stranger did not lodge in the street: but I opened my doors to the traveller—*
*Job 31:32*

# 1872

**THE WINTER SHE CAME**

# December

The rising moon paused as an icy wind poured off Brush Mountain and down into Pearl's lungs, nearly drowning her. She hurried along the narrow footpath into the evening's pewter light, pushing branches away from her face, ignoring the cold fog that rolled on the wind behind her like the crest of a wave. She glanced back into the chasing wind. Did he see her leave? Was he following?

She pulled her cloth coat together where buttons should have been, trying to create some barrier against the winter wind, but beyond sensate concern, she was too full of other worries to fully acknowledge the cold. She was racing along the thinnest thread of hope that desperation could buy. For a long time, she had thought about leaving. Now she had taken her chance.

Snow began to flurry as the moon faded into the deepening winter fog that blew through the hollow like thin cloth drifting through deep water. Cold burned her skin, and the tiny glass-like snowflakes coated her lashes and brows, alighting on the telltale signs of the invectives that had prompted her flight. As she hurried through the forest, scattered twigs and tangled brush underfoot threatened to trip her, but she was young and nimble and determined.

At least for now.

Behind her, the ravenous fog continued to swallow the moon. She stopped for a moment, winded, her breath a lesser fog pressed out in quick jetting puffs. Again, she looked back. Relief washed over her. No one was following, only the burgeoning storm, and now it was shielding her like a great magician's cloak.

*Will he come after me? Will he?* The question came to her as a perplexing mixture of hope and fear. *Will he bother?* She wanted him to want her—the way a father should want a daughter. But she knew too well the cruel spirits that taunted her and stole every tentative hope that had ever arisen out of her. She wondered what a young Indian squaw might have done in her place. She had read about them whenever she had had the chance—a scant yet rich experience—about their brave and clever and courageous lives. Bravery was a jewel to her, a shining and lovely jewel beyond her grasp. *Or was it?* She wondered. How had she fled if she had not possessed some measure of bravery?

She pulled her coat tighter across her chest and moved ahead, her steps quick and anxious in the darkening forest. All around her, the thick trees were clothed in dying light, and the wind howled through them, their bare limbs clattering like skeletons. Nothing looked familiar—even though it should have. She had walked these woods hundreds of times, yet tonight with the chasing storm, the wind and fog, the forest was transformed into a strange and opaque space full of shadowy timbers that towered above her like looming black giants.

Moving through the dimming forest, a part of Pearl relished her sudden bolt to freedom—but another part of her was fearful. She thought about the difference a few minutes could have made. *What if the snow'd come on sooner? What if he'd a come back early? Would I've took off like that? With his supper undone, his fire goin' out?*

Slipping behind a stand of ancient oaks, the best windbreak she could find, she stopped with these thoughts. She dropped her bag, an old carpet-bag she had found in a sinkhole, a depression on the edge of the woods near town that had been commandeered for a local trash dump. The bag was refined with petit point stitches. When she discovered it—tossed away with clothes too ragged for even the poorest of scavengers to wear—she marveled at the tiny threads as she lifted it, brushed it off, and ran her hand over the nappy surface—a black canvas with woven flowers of deep reds and purples and greens, all slightly faded. One corner of the bag was torn, either worn or chewed. It was the only flaw and likely the reason for its discarding. Pearl had taken it and repaired the hole with string wrapped around a bent awl; her repair was practical though not pretty. *How easy to fix a bag*, she had thought as she anchored the string into the tight wool loops; hearts were not so easy. Her fingers had bled from pricks, but this was of no matter. What mattered was that this bag was something fine for her, something all her own. Not shared. Not given begrudgingly. Not stolen.

Hurriedly, in the late afternoon before he had arrived home for his supper, she had filled the carpetbag with a few clothes, a coarse linen shawl woven by her grandmother, and the locket that had belonged to her mother. Years before, she had taken the locket and hidden it away—at a time when it was the only bright thing in her life. Pearl had never had much, so she valued these items, and she made sure to put them into her bag, wondering if she, herself, could escape, wondering if she really had the gumption to leave. She had planned secretly for weeks.

Or had it been years?

The idea of leaving had come as a gradual awakening to the understanding that her plight would not change unless she changed it herself. She was not raised to believe this way, to think this way—to think that anything was hers to choose or control. No, not at all. But softly, and at times nudged by her circumstance, the realization had arisen in her, the way a child awakens from a deep slumber or the way a man comes to understand his own destiny. She had watched and waited for the right time. And on this disappearing day, in that fleeting moment when opportunity and courage had converged, she seized her chance—perhaps her last chance. As she had closed her carpetbag and planned her route out of town—to follow the river into the hollow—she did not consider the possibility of a storm. The day had not foreshadowed it, but when did the mountains ever give fair warning? Or was it that she had been too preoccupied by the caustic mixture of fear and determination that had captured her?

After resting for only a moment, she picked up her carpetbag and continued walking until she came to a dense thicket of white pines. She crouched down in the crook of a tree where lightning had long ago split the base into two trunks, both rising, both flourishing, both determined to reach the sky. She tried to catch her breath, to calm herself. Her throat stung, and her legs ached. Rubbing her hands together, she blew on her stiff fingers and pressed her fists against her cheeks. She took shallow breaths to stave off the cold that felt as though it were eating her. A sudden burst of wind sent a shower of stiff pine needles raining down on her like rusty needles. She brushed them away. A chill rattled through her the way a broken branch rattles down through the limbs of a barren tree. Her body was beginning to feel sluggish, her blood chilling inside her veins. She tucked her hands under her arms. What she would give for gloves. Or warmth.

Or rescue.

Looking up through skeletal trees, she watched as the last light faded. The highest ridges were no longer visible. Night was free falling into the deep curve of the hollow, diving through the branches, and extinguishing the daylight's last vigor that had—only minutes before—brightened the sky as the moon had risen soundlessly above the hardening storm line before disappearing into it. Pearl began to shake—a strange and wondrous reminder that she had survived, that she had come this far, and that she might find refuge after all.

But the creeping darkness quickly rammed her mind with another fear: resting for too long would be foolish. She stood up, turned up her collar, and gripped it under her chin to peer around the tree. Icy wind coming across the nearby river stung her eyes, making them water. *Which way's the cabin?*

She retreated behind her makeshift windbreak, bracing herself to face her fears, and she dropped down again, huddling behind the tree. She was so cold, so hungry, and she was beginning to feel sleepy and confused. She looked down at the ground, blanketed with spent leaves and mosses and new soft snow that lay like a glass curtain spread out. She could lie down, disappear, where she would be absorbed into the forest floor, every concern, every fear, every hope, every dream dissolved in time. As she pondered the cycle of life and death that nourished and sustained the forested hollow—a place she had always loved for the freedom it lent her—another blast of wind jarred her, awakened her.

She peered again through the snowfall that was growing heavier. Snowflakes caught on her delicate features, melted on her purplish lips, and covered her shoulders and auburn head like a fine Honiton lace. It collected on her knuckles, lingered on her porcelain cheeks, and mingled in the translucent lashes that framed her pale blue eyes. "Weak eyes," her father called them. And then her mother had always smiled and whispered close to her ear. "Blue as the sky, my darling. Blue as the sky."

In the distance, a thin column of smoke rose from a stone chimney, and a pale, almost invisible light issued from the window of a small cabin. Pearl drew in a breath, a confession of tentative optimism, and she exhaled in a slow, measured way. What she saw ahead encouraged her—silver smoke wandering and a smudge of yellow light breaking the monochrome landscape.

Brushing snow from her face, she fanned a nascent hope that rose defiantly from the depth of her being. *Is that it? Is it?* She could barely make out the outline of the cabin through the thickening curtain of snow. Was it there? Or had her imagination triggered a winter mirage? She had read about mirages, how the mind created them from nothing. Perhaps the book she had read—the book in the house of the woman her mother had scrubbed for—perhaps it had all been a mirage, too. She squinted in the gathering darkness. Her heart leapt. Yes, it was there, the cabin she sought. Soon she would be warm—if he would take her in.

She summoned every bit of courage she owned. Ignoring her frozen hands, she tugged her coat sleeves down over her cracked knuckles and picked up her bag. She focused on battling the dispiriting air and trudged ahead, thrusting her feet through the snow. Her small leather boots were wet through, her feet numb.

Pearl mounted the steps and stood at the cabin door. Wind blew ferociously, and a sudden, frenetic gust twisted and twirled her long skirt like the untidy children of winter. All around her snow swirled, strangely beautiful and captivating. The snow's whiteness, spinning, fanning in a colorless murmuration, held a measure of reflected light. Perhaps, she thought, a snowflake has its own light. How small it must be, like a tiny, icy lightning bug.

Once again fear gripped her—a different fear. Like a boulder released from a mountain side, her resolve foundered as she stared at the door, unable to reconcile her audacity to have dared come here. She tried to detach herself from her plight, tried to reason why she had chosen this door. How dare she presume that sanctuary lay beyond this latch! She whispered in the darkness, "I'm foolish and pitiful!" *Pitiful Pearl! Pitiful Pearl! Pitiful Pearl!* The taunt she had heard so often as a child revisited her like a cruel specter. *I am pitiful Pearl. He won't help me.*

As a moan escaped from her throat, her heart fluttered, mimicking the whirling leaves that joined the spinning circus of snow. Her satchel slipped from her fingers, and she bent toward the porch floor, grabbing her knees. *How foolish I am! How pitiful!* Suddenly, she wanted to fly away into the storm, melt into the darkness—blow away and disappear forever. She turned her face into the biting wind as another harsh blast roared through the hollow. The wind blew her words away. It shook her, once again nudging her instinct to survive. She grabbed onto it, a last branch before a waterfall. She rose up. She knocked, a timid rap that quickly gave way to a desperate pounding.

Inside, a man grumbled, a chair lurched, and weighty footsteps thudded.

The door swung open. Silhouetted against yellow firelight, the old Dunkard stood before her. At first, he only stared at her. When he spoke, his words were gruff. "What're you doin' here? On a night like this?"

With her father's diatribes ringing in her ears, the balance in Pearl's spirit tipped toward humiliation. It garroted her. She was ashamed to be standing there, foolish, ashamed to be in his presence, to have disturbed him. She lowered her face. Her heart pounded inside her chest, echoing through every cold bone and muscle in her body. Whatever courage she had mustered moments ago drained out of her like a punctured wineskin. She had survived the assaults for years. She had escaped into the woods— yet it would have been better if her father had beaten her to death. Yes, it would have been better—or better if she had succumbed to the forest's cold floor, at least then to nourish some part of the universe with her rotted corpse. How could she have believed that her salvation were possible? How could she have hoped at all? With fresh regret, she stood before the man at his threshold and trembled. *I'm a pitiful fool.*

The Dunkard towered above her. He was tall and mystical and wore a gray bib of coarse hair that masked the lower half of his face and covered much of his chest. His appearance was strange, the look of a bearded owl—features that had once scared her, when she was very young. But as happens when frightening things become familiar, his form had grown ordinary to her, nearly friendly, on the occasions their paths had crossed. This night, though, only overcast eyes, protruding ears, and a stentorian voice resonating like God allowed her to judge his demeanor.

It was not his countenance, though, that distressed her as much as her own ignominy. As she stood before him, shame dissembled her. The same shame that had allowed her to endure her father's beatings, forced her to suffer them as one deserving punishment. Downhearted, she shrank into a regret that obliterated the hope she had seized only moments before. She could not look up into his face—but had she, she would have seen no condemnation, only puzzlement and confusion at the arrival of an unexpected guest in the midst of a winter storm.

To Pearl's utter relief, his next words were gentle, his voice, kind. Any gruffness, real or imagined, dissolved as he recognized the girl who had tagged along with her older brothers to his gristmill.

"Did you want grain?" he asked, confused, and not understanding the meaning of this strange night visit.

She shook her head. She looked up.

He paused and said awkwardly out of obligation—and a wish to close his door against the storm: "Come in. Come in out of the cold." He bundled her into the cabin the way a Good Samaritan receives a lost traveler.

As Pearl entered the Dunkard's modest dwelling, she passed from death into life. It was a strange sensation, as if she were somehow stepping through time, casting off everything behind her. There was no reason for this hope, yet there it was, teasing her, tempting her. Why was hope so irrepressible? She had held her breath for hours, measuring each while valiantly trying to shield her lungs from the icy air. Now, once again, she could breathe. The warm cabin air ballooned her lungs. Crucified with cold, Pearl was being reborn.

Behind her, the Dunkard closed the door against the frigid night. She heard the heavy door shut and the iron latch fall, reducing the storm to a low thrum. Lighting the cabin's interior, a roaring hearth fire caused her to squint and her cheeks to freshen. Pearl's muscles relaxed, and she felt sleepy. She was also terribly hungry.

"Sit," he said, and he directed her toward his rustic table. He offered her the single chair at it. From an iron pot craned above the hearth's fire, the Dunkard ladled a thin broth filled with root vegetables. He gave her a steaming cup of the meal he had prepared for his own supper and offered her cornpone made from grains he had ground at the gristmill, the place he intersected with other residents of the sparsely populated hollow.

"I thank ya," she whispered, without looking up at him.

She cupped the vessel the way one might hold an injured bird and drew it up to her chin, letting the steam caress her chapped face. With the warmth, the aroma, the Dunkard's kind reception, along with her gratitude, fresh tears arose unexpectedly at this simple offering. She blinked them away. Even though Pearl had found her way to this safe harbor to rest and was momentarily emboldened by his welcome, she dared not think beyond the moment.

The ordinary traveler would never have found the cabin on such a wild winter's eve. She knew of it, though, because her father had often pawned her off on her brothers when he sent them to the gristmill. Pearl, so much younger than they, followed as her brothers explored the hollow's deep woods, adventuring far and around the Dunkard gristmill before dutifully returning home with sacks filled with cornmeal or wheat flour. Often they had spied the cabin from afar, but warned off by rumors that the mysterious hermit was not to be disturbed, they had never ventured as close as Pearl had come tonight. In time, her brothers had grown up and left, leaving her alone with her widowed father—a troublesome abandonment.

Whenever Pearl and her brothers had come to the gristmill, the Dunkard had always acknowledged the girl. She had been as strange to him as he had been to her. Still, with little more than kind eyes and a thin nod of the head, he had somehow—quietly, diffidently, unexpectedly—befriended her. Perhaps he was taken by her shining hair, always flying wildly, or her blue eyes, the color of summer, or the shy and vulnerable smile hidden behind her tough facade that had to keep pace with her brothers. Tonight, it was on this man's perceived kindness that Pearl's last frail hope relied.

For several minutes neither spoke as she warmed herself and ate. He tended the fire in a manner that was self-conscious because he was wholly unaccustomed to visitors. The Dunkard had been abandoned himself though in an entirely different way. For many years, he had worked alongside his own strange brethren, serving the hollow's sparse citizenry by grinding their wheat and corn and barley. In time, his brethren had all moved on or died, leaving him to be the sole miller. He worked alone, lived alone. His solitary life—simple, chaste, modest, earnest—was a distillation of his faith.

The dry air in the cabin soothed Pearl. The timbered walls, rough and thickly chinked, muffled the storm raging outside. The only noises inside were natural ones, the crackling fire, whiffs of steam, wood on wood, fire over fire, and an occasional burst of winter wind that rattled the door and blew across the chimney like the lowest notes of a child's pennywhistle.

From the corner of his eye, the Dunkard watched her eat the soup hungrily. He judged her to be about seventeen. Had he not been a celibate man, he could have been her father, so distant their ages.

When Pearl drained the last drops of broth, he offered her more. "I have plenty," he said.

She nodded.

"Your coat? The cabin's warm."

As she pulled off her coat, he saw bruises on her jaw and neck, injuries to her soft, young flesh that made him cringe. What act deserved this kind of punishment? He wondered as he took from her the worn cotton coat, soaked through and covered with thorns and brambles. She gave nothing in the way of explanation, and he kept his observations to himself. When she stood up, he saw her swollen belly. He wondered but did not speculate.

"You have a name?"

"Pearl."

⁂

Late in the evening the wind died down, making the night soundless except for whispers from the falling snow or the occasional pop of an ember in the hearth or a burnt-through log falling into the fire, spewing sparks. To both the Dunkard and Pearl, the night seemed interminable. Separated only by space and darkness, theirs was an awkward cohabitation. Each lay awake—he on his bed and she near the hearth on a makeshift one that he fashioned from thin blankets. Neither was able to sleep for the uncomfortable and unavoidable presence of the other.

Long past midnight, by the time the embers in the fireplace diminished to a soft cat-eyed glow, the cabin floated in cavernous darkness. Pearl, temporarily unmoored from her troubles, soaked it in. She was too tired to sleep, though. Her jaw hurt, her back ached, and her legs were restless. She could not find a comfortable position, nor did she feel free to thrash about until she did, so she lay motionless, stiff, her foggy brain wakeful and overtired. Tonight, it was her body not her will that wanted to control her. It had happened before, that absence of control, and now she felt as helpless as she had on earlier occasions. It would trap her again, though not tonight. Instead, in a merger of relief and fear, she summoned the will to restrain her flesh.

The Dunkard reclined sleepless as well. Pearl's arrival had roused memories he usually avoided, but as sleep eluded him, he fell prey to the recollections that he had deliberately stowed. He relived his own youth, remembered his own family, considered his father's death that had come when the Dunkard was only a boy. He reexamined the images that time had given him the grace to shut away. He did not lift them up eagerly. Still, they hung before him and begged for notice....

*The young boy stands amidst the bearded, black-clad men and stifles his tears. He is dressed in black, as they are, a smaller version of them. He is to be solemn. He has been told not to cry—warned not to cry—because it is a poor testimony to their certain knowledge that death is a gift, a journey, merely a passage into eternal Heaven. He must heed their caution. But how can he not cry? How can he hold back the pounding tears that back up inside him like a river dammed? The boy bites his lip, squeezes his eyes shut. A small sob, a very small and innocent sob, escapes his throat. A strong hand pinches his shoulder. The boy clenches his jaw and holds his breath. He does not move or make another sound. He stares down at the grass, watching each blade line up along the perimeter of his black boots; slender green soldiers, living blades. One errant tear escapes. He watches it careen down and land on his boot. He presses his chin into his chest and his shoulders up toward his ears, muffling the preacher as the holy man reads. The drone of the deep voice is barely audible, and the confusion storming in his brain turns it into a deep buzzing sound, neither human nor compassionate. But the birds! In the dusky evening, their clear voices cut through the black monotone, the confusion, the storm of pain that pushes against the back of his face. He lifts his head enough to hear the birds chirping and trumpeting, rustling against the chaotic, traveling wind. The birds refuse to submit to this ritual that marks the collision of life and death. If only he could fly, he could escape. If only he could fly!*

*His father had sobbed when the boy's mother died—the boy remembers this clearly, for it had not yet been a year—and neither he, the boy, nor his younger brother had pinched his father's shoulder. The father had hugged them, an embrace so tight that the boy worried his bones would break. The boy had been bewildered because he had only frail understanding of the funereal rite. Would she come back? He hadn't been sure, but he hoped she would.*

*Why can't he sob now as his father had sobbed? Why does he not have the same privilege? But he dares not; he has been warned. Dunkards do not mourn their dead. It is a joy, not a sorrow. They celebrate this passage. He must do so as well.*

*".... We deliver our brothers into Your hands...." The phrase seeps into the boy's ears, stinging as if an acid has been poured in. He winces at their finality. His mother had never returned. Now they are all gone. The boy bites his lip until he tastes blood.*

*A tall thin man motions for him to approach the grave. From behind comes a gentle prod. He steps forward, touches the plain pine coffin in which his father and brother lay cold with death, and then he steps back and bows his head. This is what they have instructed him to do. This is what he does.*

*He watches the coffin begin to descend, suspended between heaven and earth, secured by ropes and belayed by four black-clad elders. To the boy, this is a curious sight. Drop, stop, jerk, drop, stop, jerk, drop—the simple, roughhewn coffin descending inch-by-inch, down, down, down. And just as it disappears behind the edge of the mounded dirt, the sun slips below the horizon. A cauldron of darkness consumes them all.*

*"Ashes to ashes, dust to dust...." The boy hears these words. And these words, he remembers ....*

In the darkness, sweat collected on the Dunkard's weathered brow as he lay awake in the strange presence of his unexpected guest. When the snow stopped, the sky cleared. Moonlight reflected off the perfect snow. The night was profoundly quiet, an absence of sound that overwhelmed him. The only resonance was the ticking of his own aging heart and the rush of his own blood, pumped out of a heart cauterized long ago by pain.

He listened to the silence and prayed for nothing in particular—and for everything he understood.

The next morning brought sunshine that barreled through the cabin windows like a jovial friend. Pearl sat at the Dunkard's table eating a breakfast he had prepared. Despite the sunshine's natural encouragement, she felt awkward and in the morning's light newly embarrassed by the audacity of her late-night arrival and by her state. Yet yesterday's trials were over, left behind along the trail where a fresh mantle of snow had erased them as surely as it had covered her tracks. The door to her past was closed, and a new and tentative door had opened.

Or had it? Was this only a temporary reprieve? As she supped the warm meal, once again she parried between hope and despair.

Wholly unaccustomed to any kind of guest, the Dunkard moved around his cabin ill at ease. He cleaned some mud off the bottom of his boots. He lifted his Bible from a shelf and set it on the table. He rearranged logs in the hearth, letting air energize the flames. He stood near the hearth with one foot propped up on the ash can and ate a bowl of gruel. He was stalling. Along with sunshine, the morning had brought him a dilemma.

"Do ya want'ny more?" he asked her.

"No. I thank ya, though," she said, and she smiled at him, a deliberate action to add substance to the genuine gratitude she felt.

"I don't find I'll be goin' to the mill today," he said. "Drifts too deep."

She realized he was asking her what plans she had, but she had none.

"Yes," she said. "Awful deep."

This was not the answer he sought.

"Do ya wantn'y more?" he asked her again, lacking any other avenue of conversation—an art in which he was poorly skilled.

"No, but it's good. I was hungry."

"Yes, I s'pose you were." He hadn't meant it in a judgmental way, though she looked up, convicted, and then dropped her gaze.

"I'll be goin' soon," she said, knowing nothing else to reply.

An uncomfortable silence fell.

The Dunkard turned away from her and stirred the fire again.

"Where to?" he asked out of curiosity and some genuine concern.

She had no ready answer. She tried to hide the fear that rushed back through her like yesterday's winds. Panic rose in her throat. She swallowed it. She had to keep her wits about her. She had to.

"Back," she said, dispirited. It was the only response she could think to offer, though it was a vacuous one.

"Home?"

"No," she whispered, barely keeping her voice intact. Battered by the full extent of her dilemma, she rested her fingers on the bowl's edge. She sat motionless, a mouse in the presence of an owl. "I'm mighty grateful fer ya kindness."

The Dunkard made no reply. He pulled on his coat and headed to the door.

"I'm goin' out to the shed for more kindlin'. Jus' stay here in the warm," he said, his back still turned. He opened the door, stepped out to the snow-covered porch, and closed the door. Maybe the cold would clear his head.

Pearl sat alone in the cabin facing the warm fire. She listened as the Dunkard swept snow away from the door and the porch. She heard frozen snow crunch as he walked out into the yard. Was this an invitation? Was it sincere? Was it mired in other intents? Did it matter? She had no alternatives. This would be her final destination, or she would face her end in the winter forest or worse yet—at her father's hand.

When the Dunkard returned to the cabin, his arms loaded with a bundle of kindling, she looked up at him.

"I kin work fer ya," she offered. "I kin do chores. I kin work. I'm good at workin'." She tried to sound earnest yet feared she was only begging. "I'm strong."

He didn't answer right away. He carried the sticks to the edge of the hearth and set them down, crouching on one knee to add a log to the fire. With an iron poker, he rearranged the logs to burn evenly, taking his time—biding his time—perplexed by this turn of events. *Is she wantin' to stay? To stay here? How long?* He was ill equipped to provide a home—and equally unable to find her one. He had only the scriptures to rely on, and they were silent on these questions. Should he turn her out to avoid impropriety—or temptation? Should he take her in, an angel unaware? He was wholly unskilled in the ways of social relations, and furthermore, except for his mother, long dead, he knew nothing of womenfolk.

He poked at the fire and watched it grow as he wrestled. *What kinda man turns out a needy girl in the dead of winter? What kinda man invites her in?* Should conviction guide? Or circumstance? Or charity?

The fire was burning strong, the chimney drafting well, by the time he stood up. His face was hot and flushed. He turned and looked at her—young, injured, and needy. In her he saw helplessness. He also saw beauty and youth. In another life, as another kind of man, he would have found her fetching, her auburn hair enticing, her blue eyes alluring. He turned again and faced the fire—and a different kind of conflagration, one easier to control.

He heard her speak. "I kin work hard," she said again earnestly. Her boldness was seeded by desperation, but her words still came out siren-like, vaporous. "I'm strong. I'd do most 'nything ya need. I'd work hard."

He didn't know what to say, what to think, how to decide.

"I'm strong," she reiterated. "Real strong."

The Dunkard stared into the fire and thought, *how strong am I? How strong a man am I?*

A cold wind burst against the cabin, causing the chimney to buzz and whine. There would be no decision to make today. Only a reaction.

"Yes," he said, and it was settled.

# 1873

## AND UNTO HER A CHILD

# March

The Dunkard stepped out of the cabin and swept away a windblown drift of snow. Lifting his broom, he brushed more snow off the cordwood stacked on the porch next to the door, and he shook snow off the wooden cover of the rain barrel, breaking up the skim ice with his knuckles. He set the broom aside and examined the sky that hung on the cusp of spring. Sundogs flanking the sun told him that snow was coming again—a tardy winter storm or an impatient spring one. Late storms, he knew from his long years, could often be worse than midwinter ones. The trees, some already laden with emerging leaves, would often break under the weight of a heavy, wet snow. He didn't know which was coming, and it didn't matter. What mattered was that snow was coming, and he must prepare. He had more than himself to consider now.

His was a habit for survival, always prepared, ready to surmount whatever challenges the hollow or the river or the heavens brought. In this way, he was attuned to his place in the universe, tied to the land not unlike the animals or the trees—as much a part of it as any other creature. The only difference was that he could calculate, reason—anticipate what was coming. They, the animals, could too, he supposed, however their understanding was innate, like breathing. His was learned from decades of practice and experience. Sometimes, though, even his most astute eye, his keenest understanding, didn't give him fair warning. Not often though.

He loaded an armful of logs and carried them into the cabin, pushing the door open and then shutting it with his foot. The iron latch clunked behind him. After dropping the logs beside the hearth, he heaved one onto the fire. The flames crackled and spewed showers of sparks as the dry wood settled down into the burning logs. He watched to make sure the new log caught fire, and then he swept up loose pieces of bark with a whisk broom—a tight bundle of reeds and switches chopped off evenly and bound around a stout hickory branch with ribbons stripped from a thick grapevine.

Pearl sat near the window, mending a garment, making stitches with a needle that was slightly rusted and dull, pushing it through the cloth with determination. She had offered to sew for the Dunkard but realized soon enough that what little he had to do, he could do for himself. Still, she had offered, and he had accepted. He could not refuse her charity any more than she could refuse his. It was the backside of grace—as important to be humble in accepting help as it was to be charitable in giving it. In this, they created a delicate balance.

Pearl began to perspire. Over the fire, a stew of turnips, potatoes, and onions simmered. All day she had been restless, on edge. She did not understand the signs of imminent birth any more than the Dunkard did.

"Fire's good'n warm," she said pleasantly, as she fanned her face.

"We'll be needin' more kindlin'. More snow's coming."

Pearl frowned "You sure? How do ya know?" she said. "Sun's shinin' bright as a bug's eye. Cain't be snow comin'."

He produced almost a half-smile, a knowing kind of expression. "Air's turning. Coming out of the north. Temperature's droppin'. Clouds are striped—and we got sundogs. Yep. Snow's comin'."

"You'd bet on that?" she teased, having grown comfortable with him.

"If I was a bettin' man, I would. But I don't count on nothin' but the grace of God."

His statement was matter-of-fact, one she had heard often during the months she had lived with the Dunkard, sharing his table, his roof, his hearth. They had discussed the weather frequently. It was, after all, a safe and convenient road for conversation. They had also discussed God, the Dunkard's singular passion. Faith was what he knew, the essence of who he was. What they had not discussed was the future. There had been no immediate need. Nothing could change until the weather cleared. This was how it was during hollow winters, as if time stood still. Winter was for holding, surviving, waiting. Waiting for the new life of spring to arrive. There was nothing to grow, nothing to plant or harvest, nothing to tend except for a few animals. Winter was a time for the forest to rest and for the Dunkard to reflect. After winter, he had thought, they would discuss the future—their future, now joined by circumstance and charity. They would discuss it later. Always later.

"Supper'll be on soon," she said.

"Thank ya." He nodded as he left the cabin again. "I won't be long."

As he stepped out the door, a brief cold wind, refreshing to Pearl, washed over her, as did her hunger. She set aside her sewing to check the stew. She pulled the pot away from the fire with the crane and stirred the mixture bubbling in the black iron pot. It would be ready when he returned. She cleared the table to prepare for their meal together.

Outside in the yard, the air was prescient, holding the damp calm that comes before a heavy snowfall. As the Dunkard gathered sticks and twigs, he prayed, reciting verses he had absorbed over his life, a life that began with faith, a life that depended on faith every bit as much as it depended on water to live or soil to plant. He was the son of a Scots Irish man, an immigrant from Pennsylvania, whose grief at the death of his young wife had driven him into the fellowship of the peculiar clan that lived apart from the hollow's other families. The Dunkards, they were called. They had wrapped the widower with empathy, and he had welcomed and absorbed it, as they gathered him into their fellowship. Thus he, along with his two sons who were suddenly motherless and far from the age of accountability, became beneficiaries of the faith. They joined the Dunkards and were baptized in the cold waters of the river that cut through the hollow—the father, by choice, and the sons, by proxy.

By the second year of their sanctification, two of the three were dead. The Dunkard had sometimes wondered if it were an unwitting penitence for the father's former life—at least that's what the young orphan had gleaned from words whispered behind heavy beards and affirmed by knowing eyes. It was the kind of referential hearing a child absorbs with clarity—but little understanding. They had never spoken to him directly about the deaths of his father and brother, yet they had made sure he was raised in their fellowship that was strange and aloof, even in the hollow's sparse collection of independent people.

When the Dunkard returned to the cabin with kindling, he knelt in front of the fire, gripping the poker to turn the logs again. The fire was both inviting and hellish. Cinders, glowing below the logs, flared up and hissed as the seasoned wood burned. The stones of the hearth and flue, already hot from a winter of continuous use, drew the smoke up the chimney with the efficiency of a vacuum. An occasional pop came from lingering pockets of moisture deep within the wood's fibers. The aroma escaping the hanging pot, the warm hearth, and the fire, all together, made a pleasant mixture of sound and scent. The Dunkard measured the ashes underneath the logs. He lifted a short shovel, raked ashes from beneath the grate, and dumped them into a scuttle. "This will give it more air," he said. He cleaned the hearth floor leaving a few large embers, fire starters for later.

He stood up to watch the fire grow before carrying the scuttle outside where he tossed the ashes across the yard. Parts of the ground, the shaded areas, remained snow covered. The rest was bare and frozen. He watched the wind carry the ashes in a gray cloud across the yard, cooling them as they dissipated. Wood to embers to ashes to dirt; this was the proper order.

He set the scuttle on the porch steps and tossed the shovel into it. It landed with a clink. He went to the shed where he retrieved another bucket and brought it to the water barrel that sat next to the porch. He dipped out enough water to fill the bucket. Back inside, he set it near Pearl's bed, which the Dunkard had built for her from the wood of an overgrown black locust tree that he had taken down because it shaded his garden too much. A stack of rags, folded, lay off to the side. These were all provisions for errant embers—and for other anticipated events not spoken of. Both the Dunkard and Pearl made their preparations as best they knew how, yet neither understood much. They were preparing by the simple instinct that they should prepare because a birth was impending.

For a week now, Pearl had been uncomfortable. Her back ached, her legs swelled, her breasts were hard and full. Her mind struggled to hold back a thousand fears and premonitions. She refused to unleash any emotion, fearing it would upset the fragile decorum she and the Dunkard had established over the past few months. This was imperative, for Pearl was wholly dependent on his good will.

The Dunkard lifted the lid from the pot hanging over the fire, stirred the broth, and filled two bowls. Pearl pushed herself up from her seat, retrieved a round loaf of bread and carried it to the table.

They sat down across from each other. He offered a prayer. It was a ritual, a habit, a necessity. She bowed her head.

"Our father in heaven, we beseech thee…"

She listened to his words that came like smooth stones covered with moss, soft on the surface yet hard, unbreakable beneath.

"…. We are thy servants. Give us strength to do Thy will…."

The Dunkards had come from Germany seeking the freedom to practice their odd religion without interference, though they would never outrun the ridicule their peculiarities invited. Dunkards did not shave their beards. They dressed in clothing befitting men of God, making their own determination of what that was. Some chose never to lie with women. Some chose never to eat the flesh of animals. Pearl's Dunkard had chosen all these disciplines. He had decided for himself decades before, inspired by the enthusiasm of youth that sought to please those on whom he was dependent. To conform, to submit, to discharge earnestly should ensure his ultimate gift, his eternal life.

The Dunkards baptized their brethren—those they brought from abroad and those they proselytized—in the river, dunking them face first, three times, branding them with water into the service of the triune God. The Dunkards lived but never flourished. Their evangelism was slim and ill received in the hollow, where pragmatic Presbyterians and strict Baptists ruled.

With their own hands, the Dunkard brethren had built the gristmill next to the river on land they laid claim, and the mill, in turn, supplied what little currency they needed. The gristmill and its deep-woods location required minimal contact with outsiders and enabled their hermitage.

Gradually, the fellowship's numbers dwindled. Some of the Dunkard's brethren, unable to master the rugged independence of the hollow, left, some returning to Pennsylvania and others traveling farther south. Others grew old and died. By the time Pearl was born in a rundown house in Galilee that overflowed with brothers and discord, the Dunkards' numbers had diminished to a handful of the most staunchly devout.

By the time Pearl fled to the Dunkard's cabin, he was the only one left.

"…Amen," he said. He broke the bread and handed her a portion. They ate in silence. Outside the wind began to blow. The temperature plunged.

By the next morning, as the Dunkard had predicted, a storm had swathed the cabin in a blanket of snow. Just before the redbuds blushed, the spring air had turned bitter, winter insisting on one last rally. He stood on the porch assessing the overnight snowfall. The Dunkard hoped it was not a bad omen, although he did not believe in such.

Pearl leaned toward the hearth with one hand under her belly, feeling the child kicking inside her. It was a sensation that was at once miraculous and terrifying. With her other hand, she stirred a pot of hominy. Her swollen womb pulled at the muscles of her back as if she were saddled. Her condition made her irritable, although she tenaciously maintained a pleasant demeanor. She could not risk being turned out for being disagreeable. Her stomach growled. Pearl craved the addition of venison or bacon to her meal, but her gratitude prevented her from imposing her desires on the Dunkard. Already a burden to him, she knew better than to make that burden heavier.

Neither spoke of the imminent event. The Dunkard had never known a woman and had no knowledge of human birthing. What fears he harbored, he kept hidden from Pearl. Childbirth had killed his own mother, so as each day passed, he struck an uneasy balance between knowledge and hope. Pearl, herself, had vague memories of following her own mother and a midwife into darkened bedrooms where pain and hysteria were sometimes followed by joy—and sometimes by grief. Neither Pearl nor the Dunkard, though, would admit anything to themselves except confidence. When fear is an alternative, confidence—even when it is false or naïve—is the better choice.

Pearl had decided to go in the woods when her time came. She had read that this was what Indian women did. They squatted and delivered children as casually as they might have picked flowers. When she was a child, she had often escaped—and lived—in the books loaned to her by her mother's employer, the minister's wife, a woman of good deeds and education. Through them, Pearl had run away to a hundred places that she would never go in body but where she could go wholly and willingly in her mind. She knew she was young and strong, as the Indian women were, and she was determined to be as fearless. The Dunkard's kindness had given her that—a measure of self-assurance, even worth. Although she worried about the sudden cold snap that the Dunkard had correctly predicted, she assured herself that warmer weather was coming soon. She would wait for it.

Yes, she would wait for it.

The Dunkard returned. He stomped his feet to dislodge chunks of dirt and ice before hanging his coat on the peg next to the door.

"You go on 'n sit down," he said, taking the ladle from her and assuming her place at the hearth. "I'll finish."

"Thank ya."

Grateful, she waddled to the table where she lifted her shawl from the chair, shook it and threw it around her shoulders, a concession to habit rather than warmth. She sat down, leaning back in the chair as far as she could with her legs splayed to accommodate her belly and relieve her back. Today she found no position comfortable. She fingered the locket around her neck as she looked through a lace of frozen crystals adorning the windowpane. It seemed as if an ice maiden had been interrupted while tatting and left it half done. *Will winter ever let up?* She swallowed a brief panic and summoned the image of a strong Indian squaw. She had no way of knowing how close her baby was to coming, although she suspected it was sooner than she hoped. Her body felt heavy, her bladder constantly full and in need of emptying—a task she accomplished behind a makeshift curtain the Dunkard had hung as an accommodation to her modesty and his conscience. And it kindly saved her the difficulty of navigating the rough outhouse some twenty paces from the cabin. What little she managed to eat floated up into her throat like a surging tide.

The Dunkard ladled two bowls of hominy and carried them to the table before he sat down across from her on an upended firkin. He had relinquished his own chair until spring when he could build another. He bowed his head. She did the same.

"Our father in heaven, bless this food we are about to eat. This is the bounty that Thou hast provided to nourish our bones and to supply us strength to do the work you give us to do." He paused, and she, wondering why he had forgotten to end the prayer, looked up to see his gray head still bowed. "And bless the child," he said. "Amen."

The Dunkard had never before mentioned Pearl's child. Neither knew what the night would bring—or that this first prayer for the child would be a necessary one.

Deep into the night Pearl lay awake, desperately tired but unable to sleep. Intermittently her belly cramped. Pain that began in her back grew more intense with each passing hour. Was it only her fearful imaginings? Or something more? The night was bitter, frozen, and wholly inhospitable for birthing. Earlier, and with great difficulty, the Dunkard had had to force open the frozen door to get more wood for the hearth. Now more snow was falling. Near midnight it turned to sleet, coating and sealing the cabin's exterior. Ice glazed the windows. It turned the trees, etched with emerging leaves, crystalline.

Pearl listened to the wind. It sounded like a lost child wandering near the cabin, seeking some open door or window to come in. The sound was unnerving and added to the weight of her concern. When the wind finally died down, a tensive quiet filled the cabin. Ice hung on the trees, pulling down their branches as if kowtowing to the heavy cold that made them creak and crack in an eerie rhapsody. Occasionally, a branch would snap and sink into the fresh snow. Otherwise, the night was quiet except for the occasional tinkle of an icicle falling across the snow-glazed roof and clattering down onto the frozen landscape. It was melodic, a cold treble chime that startled Pearl and interrupted her growing concentration.

With each strike of ice, she felt as though she were slipping into a pit. Cold wrapped her, yet heat radiated from her body as her swollen belly grew taut. Her breathing became shallow as searing pain cleaved her. This had happened before, off and on in prior weeks, but the pain had always subsided. It must do so this night. She willed it so. How could she go out as the Indian women did on a night entombed in ice?

Outside more snow began to fall with a whispering cadence. Pearl lay still, enduring the increasing pain. She listened to the shrill wind begin to blow again past the cabin and through the trees, making its haunting crescendos. She listened as snow whished against the windows, a delicate and icy fan. If she could have fallen asleep, she would have slept well on the sound. Instead, she mouthed into the night the scriptures the Dunkard had read to her the prior evening: "In that day the Lord will whistle for the fly which is at the sources of the streams of Egypt, and for the bee which is in the land of Assyria. And they will all come and settle in the steep ravines, and in the clefts of the rocks, and on all the thorn bushes, and on all the pastures."

Pearl had not understood the passage, but its poetry had appealed to her ear, the image to her eye. Its softness now assuaged her pain. "…and on all the pastures. And on all the pastures. And on all the pastures…" she recited, as if it were the cleansing breath that might ameliorate her suffering.

As dawn approached, the pain eviscerated her like the claws of a bear. She found it hard to breathe. She gripped the edge of her bed as she steeled herself for each fresh onslaught. Her pains were coming one right after another. She willed them to stop. *They gotta stop. They gotta stop.* Pearl glanced toward the window wishing to see first light, fresh green colors. All she saw was darkness and all she heard was the wind and the snow pecking on the windowpanes, both sounding as if they were mocking her.

Intermittent waves of pain soon became a flood, every nerve ending electric, every muscle drawn taut, every movement of Pearl's body excruciating, every movement of the infant inside her, terrifying. As long as she could, she stoically suffered the devilish stabs until she could no longer hold onto her silence. The Dunkard awoke to her groans. He came to her bedside.

The Dunkard dampened a rag with water from the bucket. He knelt beside her bed to wipe her face. Although he tried, he could not avoid the fear in her eyes, and he averted his gaze so she would not see his own panic that was rising as quickly as a summer storm.

"What can I do?" he said, not knowing what else to ask. She gasped, shook her head, and clenched her teeth to endure another wave of the pain. All he could do was watch and listen to the unfolding spectacle so utterly foreign to him.

It was awkward at first, but before long they both were swallowed up in the work. Pearl's breathing was rapid, her eyes closed, her face drawn. He saw the depth of her agony. When the Dunkard touched her hand timidly, she grabbed onto it. Her grip was vise-like, desperate. Since his mother's death, the Dunkard had not touched a woman's flesh, but this was an act of empathy.

When she turned and retched, he barely avoided the stream of foul liquid.

"I'm sorry," she whimpered, and she began to cry.

"Shhhh," he said. For the Dunkard, it was a welcome distraction. He tossed a rag on the floor, a makeshift mop, but he did not leave her side or release her hand. He wiped her mouth, wiped her face, stroked her arm. As he leaned close to comfort and encourage her, he marveled at the softness of her skin and the warmth radiating from it. It felt strange and wonderful as her heart beat against his calloused palm, and he battled the illicit thoughts that might have drowned him had he not been focused on a mission of such import. He offered gentle words and whatever physical comfort he could. What distance that had lingered between them through-out the winter was consumed like a feather in fire.

Suddenly Pearl groaned and her back arched. She threw off her cover-ing and drew up her legs in a brazen motion that was wholly shocking to the Dunkard, but her desperation pre-empted all embarrassment.

"Help me," she screamed. Her eyes were wide. "It's comin'. Help me."

Led only by the instinct born into human beings and ignoring the impropriety scorching his righteous soul, the Dunkard rounded the bed. He grabbed Pearl's naked legs, holding them as he watched the baby's head rip through her flesh. He could no longer avert his eyes. Pearl let out a chilling scream as the Dunkard saw the infant's head emerge. Moving close—closer than he had ever been to a woman—he cradled the head as Pearl's body contorted. She strained and in one final push, her body thrust the child into his waiting hands. Immediately, Pearl relaxed. Everything in and out of the cabin fell shockingly quiet. The Dunkard held the baby, a boy, covered with a milky film, bloody and bluish, silent and unmoving. Warmth escaped from the tiny body and steam rose from it like a specter hanging in the cabin's cold air. There came no sound from the infant, no movement, until the howl of the wind returned as if a banshee were bleating at the door.

"Rub," Pearl whispered, as the faraway memory of a midwife returned to her like a good psalm. "Rub."

The Dunkard cradled the lifeless body and put his rough hand on the infant's wet chest, massaging vigorously until all at once a cry pierced the night. At that, tears and laughter broke from Pearl, a strange and wondrous amalgam of relief and elation. From the Dunkard also came emotion that he had long suppressed. He laughed aloud, hearty and unbridled, and with it came an exultation he had not felt since he was a boy—a kind of emotion that came as if joy had been reborn in him or had echoed from a prior, forgotten life.

All decorum, shattered by necessity, vanished as together Pearl and the Dunkard celebrated—and between them passed an immaculate communion, a fleeting union, a brief and intense intimacy that neither had ever known before. Pearl, from a woman's most vulnerable state, looked into the Dunkard's eyes and through their shared joy passed a gaze of total surrender, as if they had been joined body and soul.

The Dunkard wrapped the squalling boy in Pearl's shawl and handed him to his mother who put him to her young, full breasts. The baby quieted. The Dunkard longed to lie down beside her, to hold her and the child, to pull them close to his own body, to envelope them, to caress them, to consummate the moment that had overtaken them both. But as surely as if a wind had careened down through the hollow, blown open the door, and filled the cabin, his religion, his restraint, his well-trained sense of propriety, returned to him in a rush and pulled him back from her, from the abyss of temptation.

With regret that only righteousness can create, he covered up her nakedness, and with a kind of joyful obedience only the devout understand, he turned away.

"I'm gonna call him Ned," Pearl said as dawn began to break.
This was the Dunkard's Christian name.

# May

Pearl held the infant to her aching, swollen breast. As the baby suckled, she felt her milk come and her breast gradually become flaccid. Together, they were a Madonna and child cuddled in the bed that the Dunkard had made for them and softened with dried grasses, weeds, and whatever else the forest gave for comfort. Early morning light flickered through a flush of newborn leaves, casting shadows across their faces. The cabin was chilly, but the air had grown warmer, fuller of moisture and life, and it was overtaking the knifelike cold of the winter now finally past.

Momentarily, Pearl heard the Dunkard stir. She listened to him go out the door for wood to stoke the fire that had diminished to embers during the night. Soon, they would only need wood for cooking. Pearl was eager for summer.

She shifted the infant to her other breast and felt him latch onto her nipple, felt her flesh meld to the shape of his tiny mouth, felt the tug on her body and felt her own belly constrict as her milk flowed.

The Dunkard returned to the cabin, coughed, and dropped logs onto the fire. She listened to the rustle of dry wood and the sound of the poker stirring the cinders awake. Next came the sudden and welcome whoosh when the dry bark caught fire and flames licked the throat of the hearth. Soon the cabin warmed. The Dunkard went out again.

Spring had come late, yet it had come. By the time it settled in and carved back the ice from the riverbank, Pearl, her son, and the Dunkard had settled into a comfortable but fragile routine. Decorum had returned like a stern schoolmaster, but in the wake of the child's birth, in the aftermath of the event that brought them together, a new closeness existed, an unmistakable—yet unacknowledged—intimacy.

Over the months that followed, the Dunkard became the surrogate father, yet not a surrogate husband because he held to his religion fiercely—and at times desperately, when the temptation to embrace this young woman rose in him. Although the momentary thought—a stubborn and sinful one for him—would sometimes cross his mind, he dutifully subdued it. To abandon a single tenet of his faith was to lose it all. After years of practice, of playing out his beliefs on the narrow parameters of his strict religion, it had become a religion unto itself, the original intent obscured by the practice of certain and specific rituals. Celibacy, his gift, was paramount. He could not risk eternity on passion, although desire never left him. What he could not have in the flesh, however, was satisfied by the relationship that developed with Pearl. It would have to suffice.

When Ned was satisfied, Pearl sat up and basked in the light of the spring morning. She held her son in her arms with a mix of joy and remorse. As a child, she had watched as her brothers' wives cradled their own babes. It had seemed foreign to her then, yet strangely appealing, as if holding a baby were the perfect destiny of every woman. So long ago, she had thought it was the magic of marriage vows that produced babies, the same way that a word from Mr. Pulaski had produced credit for her father and thus any number of items in his hardware. Perhaps if her mother had lived, Pearl might have learned differently. Correctly. But would knowledge have spared her? Would she have wanted to be spared?

Pearl looked down at her sleeping son whose dark eyes would always remind her of him—the dark-eyed boy who paid her what attention her father and brothers had not, who told her about love and how it was their destiny together, whose body she had eventually absorbed. He had been so persuasive. She had believed him—she had wanted to believe him—if only to salve the wounds of neglect she had long suffered. But she hadn't known that love has different forms or that what one sees and what one wants to see—like a mirage—can be two different things altogether. His touch had stripped her of her inhibitions and left her joyful yet confused—and with a privation she would never resolve.

Pearl thought of her mother. And how she, the daughter, had once confided to her mother her wish to be like the pretty girl who lived in the Presbyterian manse—the house where she and her mother had cleaned exhaustively before the wedding of Miss Louisa Cross to Mr. Robert Leaberry. Pearl had helped her mother polish the family's silver, dust the corners and tabletops in the simple but dignified rooms. She had helped sweep off broad, welcoming porches, and change bed linens that felt like silk, so different from the coarse blanket that covered her own bed. Pearl had been only a child then, not yet eight, shadowing a kind mother who worked quietly, earnestly, and out of sight of the manse's family. Pearl was curious, as all children are naturally curious, and she had been drawn by the elegance and order of the tall, well-appointed house with all its finery. She had been enchanted by all the excitement that spun through the rooms in anticipation of a wedding.

A wedding.

On one afternoon days before, her mother had taken her by the hand, and together they tiptoed to the upper floor of the house whose long, elegant windows flowed with lacy tambour curtains and whose wood floors were polished and gleaming. Together, like tiny, out-of-place mice, Pearl and her mother, hand-in-hand, had peeked into Miss Cross's bedroom. The walls were covered with pink and aqua wallpaper, fresh and clean, and the scent of lilacs wafted from a tall, slender vase filled with the deep lavender flowers. Hanging on the front of a massive wardrobe was a dress. It was green silk, the color of magnolia leaves, and decorated with lace that her mother told her had been imported from Belgium. *Belgium! Can you imagine?* Her mother had whispered so close to her ear that Pearl had felt her breath. *Ain't it pretty, Pearl? Someday, I hope....* Her voice had trailed off, and her mother never finished her sentence, as if she realized midway through that the grandest hope for her daughter was probably impossible.

It was a week later when Pearl hung off the wooden railing near the front of her father's livery to watch the wedding party proceed down the street toward the church. She dreamed that someday, one day, she would be that bride, every bit as beautiful as the lovely Louisa Cross, and that she would someday have a husband as handsome as Mr. Leaberry. Louisa Cross Leaberry. She had mouthed the name as she fell asleep that night. It was the last time Pearl had dreamed.

Her mother had died soon after, and all of Pearl's childish longings—those that were impossible and even those that might have been realized—vanished. They vanished like stars overtaken by clouds, like a moon eaten by fog, her dreams buried along with her mother. From that moment on, Pearl's life became about escaping her father's unrelenting discipline that would spiral down into a singular madness brought on by sorrow, drink, and the hard times that marked his life. Only the dark-eyed boy had offered her any reprieve, and she had swallowed it like one dying of thirst.

Pearl touched the locket around her neck, her amulet of goodness. It was the only link to her mother.

The child in her arms stirred. She stared down at his small, pink face, his dark and downy hair. This was her child. How her mother would have cherished him! Pearl rose, tucked the infant into the warm spot of her bed and dressed.

Youth favored her, and she had recovered quickly from the birth. Without the burden of her heavy womb, she felt light and energetic and happy. She slipped out of the makeshift room the Dunkard had fashioned for her in a corner of the cabin and began preparing a breakfast.

Just then, the Dunkard returned to the cabin. He was smiling and for an instant, Pearl saw in his face a youth and vitality that must have been his once. As their eyes met, they exchanged a desire—a powerful, mesmeric desire. Pearl blushed. The Dunkard looked away.

"I'll stoke the fire," he said. He was as hungry as Pearl.

# June

The Dunkard sat at the table reading his Bible as Pearl set down two plates of hominy. A momentary wish for meat washed over her once again. The Dunkard steadfastly refused to eat the flesh of animals, a sacred choice he had made, and a practice Pearl longed to change. Hunting had been the primary source of her family's sustenance, an economy of survival that she understood, that she had learned. From her mother, she knew how to preserve and prepare meat. And from her brothers, she knew hunting.

"Let the damn girl go on with 'em," her father would command, ignoring her mother's objections and her brother's vocal protests. "Get her out from under my feet—she's jus' in my way here. I don't wanna hear it! You boys, go on. Take the girl with ya. Get her outta here." So, as she tagged along behind them, she watched and learned.

Pearl sat down across from the Dunkard and waited for him to finish reading. She always followed his lead, his ritual, choosing never to take any action that might jeopardize the safety she had found with him. Slowly, though, she was learning how to engage this quiet and outwardly austere man.

When he looked up at her, she smiled and said, "Bacon would taste awful good this mornin'." She longed for the taste of a hunk of bacon or venison or even a plump squirrel.

He smiled back. "You don't like hominy?"

She leaned toward him over the steaming gruel. "Don't matter if I like it or not. I'm thankful fer it," she said, and after a moment's hesitation, added, "and fer your endless kindness."

The Dunkard looked away, embarrassed. "To God be all Glory," he said. "He is the provider."

"Then God be thanked 'cause I'm hungry as an ol' sow," she said as she lifted her spoon, ready to dip into the bowl. "Seems like I'm hungry all the time. Ned's the reason, I 'spose."

The Dunkard looked toward the child who was beginning to coo. "He's a fine boy. You should be thankful to God—a fine boy."

"I am. And thankful God made me strong—and hungry."

He laughed. And then he bowed his head, laid his hand on his open Bible, and prayed.

When he finished, Pearl persisted. "I still say a little bacon would taste mighty good," she said, as she stirred her hominy to cool it. "Why'd God give us all this—everythin' in the forest? Seems like we oughta use it, all of it. Don't it?"

He thought for a moment. "I use it. The forest's bounty—and the land's."

"But the Bible says we're s'posed to subdue the land," she said. "Look here." She reached for his Bible and slid it across the table. She rifled through the pages. "Listen what it says here… 'and multiply and replenish the earth. And subdue it: and have dominion over the fish of the sea, and over the fowl of the air, and over every living thing that moveth upon the earth.' "

He paused to think. "Subdue does not mean to kill. We are command-ed not to kill," he rebutted. Remember Deuteronomy 5:17: 'Thou shalt not kill.' "

Her eyes twinkled. "Killin' a deer ain't like killin' a man. 'Course it ain't," she said, her voice emphatic. She flipped more pages and read: "When Isaac was old, and his eyes were dim, so that he could not see, he called Esau his eldest son, and said unto him." She paused and ran her finger along the line. "Here it is," she continued. "Now therefore take, I pray thee, thy weapons, thy quiver and thy bow, and go out to the field, and take me some venison; And make me savory meat, such as I love, and bring it to me, that I may eat." See there—Isaac told Esau to go hunt."

The Dunkard was delighted she took interest in this book, this Bible that gave him strength of mind and body. He knew its power. He knew the words when spoken would land on fallow ground. He depended on the promise of Isaiah 11:55, one of the first verses he'd memorized as a young boy, sitting in the circle of the fellowship. His prayer was that the words would root and produce life.

"It's right there in the Bible," she said. "They hunted. And I bet they ate good."

He listened patiently but was not persuaded.

"Perhaps Isaac was wrong. Isaac wasn't God," he said after a moment. "God said 'Thou shalt not kill.' This we are commanded…and killing is taking a life, isn't it?"

This question always stumped her. She smiled at him and lifted a spoonful of hominy. "I still like bacon, but I can be jus' as satisfied with this."

They never resolved their difference. Happily—though often hungrily—Pearl acquiesced because the debt she owed the Dunkard was great. As determined as she could be, she only pushed so far. She owed him too much, and whenever her persistence seemed to make him uncomfortable, she let the subject drop. Their discussions over meat were always good-natured. Still Pearl longed for more, especially bacon, and especially in her state of heightened hunger after Ned's birth. Although she never lost her taste for meat, Pearl came to understand that the Dunkard was content to live as the winner of his peculiar tontine, and part of that reward required that he adhere to every doctrine. Refusing the flesh of animals was one of the doctrines that made the Dunkard feel heavenly legitimate; it brought him joy. Pearl would never take that from him. Yet she could argue with her strong will—the same will she had mustered to leave her father. The same will she had almost lost in the forest on that first night she came to the Dunkard's cabin. The same will that motherhood had braced.

Perhaps it was because he was the last of his kind that the Dunkard himself felt duty-bound to honor and maintain the doctrines that had guided his late brethren. Practicing his beliefs was a compulsion to history, loyalty, devotion and duty, a simple and unyielding dedication to faith. Living his convictions was also habit, the kind that gave meaning and rhythm to his life. Each of his brethren's lives had testified to their beliefs;

this is how they lived, how they related to all other humans, despite the isolation and ridicule it had spawned. How could he, therefore, being the last of them, ever fail them by abandoning their creeds?

For his part, the Dunkard had found an unexpected reward in outliving all his brethren. He often wondered what would have happened to this cast-off girl had he not been alone when she came seeking shelter. Where would she have gone if he still lived in the community of other Dunkards? What would have been the tenor of their corporate discussions? Didn't their living arrangement constitute an evil? What would have been their decree?

He knew. He knew it was her good fortune that he was the last, that he had been able to make the decision alone. When he had been presented with the task of turning her out into the raw world, back to her father or into the wilds, what choice had he? None, he believed, and thus Pearl had taken up residence with the Dunkard.

In the warmth of the crackling fire, they ate together in a comfortable companionship, each glad to have the other but neither so bold as to voice it. The Dunkard looked across the table at Pearl who was eating hungrily. He had grown tender toward this girl—this young woman. In spite of himself, he loved her deeply.

# July

Patches of fog hung along the mountain ridges. Pearl bustled around the cabin completing her chores one-handed. With her other hand, she held Ned on her hip. She had fashioned a sling for the baby that wrapped around her neck, crossed her chest, and opened to support the child. Still the mother's arm surrounded his back as if to ensure that nothing would separate them.

When Ned began to wail, she dropped the broom, pulled open her shirtwaist and twisted to give him her nipple. Immediately, he quieted and when his stomach was filled, he fell asleep. She swaddled her son and tucked him into the cradle the Dunkard had pulled down out of the shed. She grabbed a bushel basket off the porch and went to join the Dunkard who was hoeing the garden. Planted early, the corn would soon tassel out.

The morning was cool and windy for July. The Dunkard wore a worn straw hat that shielded his face from the sun. He looked up when he heard her coming.

"Ned?" he said.

"Sleepin'."

Pearl crouched down on her knees and joined the work, picking beans, gathering them in her apron. All around, the earth was fresh and vibrant in the early morning, the best time of day to harvest, before the sun and heat drew moisture out of the plants and back into the roots.

Usually, they worked silently. Today, however, the Dunkard seemed to want to talk. "My mother died young." He drew the hoe through the black soil. "I barely remember her."

Pearl looked up. The Dunkard had never offered her this kind of information, though she had wondered why an elderly, childless man would have a cradle to offer her son. Pearl slowed the pace of her work.

"I had a brother. When my mother died, my father couldn't care for us alone. The Dunkards took us in. Eventually my father joined them."

"Them?"

"The fellowship. And I with him. My brother was younger."

"How ol' was ya?"

"Old enough to obey. And not to question."

"You didn't question?"

He didn't answer at first. Her question stung him.

"Had no reason to," he said finally. He set down the hoe and took hold of a handful of beans, tearing them from the stalk and dropping them one-by-one into the basket.

Pearl dumped her apron-full of beans in, too. She wanted the Dunkard to stop, to not tell her more of his life, to preserve the mystery that shrouded her savior. She depended on him. Still, she was drawn in by the pull of his humanness, which was stronger than she had earlier supposed. He had always seemed so stoic, so distant, so upright, so spiritual—and then this.

"You remember your father?" she asked.

"Yes. He didn't live much longer than my mother. The grippe took him—took them both. My father and my brother. Same time. They said it was punishment for his sinful life."

Pearl looked up at him, puzzled.

"My father had taken a wife, and she'd born two sons—me and my brother. I don't know what other sin he'd a done. Jus' don't know."

"It was a sin to have a wife?" Pearl was incredulous. *Was this why you live alone? Is this what you fear?* She could do without meat, but not without this kind of hope. She persisted. "Was it?"

The Dunkard didn't answer at first. It was a rhetorical question too complicated to explain—and more than he thought Pearl would understand. He wasn't sure he understood himself, but he didn't need to understand. He only needed to obey. He would leave it at that.

"I don't know," he said with stark honesty. "I only know we are all sinners."

Pearl did not understand. The Dunkard was a good man. She had a passing thought about Miss Louisa. About her mother. The good people. "You musta misunderstood."

He was quiet for a moment. "No. We are all sinners. God is just—and merciful."

To this she made no reply. Merciful. The word enfolded her. She had begun to understand mercy the moment she had entered the Dunkard's cabin. Mercy had saved her life.

That night after they ate supper, the Dunkard stood in the side yard, his back toward the setting sun. He raised the axe and let it fall into the groove of the log, which split open into two nearly equal halves. He had tried to forget about his mother, but Pearl's presence often brought her to his mind. The pain of her death had spoiled them all and sent his father into the arms of the Dunkard brethren, who were eager to embrace him in his sorrow, eager to assuage it with their encompassing faith. Yet after all these years, the Dunkard still felt his mother's touch, how she had stroked his cheek, told him he was a good son, his father's son. He grappled with thoughts long dormant, with questions long ignored, and with memories that were much easier left undisturbed.

In the evening's lingering heat, he paused for a moment, wiped his face, and leaned against the pile of logs. From this vantage, the Dunkard stared at the river that ran along his land only a few dozen paces from his cabin. It was a strong river, filled with rapids and wide sweeping bends. The cool waters beckoned him. It had been a long time since he had slipped into the river's waters and let them cool and comfort him. It would refresh him, he knew, but he had work to do. To the west, the sun was dipping toward the ridge. He needed to finish before dark. He pulled another log from the pile, set it on end atop the stump, raised the axe and, in one motion, split the log. His strong, calloused hands hardly felt the vibration that transferred the force of the axe to the log. He kicked aside the halves, upended another log on the stump, and raised his axe.

The Dunkard no longer knew his own mind. He had taken in a girl, a woman, and was living with her. And now she had a son. One half of his sensibilities, those that were compassionate and generous, applauded him. Another half, the one riddled with judgment and temptations, niggled his soul like a persistent fly. In his quietest moments, he heard the brotherhood's unbending declarations. He could not silence their whispers or manage his own thoughts any more than he could blot out the sun. The arrangement with Pearl—that he had allowed—presented a perplexity that scriptures did not solve for him, that confused him further, that caused him to juggle them both as equals. He stood atop a high branch, balancing the conundrum. If he were to tip either way, he would tumble into an abyss of doubt. The Dunkard could not allow either belief to prevail since his faith was the source of his very breath. He could not abandon it—not after structuring his entire life around it. It would be like eternal death. So, he balanced and waited; someday he would ask. Someday he would know.

He looked toward the cabin and wondered if Pearl would leave him now that she had her son and her health back. She was young and strong. Why would she want to stay? He could offer her only shelter and food. Was that enough? No matter the conflict that raged in him, he could not deny how very much he hoped it would be enough.

From inside the cabin, he heard Pearl humming. He set down the axe to listen to the seductive music of her voice.

# 1880

## SEVEN YEARS PAST

# March

An air of anticipation swirled about the cabin. Ned sat on the cabin's stoop tapping his foot, his patience sorely tested. He had been up since the first fissure of dawn, unable to sleep from sheer excitement.

He had grown tall and lanky over the last few winters, and his increasing appetite had tested the Dunkard who had forgotten what it was like to be young and growing. Ned was energetic and clever and interested in learning everything the Dunkard could teach him. He was curious, thoughtful, and he often posed questions that neither the Dunkard nor Pearl could answer. The Dunkard would always retreat to his Bible for answers, and Pearl to her considerable reason and common sense.

Pearl had taught her son to read using the Dunkard's Bible in the same way the kind mistress of the Presbyterian manse, Miss Louisa Cross's mother, had taught her in lessons when the opportunity had intersected her mother's employment. The lessons, offered in exchange for special tasks such as beating rugs or washing windows, had supplemented Pearl's poor schooling in the local one-room school. Sitting in the spacious parlor with the lovely tambour curtains, Pearl always paid close attention to the words and instructions. Everything she had learned at the manse, she passed on to her son.

The Dunkard listened to Ned's regular recitations. Pearl had often wished there were other books—entertaining ones like those the minister's wife had loaned her as a child. Once Mrs. Cross had given her a set of books about a girl named Little Prudy, but her father, incensed by the charity, had thrown them into the trash barrel, burning them. She had lied to the minister's wife and told her that she had lost them.

Had Pearl asked the Dunkard for other books, he might have brought some on the few occasions he left the cabin and ventured into town. She had never asked though, thinking it might have been an imposition. Her habit of considering his ways and never pushing too hard guided her. Even after seven years, she had never lost the troubling worry that he could turn her out.

On one point, however, Pearl had earned a compromise.

Ned picked up a twig lying on the porch. He broke it into four even pieces, tossing them into the yard in the direction of the path that led to the river. Shortly, the Dunkard emerged from the shed with two long poles. Ned hopped up. The Dunkard handed one to the boy, then turned to Pearl who had stepped out onto the porch.

"We should be back by noon," he said to her, and turning to Ned. "You got your bait?"

"Right here," the boy said, patting a small basket hanging from a rope over his shoulder. The basket was lined with moss and filled with black dirt, bedding for a generous collection of night crawlers that the boy and the Dunkard had dug up the evening before.

"You bring me a big-un, Ned. A big 'ol bass," Pearl said, wiping her hands on her skirt. "I can taste it already."

"I will, Mama," he said grinning, as he followed the Dunkard toward the river.

The Dunkard looked back over his shoulder at Pearl and gave her a wry smile, as if to say with a mixture of accusation and gratitude, *you're responsible for this*. She smiled to acknowledge her small victory though she was careful to do so with humility because it had been his one acquiescence to her culinary desires.

"He told his disciples to be fishermen, didn't he," Pearl had argued, persuasively. "Well? Didn't he?"

"Yes, he did. Fishers of men."

"Well, what's the difference? Ain't no different. A fisherman's a fisherman. If you wanna be obeyin' God, then you oughta fish. I can show ya," she had argued, adding one last salvo—the one that tipped the scales. "Ned's growin' fast. My boy needs this. Look how he's growed!" This was one argument the Dunkard could not counter.

Although his religion remained paramount, Pearl had softened him, and he, like a lover succumbs, had eventually given in to this one modification when he agreed to let Pearl teach him and Ned to fish. The Dunkard only caught fish for Pearl to prepare for herself and the boy. He steadfastly refused to eat it. Part of his conscience was seared, and he worried about the consequences or whether this one act would further weaken his resolve—and yet, he, without ever admitting it to Pearl, came to enjoy fishing with the boy.

Pearl watched them turn downriver, heading toward a cove that she had correctly identified as a good fishing hole. She watched them go, walking side-by-side, talking. To any unknowing onlooker, they might have been an ordinary father and son. Watching them together, Pearl was overwhelmed with a gratitude that brought her to tears. She had come to love the Dunkard, a love far greater than mere gratitude inspires, a love beyond need—a love that no validation of flesh and bone could increase.

# April

The gate on the sluice swung open, and the Dunkard watched water rush onto the paddles. The huge wooden wheel creaked and began to turn. The sound was one he liked; a full-bodied whoosh below the high chiming sounds of falling water. How many days had he stood here alone before Pearl had arrived at his door? How many days had he worked and returned alone to his deep woods cabin? Instinctively, he looked in the direction of the cabin they kept together. How could seven winters have passed since he first opened his door to Pearl.

The Dunkard had always known the love of God. He had rested on it at night, leaned on it during his days, and communed in it with his late brethren. In still mornings, especially when the forest was quiet and the heavens scattered hoarfrost like ashes, he felt his brothers' presence—it was as if he could turn and see them with him, side by side, grinding grains. While they had lived, they had formed a confederacy of faith against the outside world, a kind of shield against all things opposed to their rigid beliefs. When they were all gone, and he had been left behind, he found comfort in solitude and in a strange and comforting notion that he was alone now by divine purpose.

But he was alone no longer. Not for these last seven years.

The Dunkard tipped a barrel and rolled it along its metal hoop toward the hopper where he would dump the contents, shoveling out enough at first so he could lift the barrel.

Pearl had not taken the place of his brethren. At first, she had been a burden, one he had accepted reluctantly out of his Christian duty. What else could he have done with a young girl in her state? In the middle of winter? Short of a divine answer delivered on stone tablets, circumstance and the long, harsh winter that followed had made the decision for him. Perhaps that had been his divine answer after all. He often wondered.

Pearl had found her way into his heart. In the beginning, he had loved her as deliberately as any sinner is duty bound to love another sinner. Duty. Responsibility. Obligation. Gradually, though, through the simple and consistent drumbeat of everyday life, and because of the natural longing that imbues men and women, Pearl had dug a hole in his heart, a place he had once reserved only for God. And she had settled there. He had resisted love at first until he gave up, gave in, and loved her completely. When he was alone at the gristmill, away from the temptation, he wondered what might happen if his faith failed to cordon him.

The Dunkard laid his grizzled hands on the stringers of the barrier fencing the wheel. Age was a barrier, yes, but one that might have been surmounted. He was, after all, a man—a mortal, sinful man. And though he struggled mightily to subdue his mind, when he was here, alone at the gristmill, he sometimes imagined what it would be like to take Pearl to himself and to treat her not as a companion but as a wife. His imaginings, though, only emerged here at the mill, where distance protected him from desire and kept his resolve intact.

The Dunkard breathed deeply. High above him, the wind blew through the trees. He hoisted the barrel and dumped the dry corn into the hopper.

# May

The crying cow awakened the Dunkard and Pearl. The old man threw on his coat and shook Ned. "Wake up. I need you out'n the shed," he said to the boy, who sat up and forced open his eyes. He dressed quickly, pulling his pants up over his grasshopper legs—a label given them by the Dunkard for their length and flexibility. Ned followed the Dunkard to the shed. Pearl, coming behind, carried a lantern.

The cow lay on her side near the shed door, her belly distended, her legs bent in an unnatural fashion. She bellowed pitifully when the Dunkard and Ned came near. Pearl lifted the lantern as the Dunkard knelt beside the beast to assess her progress. He stroked the animal, whispered to her. Ned watched the Dunkard's face for signs of confidence or worry to determine which emotion he should mimic.

"Don't think it will be long," the Dunkard said. He pulled a milking stool over, sat down and gave the boy a smile barely visible in the sallow lantern light. The Dunkard soothed the animal. Ned crouched down near the cow's back. The lantern gave off a quiet "sirrrrrr" and except for that and the work of the animal, the night was bereft of sound. It had been a late spring. Leaves were just beginning to green and the Dunkard's few animals had started to foal and calve and lamb. The night air was cool, and the night bugs had not yet begun to chorus. Ned leaned toward the cow for warmth. The smell of hay and manure was potent but comforting. They all waited. There was a muted excitement at the event's unfolding. To Ned, the air felt electric. The Dunkard spoke placid words to the cow as he gently rubbed her rump.

When the bag of water presented, the Dunkard, noting the angle of the moon, pointed toward the shed's opening. "Look up there, Ned. See that. Oughta be soon. When the moon crosses that lowest bough of the white oak, we should have us a calf."

Ned watched the cow and the moon, one, then the other. When the calf's legs began to emerge, Ned, wide-eyed, stood up and came around beside the Dunkard for a better view. Soon the calf's nose was visible. The Dunkard took the mouth and pinched the tongue. There was no retraction, as he would have expected. A look of concern creased his brow. Once more he noted the angle of the moon. It had crossed the bough and was falling so that moonlight was now shining into the shed.

"We might have to help her, Ned," the Dunkard said as matter-of-factly as if he had said she needed feeding. Ned was pleased to hear him say "we."

When the moon disappeared below the tree line and dawn began to erase it, the Dunkard knew to wait no longer.

"Git over here beside me," he said, motioning to the boy. He tossed him a rope. "Tie that around the calf's legs. Cinch it tight. Now, when I tell you to, you pull. You're gonna have to pull hard. Wait till I say. You understand?"

Ned nodded.

The cow bellowed. Ned saw the muscles under her thick, brown hide rolling and contracting. He watched the Dunkard push back his sleeves and gently work his hands inside the cow's warm body on each side of the calf's head. He massaged gently, working the head all the way out. Even in the cool night air, beads of sweat glistened on the Dunkard's forehead.

Suddenly and urgently the Dunkard spoke. "Now, Ned. Pull hard and steady."

Ned gripped the rope, dug his heels into the loose soil and straw of the shed floor and tugged as the Dunkard guided the calf. The cow raised her head and bawled pitifully. Any revulsion Ned might have felt was blinded by excitement. Within a minute, the whole calf lay in the hay, unmoving.

"It's dead," Ned cried, his voice cracking.

Calmly, the Dunkard lifted the lifeless animal, and as Ned watched, he rubbed her chest vigorously. Right before Ned's eyes, the calf heaved air and came to life. Within the minute, the calf, wet and shaky, stood up on spindly legs.

"Thank you, Ned. You done it jus' right."

Ned started to laugh.

⸎

The Dunkard carried a milk bottle with a large black nipple attached to it as he traipsed from the cabin toward the shed. The birth had been too much for the cow. She had died the next morning, leaving her calf hungry and crying. Pearl had wanted to butcher the cow and preserve the meat, but she said nothing. It was too much to ask.

Ned and the Dunkard had dragged the cow to the edge of the woods where they buried her in a shallow grave that they covered with river rocks to keep scavengers from digging up the carcass. The older man was grateful for Ned's youth and strength.

"Can I feed her?" Ned said, as he came out of the shed where he had stayed all night with the calf.

"Come 'round this side," the Dunkard told him.

The Dunkard assembled the bottle, which he offered to the hungry animal. Soon she was sucking a thin mixture of water and grain. Ned stood alongside with his arm slung over the doe-eyed calf's back.

"She's hungry," Ned said.

"That she is. Good sign. Here, you feed her." The Dunkard handed the bottle to Ned. "Hold it tight." He stood to the side and watched. The Dunkard's father had given him charge of a calf once. He had been even younger than Ned. As he watched Ned and the calf, he savored the bittersweet memory.

For the next week or so, the Dunkard and Ned went to the shed every morning and evening to feed the calf. As soon as she was old enough for grass, the Dunkard turned her out into the yard.

Ned's calf would grow into a fine heifer.

# June

The Dunkard stood in the cabin's doorway silhouetted against the morning sun. The light bent around his shoulders and erased the lines from his face, leaving him to appear as if he were glowing. He held his Bible draped over his large hand like a communion cloth. Ned sat at the table eating a simple breakfast. Pearl was sweeping the cabin floor. When she looked up and saw him, she started.

"Why, I thought 'ol Gabriel'd come through the door!" She stopped sweeping and planted the broom squarely against her chest.

"Today, we should baptize the boy," the Dunkard said with a determination that Pearl knew would be useless to oppose.

"Why today?" she asked, not defiantly but with a genuine interest.

"I mark that we're into the boy's seventh year."

Pearl looked at her son. Could it have been seven years since she came to be with the Dunkard, seven years since she bore her son? Hadn't Ned always been with them? At the same time, it felt like only yesterday that Ned had suckled. It was a strange collision of memories that rushed through her like a sun shower. She had tried to let go of her past, and she had succeeded—happily—devoting herself to the Dunkard's care and the rearing of her young son. For seven years, she had cared for her boy with the instincts of every mother. For seven years, she had served the Dunkard the way one serves a savior, with gratitude that has no end.

But Pearl had her own mind as well, and the Dunkard had never discouraged her from using it or expressing what she thought. Had he done differently, she might have been tempted to leave, but he had only taken care of her, never demanded of her, never given her any reason to want to leave—and every reason to stay.

Until Pearl had come to know the Dunkard, she had never known enough goodness to conceive of a heaven. But the Dunkard and his kind ways had persuaded her. She revered him, and she feared his devotion to things she could not see or understand. Such kindness had provided great comfort and a bridge for her—much like the one that had vanished when her mother died.

"Seven?" she said. "You sure?"

"Yes. Seven. A good year." He looked at the boy the way a father admires his son.

Pearl had known this day would come. The Dunkard had encouraged her on numerous occasions to submit herself to this ritual that defined his faith. Every time, though, she had said no, and he had never insisted. She could not speak to him of her fears or her belief that she would never be worthy. Such a ritual was only for those deserving. He had sensed this, and whenever he asked her, it was spoken gently. The Dunkard had no overbearing tendencies, only the type of influence that is so kind that one is obliged to consider. She had considered. She had been grateful for his concern, and she had also worried. What if this were a requisite to the eternal life her Dunkard sought with such fervency? Would refusal abrogate that for her? Still, time and again, Pearl declined.

"I'll baptize him in the shallows," the Dunkard said. "At the upper bend. Above the rapids where the river's calm."

Not wanting to refuse the Dunkard's desire for her son, Pearl voiced no objection. She nodded. Ned listened as they talked.

The Dunkard turned to the boy. "Ned. Today, I will baptize you."

Ned smiled. "Right now?" he asked. Unlike his mother, Ned was not afraid of the Dunkard's faith. He was eager to embrace it and anything else the Dunkard recommended. It was a son's desire to please a father.

Ned often sat at the Dunkard's knee, listening to his instruction. He sometimes found the scriptures confusing and asked questions.

"Ya mean God told Abraham to kill his boy? To kill Isaac? And then he told him not to? Why couldn't he make up his mind?"

"God is God. We can't always understand." The Dunkard smiled.

Ned's interest heartened him. He knew it was impossible to explain the will of God, but he would try. "God is all powerful—and all merciful."

Ned was perplexed. "But why?"

"It was a test, son. A test. God wanted to know who he loved best."

Today, though, there were no questions. Ned quickly took another spoonful of his breakfast and jumped up.

On the Dunkard's face was an expression of absolute delight. He loved this boy as if he were his own.

Sunlight bounced off the river as they made their way along its bank, passing the rapids and rounding a bend where the river had carved out a narrow cove. The Dunkard led the procession, his hand resting lightly on Ned's shoulder. Pearl followed. The day was mild—so different from the one into which Ned had first entered their lives. All the trees were thick with leaves, the grasses greening. The water would still be cold. Pearl carried her shawl to dry her son's face. The sun would do the rest.

They followed the river until they reached a point where the land flattened out and the grade of the riverbank became easier. The Dunkard removed his boots and set them aside. Without being asked, Ned did the same. Together Ned and the Dunkard waded into the shallow part of the river, sinking into the silty bottom, their clothes darkening in the water, until they both stood waist deep in the river. Ned shivered and smiled. Pearl stood nearby anchored to a tree, watching.

The Dunkard didn't smile often, at least not as broadly as he did just then. There was a radiance about him, as if an immaculate joy had embraced them all. Pearl found herself smiling as well, sparked by a gratitude she only barely understood. Here was the father for her son, infinitely wiser and kinder than the dark-eyed boy would ever have been. This fact alone gave her a small glimpse of eternity. If providence had indeed given her over to the Dunkard's rescue—as the Dunkard had often conjectured—maybe she was witnessing the reason.

The old man raised his hands heavenward invoking faith, and then he lowered his hands onto Ned's shoulders. Turning the boy so that he faced upstream, the Dunkard began. He placed one hand on the boy's forehead and the other on his chest. He lowered him into the water face-first, three times.

"I baptize thee in the name of the Father….In the name of the Son…. In the name of the Holy Ghost…."

Pearl watched. Part of her wanted to join them, to wade into the water and submit to the ritual that was so simple yet so profound. But she could not. She could not see herself any way other than by the descriptors so early attached to her. She heard children taunting her. *Pitiful Pearl.* She heard her father. *Take the damn girl with ya. Get her out from under my feet.* And faintly, but not loud enough to silence the others, she heard her mother whisper. *Blue as the sky, my darling girl. Blue as the sky.*

The sound of the water lapping against the riverbank at her feet, though, began to drown out the haunting voices from her past—and another voice, a strange voice, touched her ear. *I am greater than all your pain.* She did not recognize this gentle voice, and it startled her. She looked up as if someone had stepped out of the shadows. She shuddered. No one was there. But an unexpected warmth crept into her. She raised her hand to her chest and inhaled deeply.

As the Dunkard and Ned climbed out of the water and up the bank, Pearl handed her shawl to her son. "Wipe your face."

"Did you watch, Mama? Did you see?"

"I saw, son."

When it was all over and done, the boy embraced the Dunkard in a fit of youthful enthusiasm. The Dunkard responded in kind. Pearl met the Dunkard's eyes. Once again, as it had on the night Ned was born, something precious and intimate passed between them.

As the trio walked back toward the cabin, a peace settled into Pearl that she had never known before.

# July

The Dunkard emerged from the woods slowly and crossed the yard to the cabin stoop where he sat down momentarily to catch his breath. Pearl watched him while she hung clothes on a line strung taut between two blackjack oaks. The wash bucket, upended, leaned against the backside of one of the trees. She tried to keep her observation from being conspicuous. Deep in her soul, she worried he was ill, though neither of them would speak the words. Some fears were best left unspoken. If she didn't voice it or think it, maybe it was not true, maybe it would not come to pass.

His cough had come on early in the spring. He could not shake it. He would fall into fits that racked his chest, and a thick mucus often choked him. Neither Pearl nor Ned could do anything more than stand with him until a fit subsided. Afterwards, he would always apologize, and Pearl would offer him a drink of water. Ned would sit with him, displaying a patience and tenderness far beyond his years.

As the Dunkard struggled with the cough, his hands and feet began to swell. His trips to the gristmill became harder and harder. He went anyway. Life was work and this seeking of normalcy would cure his ills; he was certain it would. More and more, Pearl insisted on sending Ned to the gristmill with him to lift the barrels and the heavy bags of grain. It was part help and part education.

"I can teach the boy to run the mill," he said in agreeing to the arrangement. But privately he wondered if he would have the time and strength.

The Dunkard struggled to pull himself up from the stoop. Pearl tossed the remaining wet clothes over the line and hurried to help him. Once he would have refused her help, but no longer. "Thank you," he whispered, as he leaned on her young arm. She could feel his grip. His hands were still strong. His body, though, seemed to be wasting away.

The Dunkard had taken Pearl in, believing God had given him this mission. Now he knew the same gracious God had blessed him with a companion. Though he never voiced it except to his God, he was intensely grateful for Pearl and for the son she had born. Having known solitude, he no longer wanted to be alone. And now, with his end near, he would not be alone.

Still, he was conflicted. Dying was not his fear—dying meant receiving his heavenly reward. This was his great expectation, his lifelong hope. Yet his hope of a simple departure now held a sting— leaving behind Pearl and the boy

Pearl helped him to the door and to the table already prepared for their evening meal. She handed him a cup of broth. He sipped it while he watched the boy through the cabin window. Ned was hard at work, rebuilding the sides of a broken cart. *A fine boy*, the Dunkard thought. This was the son of his heart, even though he came from another man's loins. He had never asked Pearl about the boy's natural father or whether this child was the product of sin or crime. It did not matter to him.

It did not matter at all. *A fine boy.*

The Dunkard's swollen hands shook as he drank the broth. A few drops landed on the table. He wiped them away with his sleeve. Celibacy was the gift God had given him; the gift he had accepted. In the fervor of his youth, he had embraced it without understanding all its ramifications, only his earnestness to please God. As a young man in moments of weakness, he had imagined lying with a woman—images he had dismissed as sinful and beat back with heavy doses of the Holy Word. He had found support in the unbending teachings of the Dunkard fellowship and in their corporate agreement. Now, as he watched Ned, he wondered what kind of God would deny any man a son.

Or perhaps his God had not denied him at all, only the pleasure, the temptation, the act of making one.

# August

Pearl sat next to the Dunkard's bed. The air was hot, insufferably so, and damp as steam. The course bed clothes had been freshly washed. Still, they barely masked the stench of illness that pervaded the cabin. The odor hung on the sparse furniture and clung to the bare log walls. Pearl had opened the windows and door, but the air, sluggish and heavy, barely stirred and brought only occasional relief.

The Dunkard had declined quickly through the summer, yet he had persisted in doing the work he had always done, gladly accepting Ned's help. The Dunkard's chest had caved and was often racked with violent periods of coughing. When his strength waned so precipitously that he could barely stand, he had finally taken to his bed.

Today was like every day had been for a week. Pearl watched the Dunkard carefully. He was sleeping for the moment, his mouth slightly open, his sunken eyes closed, his hands limp beside him.

Ned, who was only partly aware of the gravity of this moment, tended to chores outside. He did not understand death. Except for the cow's demise, the curse of life had not yet fallen on his young shoulders. Pearl understood it though, all too well. She recognized death's pallid face. She had watched her mother go soundlessly, like a breeze that wavers and dies. And in that moment, in one daring act, after the others had left the death room, after the others had left the only daughter alone to weep for her mother, she had stolen the locket from around her mother's lifeless neck. Pearl, who had been overlooked as the recipient of any maternal legacy, had unclasped the chain and hidden the locket. She had wanted this one object so desperately that she had dared to take it. To her relief, no one noticed until just before the burial when a brother's wife asked about it. Pearl said nothing. She let them assume it had fallen off and was lost. As she sat with the Dunkard, she fingered the locket.

The air was heavy and summer laden. Heat and insects, along with all the rhythms and aromas of living, pulsed through the hollow and effervesced in a cheery yet contradictory way. Outside, crickets clicked, squirrels chattered, and birds chirped. Pearl brushed a fly from the Dunkard's brow. It buzzed, circled, and came again, drawn by the stench of death creeping closer. When the fly landed on the bed covers, Pearl positioned her hand five inches from the back of the insect and with one sweep and grasp, she captured the fly in her hand. She felt it flying inside her fist, desperately trying to escape her hot palm. Pearl squeezed—hard—and tossed the lifeless insect to the floor, as if to say to his buzzing brethren: "Be warned."

And deep in her ear, a memory surfaced. It was the Dunkard reading to her: *In that day the Lord will whistle for the fly which is at the sources of the streams of Egypt, and for the bee which is in the land of Assyria. And they will all come and settle in the steep ravines, and in the clefts of the rocks, and on all the thorn bushes, and on all the pastures.*

Quiet, Pearl listened to her memory, yearning to hear his voice strong again. She took the Dunkard's calloused hand in hers as he slept.

Despite the heavy summer heat, she watched her Dunkard shiver. Small beads of perspiration gathered on his leathery cheeks—*the dew of heaven*, she thought, and wondered why such random words would come to her mind. Perhaps she had heard it in a Bible passage he had read to her once. It must have been. How else would she have known it? She started to stand up, to get his Bible and read to him, but she changed her mind. She didn't want to let go of him for even a moment. She had to stay. She wanted to stay with him, as if her presence might hold him on this broken side of eternity.

The Dunkard's breathing grew increasingly labored. His hands and feet had swelled into grotesque caricatures. His face was the color of a fading dogwood blossom. His tongue was thick and dry, his owlish eyes sunken.

"Take this," she said, and she encouraged him to drink some water. His colorless and cracked lips parted to receive this small offering, but he could lift his head only inches from the bed.

"Let me help," she said. Pearl cradled his shoulders, brought her face close to his, touched her cheek to his head, and held the cup for him. "Drink."

She thought of the night he had first handed her a cup, how it had saved her life. This was the same cup. The memory stirred her tears. Could she do the same for him now? Could she save him as he had saved her?

"Thank you," he said, his words barely audible, more shaped than spoken. Pearl understood them though, as she had come to understand all his words, all his actions.

His thirst slaked, the Dunkard grew still. The effort to drink had exhausted him, and he rested on the bed, closing his eyes so that Pearl would not have to suffer more, so that she would not have to watch the life ebb from his body. He understood what was coming even if she denied it. She stroked his face where it met his coarse beard. She took his hand again and held it. Though his grip was weak, she felt him respond to her touch. How few times in these many years had their flesh touched, she thought. How good it felt to cradle his hand in hers.

Pearl watched him carefully. She saw a serene acquiescence in his face. She was comforted that he was at peace, but she did not understand his passive acceptance of death. She knew that one day she would rail against death, hold it back with every ounce of her being. Her faith in eternity was only borrowed.

After a few moments, he was once again racked by a deep and painful cough. She squeezed his hand and offered him more water. When the fit subsided, he opened his eyes and whispered. At first, she did not understand him. She leaned in close. She could smell his breath, sour but sweet to her, and she could feel the warmth of it on her cheek. She remembered again the broth he had given her that first cold night. Tears stung her eyes.

"Take me to the river." He could barely speak, but his words were emphatic. "Take me to the river."

"The river? I don't understand."

"When I die. Take me to the river when I die..."

"No!" she said, repulsed by his blatant acknowledgement of his fate. "You ain't gonna die."

"Yes, Pearl. It's my time." He tried to smile at her, but the urgency of his message pre-empted it. "The river. Put me in the river." Each word spent one more breath of the few he had left. "They'll find me. Downstream. That way…" He paused as pain and breathlessness caught him. "They'll not bother you and the boy. You keep here. In the cabin."

"No." Defiance fogged Pearl's eyes. She clenched her teeth to keep from sobbing. She wanted to scream out a denial and halt this process. Her own breathing was quick and desperate. "No!"

"Yes, Pearl. You must." Through pain, he turned his head and looked up at her. "You must. Please. Take care of our boy."

"No! You're not going to die," she whispered with a desperation that made him grimace. Embracing his gnarled hand in her own, she leaned down and kissed his hand. "You can't leave me. You can't."

When he felt her tears drop on his cheek, he struggled with his own longing to stay with her—with his desire for her that had formed a deep and abiding love. But he was resolved to the greater will of the God he had followed so long. He was silent for a moment. He called her closer and whispered.

"Please, Pearl. Promise me," he said, his face contorting in pain. "Promise me." His voice was little more than a wisp. He was pleading.

Pearl stifled the sobs that welled up in her throat. *He shouldn't have to beg.* Here lay the only person who had been kind to her, the only person other than her mother who had valued her, who had taken in a broken girl and loved her. For a fleeting moment, Pearl understood real love, and in that moment, she could return it as best she could—she could promise.

The Dunkard closed his eyes. She opened hers wide and wiped her face with her hand. She stared down at him, lying before her, tangled in the last throes of living. She wanted to memorize every inch of his face, burn it into her brain. What other way was there to hold onto him?

The Dunkard's instructions were plain, his request genuine. He opened his great gray eyes, now yellowed and weak and sunken yet still full of the kindness he had always offered her. "Please, Pearl. I won't be here. This ol' body—remember? Ashes to ashes…"

"… Dust to dust," she finished.

"Drag me to the river. The current will do the rest."

Pearl put aside her own selfishness and promised. He sank into his bed, relieved. She watched as a peace washed over him like water over the mill's wheel.

As she sat with him, his breathing grew weaker. Outside the cabin, the summer air thrummed, an ordinary day.

The Dunkard had explained to her that she should not be bothered with his earthly body. He would be elsewhere, healthy again and whole and joyful. She should rejoice too, but every part of her rebelled. How could she rejoice? It was a confusing, overwhelming request. How could she possibly rejoice?

As she watched the Dunkard struggle, fractured passages of the scriptures he had read to her swarmed her mind, as if she were hearing them from his lips. *For he that soweth to his flesh shall of the flesh reap corruption; but he that soweth to the Spirit shall of the Spirit reap life everlasting…*

His voice floated through her memory with such vitality that she looked up, but it was her own voice this time, and in her hands, his Bible lay open. She had not realized she had stood and retrieved it.

"We know that we have passed from death unto life because we love the brethren...." She choked back tears as she continued reading to him. "…death hath no more dominion over him." She willed it to be true. At these words the old man stirred, but only his spirit. Fever had overtaken his mind.

The Dunkard died in the late afternoon. Although one part of her expected it, knew it was coming, another part of her was stunned, as if a paralyzing blow had struck her. Numb and struggling to reconcile her grief with her duty, Pearl sat beside his vacant body through the last of the infernal afternoon into evening until the heat of the day abated. Only then did she call Ned.

"He's gone," she told her son. "Bring me a rope."

At dusk, she and Ned tied the old man's feet together and lifted his body from the bed and carried it out of the cabin. A cool breeze wandered off the river; still they both perspired heavily. Already, the scent of death rose from the corpse while above them buzzards circled.

"This is what he wanted," Pearl said. She was answering the question on her son's face. "He told me to do this. I promised him." In her voice was insistence, and with her eyes, she pleaded with her son not to challenge her.

Pearl dug her hands under the Dunkard's limp arms. She was moving only by some inner strength wholly unfamiliar to her. Perhaps this was the grace that the Dunkard had promised her she would find.

"Get his feet, Ned."

It took both mother and son to drag him the few hundred yards downstream past the bend to the broad part of the river. A part of Pearl felt ashamed that she was dishonoring the Dunkard this way, but there was no caisson in the offing, not even the cart sitting next to the shed, which had a broken axle. *He had insisted, hadn't he? And I promised.* In this she took comfort. She moved with obedience and an obligation to gratitude. To him above all others, she owed the honor of keeping her promise. One final promise.

"We should bury him," Ned said, as they approached the river. There was grief and confusion in his voice. "Aren't we going to bury him?"

"No," she said, avoiding her son's gaze. "This is what he wanted. I told you. He had his reasons."

"But we buried the cow," said Ned, his voice strident.

"I don't care what you done with the cow. He said the river. He tol' me, Ned. He tol' me to put him in the river!" Pearl avoided her son's gaze and with supreme effort kept herself from sobbing. "I cain't do less than what he wanted. I cain't!" Her eyes burned.

"But why?" Tears drew jagged lines down Ned's face. He swiped them off with his hand. "Why?"

Pearl didn't answer his question. Explanations would have to wait. "Don't argue. Jus' help me," she said. Her tone was insistent, impatient. He heard anger, but it wasn't anger; it was the deepest kind of conflict a woman knows—to be torn between the desires of two people she loved—to want to please one without hurting the other. But it could not be done.

When they reached the right spot along the riverbank, a spot where the current was swift and the banks smooth, Pearl knelt beside the Dunkard's empty body. She straightened out the worn shirt that dragging him had displaced, covering his cold back. She folded his arms across his chest.

"Go get his Bible, Ned."

Ned ran back to the cabin, eager to flee if only for a moment. He returned, still running, with the Dunkard's holy book clutched in his hand. Pearl took it, opened it, and found the verses—those he had shown her earlier, those he had chosen, those he had marked with the black crow's feather. She read with difficulty, stopping every few words to stanch tears.

"But God be thanked, that ye were the servants of sin, but ye have obeyed from the heart that form of doctrine which was delivered you. Being then made free from sin, ye become the servants of righteousness. I speak after the manner of men because of the infirmity of your flesh; for as ye have yielded your members servants to uncleanness and to iniquity unto iniquity; even so now yield your members servants to righteousness unto holiness. For when ye were the servants of sin, ye were free from righteousness. What fruit had ye then in those things whereof ye are now ashamed? For the end of those is death. But now being made free from sin, and become servants to God, ye have your fruit unto holiness, and the end everlasting life."

She closed the book and laid in on the ground. Mother and son stood beside the Dunkard's body. Flies gathered on it. Buzzards hovered in the sky. Below them, down the steep riverbank, the water flowed with a quiet reverence.

"You pray, Ned."

He looked at his mother. Ned did not know what to say, how to pray over death, how to sanction this ritual he barely understood. But his mother's head was already bowed, and tears dripped from the edge of her clenched jaw. Ned opened his mouth to protest but stopped. He searched for words, thinking hard about what the Dunkard might have said. He stumbled through a prayer. "Bless him, O God Almighty," he began, invoking the salutation he remembered as true. "The Dunkard, he was good—a good man. He was good to us—me and mama. He's coming back to you now. Take him. And help us go on without him. Amen."

This was all Ned knew to say; it would have to do. His voice didn't break, though he spoke quietly as if one more syllable would shatter his vocal cords already stretched tight. He was suspended in that moment of disbelief that swarms around those closest to the deceased. That moment, coming as a kind of cloud that muffles the sound of death and softens its pinch—inasmuch as death can ever be muffled and softened.

Pearl, however, felt no such softness. Every muscle and bone in her body felt the agony of his loss as if her own limbs had been pulled from her.

She knelt and unbound the Dunkard's swollen feet. Together they rolled his limp body down the bank where it slapped the water and sank out of sight. The sound of the splash exploded in Pearl's ears, a concussion she could not bear. She raised her hands to her head in a gesture of alarm and covered her ears, watching. Silently, the current, the Dunkard's funeral barge, would ferry him down river. At that moment, the sun dipped behind the ridge. Darkness devoured the hollow as completely as death had devoured the Dunkard.

Eventually Ned wandered back to the cabin. He was hungry. But Pearl sat by the river in the darkness until moonlight bathed the surface, and she saw again the spot where the Dunkard's lifeless body had disturbed the silt and disappeared beneath the black water. The water seemed to glow. As the river groaned, following the course of a thousand years, the night creatures sang an elegy.

Pearl heard Ned calling her from the cabin. She turned briefly, but she could not leave yet. She felt compelled to linger, as if she were prolonging her duty to her lost friend, to her purest love. It was duty, but it was longing too, and it was regret, sadness—a deep and unrelenting ache she could not shake. She did not want to shake it, for as long as the hurt remained, she was tethered to the Dunkard. She hoped to hurt forever.

Pearl had been born seeking love the way one seeks light out of darkness. Want of it had sculpted her, and lack of it had tainted her like vinegar curdles sweet milk. If she could have created love, held onto it, and stashed it away to have whenever the need arose, it would have blotted out all the dark places in her life, like an inextinguishable flame. But she never found it on her own because no one can conjure love on demand or hold onto it any more securely than one can grasp sunlight. Love cannot be managed like a garden or painted like a portrait—or summoned the way one seeks a friend or shelter from winter. Love is given, stumbled upon, lost—but it is never created. No, never created. Love simply shines on us—or it does not.

And briefly—ever so briefly—love had shone upon Pearl. Through pain and loss and sorrow, she now had some inkling—if only a trace—of the otherworldly love of Heaven. Now it was gone. And Pearl would once more live with the longing, as if a permanent and stubborn shadow had fallen over her life, and no matter how she sought to find her way into the light, she would invariably choose the wrong door or go in the wrong direction. Love would elude her like a precious necklace caught in a branch, dangling just beyond her reach.

Pearl lifted the axe and threw it with all her might into the crease of the log. It split in two, and fell on both sides of the hard, broad stump that the Dunkard had used for decades to chop wood. The moon hung in the sky, a lost coin, lost like every dream she had ever had.

For three days after the Dunkard's death, Pearl had not uttered a word. Her heart and mind were consumed as though she were burning on the inside, like the inside of a hollow log can harbor a smoldering fire for days. Whether sleeping or waking, she could not escape the inferno. Memories consumed her, and the loss of her beloved Dunkard overwhelmed her.

She refused to cry in front of her son, so her tears backed up in her soul—a river dammed—until she was drowning in sadness. Tonight, one by one, she released them with the axe. Through the long, lonely nights that followed the Dunkard's death, while Ned slept, Pearl split the logs beneath the watchful moon—all the logs, until there were few to be cut. In an act of sheer desperation, of fearing the future without the Dunkard, of unbearable grief, Pearl wielded the Dunkard's axe.

The moon sank low in the sky. On the eastern ridge of the hollow a hint of dawn appeared through Jasper's Gap and began to glow. Except for the thud of each axe fall and the rip of the splintering logs, the fading night was quiet and cool, muted by an early frost that would soon bring the deathful summer to a close.

Pearl tossed the axe against the stump and collapsed nearby, sobbing.

By the fourth day, she had recovered enough from her shock and grief to speak to her son. His presence and his need of her soon became a welcome balm, a distraction. Still, her days stretched out long and lonely without the Dunkard's companionship. The void that his absence created was far deeper and wider than she had ever imagined it could be. She struggled through each day's chores—harvesting, preparing food, eating—with rote effort. The Dunkard's shadow followed her everywhere. In the blackness of the nights, she wondered what would become of her and her son without his company, his guidance, his protection. This worry compounded her grief. What would happen to them now? She had no source of income, no connection to the world beyond the Dunkard's cabin, no knowledge of the gristmill. How would they survive? Ned knew the gristmill, but he was too young to run it. Who would fell the trees to dry and split for heat during the coming winter? Had she put away enough food?

In the days and weeks that followed, what little joy Pearl could muster from her shattered heart, she offered to Ned. She tried to absorb all the pain to spare her son the death and separation of the Dunkard.

# September

Three boys with long poles walked along the riverbank at the north end of the hollow outside of Galilee. They were heading to a spot where the river curved and began a slow meander around the town. The boys, not more than ten, were suntanned and barefooted. They wore rolled-up overalls with straps that crisscrossed bare freckled shoulders. Fishing poles were slung back like rifles. Chatty and carefree, they laughed as they walked. One carried a creel basket filled with three smallmouth bass and one brown trout no bigger than a fist. They had fished all morning and now they were heading to the curve of the river to test their balance on logs and debris that washed in and collected.

"Come on," said one. "Race ya."

They dropped their poles in the grass and ran. Reaching the riverbank, they slid on their backsides down toward the water, using their heels and hands as brakes. Brush, half-submerged logs, and trash littered the water, along with broken tree branches, frayed ropes, and discarded boards, all rocking casually back and forth. Many times, in the tangled debris, the boys had found dead beavers or raccoons to poke, or a large, rotting carp floating belly up, festering in the sun—the kinds of things that boys like to discover.

The tallest boy, balancing on the back of a large oak log, yelled, "What's that?" He pointed to something white lodged against a log and half-covered with brush.

"Possum's belly, I bet," the boys on the bank guessed. "Gotta be a possum."

The tall boy leaned toward it and kept his balance with a branch sticking up out of the log. "Ain't a possum. It's too big. Get a stick."

Another boy scurried up the bank and dragged back a branch some two yards long, long enough to reach whatever it was they had found.

"Hand it here—and ya'll hold onto me," said the tall boy as he leaned out over the water. Two smaller boys grabbed the straps of his overalls and planted their heels in the mud, water swarming around their ankles. Their discovery looked like a downed sycamore tree at first but as they got closer, it resembled a huge, waterlogged mud cat bleached by the sun.

The tall boy snagged it with the branch and pulled it closer.

"It's a body!" he yelped. A body, floating face down, stripped naked and pummeled by the rapids upstream. The boy with the stick dropped it and fell backwards, scrambling back across the log. Spooked, the boys bolted up the riverbank, yelling as they headed into town, leaving their poles, fish, and courage behind.

Shortly, two burly men, alerted by the boys' wild tale, waded into the water to pull the body from the river while another walked back to summon the undertaker. Huddled on the bank above, the boys watched. One turned and vomited. The others, shaken, were silent.

"Who you 'spose it be?" one man said, as they lugged the waterlogged body up the bank and hauled in onto the back of a wagon. "Cain't tell much. Been in the water right long. Too long. Don't really look human no more."

Because of the length of the beard, they speculated it might be the old Dunkard. There was little else to identify the doughy mass of waterlogged flesh. They covered the body with a tarp and hauled it back to town without ceremony, the way they might carry logs or sacks of grain. The boys regained their courage—their curiosity overtaking them—but they were sent home, protesting mightily.

It was the Dunkard. And this was exactly what he had hoped for, what he had prayed for—his one final entreaty to his Heavenly Father before he met him face-to-face. Pearl and her son would be safe and sheltered in his cabin, unburdened by his earthly body—and hidden away. If Pearl could get him to the river, the Dunkard had known the current would take his remains downstream to where the river curved and fallen logs and trash accumulated. They would find him there. They would surmise that the Dunkard had died, fallen into the river, and floated down into the world he had long avoided, an empty remnant of his earthly life. Surely some compassionate citizen would take his remains and bury them in the potter's cemetery, which suited him all right. Or if they mistakenly burned him along with the river's debris, an annual chore, that was no matter either. One way or another—ashes to ashes and dust to dust.

And indeed, the Dunkard's demise at the hands of age and the river was thus presumed by the locals. There was no kin to notify.

Early the next morning, just after dawn, Elijah Felts, a lanky, leathery-skinned man with a shovel and pickax slung over his shoulder, ambled up to the church cemetery heading to a line of plots designated for the poor and destitute. Backed up against the western periphery, the plots ran along the front of a scraggly field fence that delineated the church property from the surrounding farm fields. Paupers' graves, each one neatly, efficiently, and anonymously tucked away, were marked with large river rocks, one at the head, one at the toe. A handful of the stones had names scratched along the smooth surfaces, but most had none. The stones represented what the Bible called "the least of these," which made the final rest for the unremembereds the responsibility of the church.

After the Dunkard's body was found, the undertaker had made the arrangements. He had done this before, often, usually for passersby whom no one knew and who met their ends near and around the town. It was a civic duty, this ritual nod to death and resurrection.

The gravedigger opened the earth with one hard thrust of his boot heel on the shovel. Over the next few hours, he dug a hole deep enough and long enough, but no deeper or longer than necessary. Six by three by six. When finished, he leaned his tools up against a tree and lay down in the grass, tipping his hat over his eyes, and he waited. Sometime after midmorning, before the full heat of the day arrived, the undertaker, driving a horse and cart borrowed from a local business, delivered the body.

"Who we be burying today, Mr. Pratt?" the gravedigger asked.

"We're thinkin' it's the old Dunkard. Hard to tell, Elijah. But that's what we're thinkin'. Boys found him in the river, down where all the trash collects."

"I bet them boys was surprised."

The undertaker chuckled. "Sure was. One of 'em was so spooked he asked his mama if he could sleep in her bedroom that night. She tol' him she wadn't having none of that nonsense—but he was so shook up, she had to give in an' let him."

The undertaker took off his coat and tossed it over the side of the wagon. "Come on, Elijah. Gimme a hand."

Together, the undertaker and the gravedigger lifted the body out of the open cart and carried it to the grave. The body was wrapped in a makeshift shroud, a piece of discarded canvas from a torn awning that had blown off the local hardware store in a windstorm, and it was tied up with bailing twine.

Straddling the freshly dug grave, the two men dangled the body over the hole and dropped it in with little ceremony. It landed with a thud. Clods of fresh dirt and pebbles rained down on the canvas. The undertaker brushed off his hands.

"I'll go git the reverend," he said to Elijah.

The undertaker walked to the tall, white clapboard manse—a companion to the tall, white, clapboard church that shadowed the cemetery. He knocked. Folding his arms, he did a half turn and stared out toward the road as he waited.

"Sorry to interrupt you, Reverend," the undertaker said when the preacher came to the door wiping his mouth on a napkin. In the middle of work on his Sunday sermon, he was finishing a late breakfast. "We're ready fer ya."

"Be right with you, Mr. Pratt. Let me get my coat."

The preacher lifted his Bible from his desk, rolled down his shirtsleeves, and slid his coat on over his waistcoat before he walked out to the cemetery where he joined the undertaker and the gravedigger. The three men had gathered here many times at this eternal precipice for this same purpose.

As the reverend opened his Bible and began to read a passage, a breeze swept in, rustled the pages, and lifted his words onto the wind, carrying them away. High above their heads, leaves waved, but otherwise the world took little notice of this passing. After a few minutes, he closed the book and bowed his head to pray.

"Heavenly Father…" he began.

The sun was shining bright, the day warming. A trace of honeysuckle lingered in the crisp fall air. The three men stood respectfully, each with his hands clasped behind his back and his head bowed. It was the end of a quiet life. No one knew the departed well enough to offer more than generic sympathies. It was an oft-repeated recitation, a civil ceremony with little other import than ritual. What mattered had come before, in the Dunkard's cabin, and remained there, hidden by design.

"…Amen," the reverend said.

"Amen," the others affirmed, in unison.

"Thank you, Mr. Pratt," the preacher said to the undertaker as he shook the man's hand. The reverend walked back to the manse to continue working on his sermon. The undertaker handed the gravedigger a small payment. "Thank ya, Elijah." The undertaker left in the empty cart.

With the heel of his boot, the gravedigger again drove the shovel deep into the pile of dirt and stones. He began to fill the grave. The finer dirt poured down like sugar and nestled around the Dunkard's remains; larger clods hit with thuds until there was nothing to see but dirt. When the gravedigger finished his job, leaving a mound of grassless dirt that rains would flatten and weeds and grass would cover, he collected his tools—the pickax and the shovel—and he left as he had arrived, walking with his tools slung over his shoulder.

He was whistling.

# October

nside the cabin, Pearl dumped a chopped onion into a stew of beans and potatoes. On the table, a loaf of bread rested, and the smell of yeast filled the cabin. Ned, sitting near the hearth whittling, noticed the aroma. His stomach growled. Pearl did not notice the aroma or much else. After a heavy freeze, autumn had rushed in as a strange suitor bearing color, but this year, the season brought her little joy. While she stirred the pot, her eyes wandered to the open door, to the river, to the current that had carried the Dunkard away. More than a month had passed, but still she suffered from the hope that follows death—an incongruous, illogical hope that death is only a mirage. At night she dreamt of the Dunkard, and she expected him to walk through the cabin door and sit down at the table to peel an apple or a peach, to break bread with her, to talk to her.

As the Dunkard had predicted, no one bothered Pearl and Ned. No one knew that they had been abandoned by his death. The mother and son would have to survive on her wits and skills now, sheltered by the Dunkard's cabin, his gift of anonymity, and by the fervent memory of his spirit.

Through each successive day of that autumn, Pearl existed as if she were only flesh and bone, a body bereft of spirit, as if her soul had drowned in the river when she had watched the Dunkard's lifeless body submerge and slip away from her. Loneliness possessed her and swept through her everyday tasks. Coveting her grief, she hovered somewhere along the edge of living, a body out of mind, clinging to her pain as the last bond to her Dunkard.

Gradually, Pearl sank into routine, and just as gradually, the pain began to fade, though it would never fully leave her. She longed for the Dunkard's companionship, for their shared conversations, for his words to meet her lonely ears, and for his smile, so fresh in her mind. She desired him the way a parched throat obligates water. She did not understand the depth of her grief any more than she understood the autonomics of rising, moving, and working that ferried her through each day. Her bones ached. She found it difficult to meet her son's eyes or his half-spoken questions, which she often answered with her hand clasped across her mouth—and sometimes his.

Perhaps it was all a horrible dream. She wished it were so—a nightmare from which she could awake to find her friend, her protector, the one who had loved her, restored to her. Alive again. Perhaps she would look up from her task one morning to see him emerge from the woods once more, to watch him stride across the yard to meet her. Perhaps. It was his presence she missed, but his presence had lingered with her, too. It was as if they were trapped together yet separated by a strange and impassable fog.

Pearl added a pinch of salt to the stew and continued to stir. Ned looked up, eager for his supper.

"Is it almost ready?" he asked. "I'm hungry as a bear, Mama."

Pearl continued stirring.

The Dunkard's bed lay empty but carefully made. Pearl had no desire to dispose of any of the relics of his life, nor erase any of its markers. His coat still hung by the door. His boots still sat by his bed. His Bible remained on the table. She drew closer to these objects as she drew closer to death, made a friend of death. Keeping all his earthly things close was all she could do. When Ned had asked if he could take the Dunkard's bed, she had snapped at him. He had intruded in some inner sanctum, stolen a private wish, as if he were proposing to replace the Dunkard, which he could not. Pearl had found it impossible to dispose of even the simplest object the Dunkard had touched; how could she possibly violate his bed?

While Pearl leaned down at the hearth mindlessly stirring the stew, conversations with the Dunkard returned to her, a private reverie and a private longing. She remembered so well their discussions about meat, how he had read to her from the Bible, how she had turned the text around to read to him, how she had flipped to passages she knew—passages that would bolster her own viewpoint. How they had talked and laughed and argued.

But it was a discussion no more, only the echo of conversation. And sometimes, it deafened her...

*It is not right to kill any living thing, Pearl.*

*Well, then why'd God have give us all this—everything in the forest? To go to waste? Cain't jus' go to waste.*

*But I use the forest's bounty—and the land's. This is how I live, off this land.*

*But don't the Bible tell you to subdue the land? Don't it? And take dominion over every livin' thing. That's what it says.*

*Subdue does not mean to kill. We are commanded not to kill. Remember Deuteronomy 5:17. Thou shalt not kill.*

*But killin' a deer ain't like killin' a man. Isaac told Esau to go hunt. Now, didn't he?*

*Perhaps Isaac was wrong. Isaac wasn't God, but God said, 'Thou shalt not kill'....*

"Mama?" It was Ned, disturbing Pearl's reverie. The mother looked over at her son, but she didn't see him. She only heard the interruption, a sound that made no sense, a disembodied voice that she would ignore if she could. Ned recognized her absent gaze and knew her mind was on the Dunkard. It hurt him to see her pain. He wondered if she would ever be right again.

Ned stood up, resigned. "I'll bring in some water," he said.

Pearl continued to stir, turning the spoon, slowly circumnavigating the pot.

The boy slipped out of the cabin, away from the pall of his mother's loneliness and grief. Ned, a tender youth, tried to understand as best he could for one so young, and he filled in where his mother in her anguish left life alone.

After the Dunkard's body had been buried, it was the general consensus that he was indeed the one found in the river. His absence from the mill was further confirmation. A young farmer named Malcolm McCleary proposed to take over the gristmill. The community welcomed his enterprise; it would keep their cornmeal and flour and cracked rye coming. Malcolm was welcome to have it.

# December

Winter started gently and with it came a short but energizing Indian summer. It lasted barely a week, but it infused Pearl with some strength, some measure of reason and calm that began to flow back into her with the warm winter sun. It allowed her to breathe deeply and take stock of her life. Though fleeting, it prompted Pearl to prepare for the coming winter, the first winter without the Dunkard's care.

With Ned's help, she carried logs onto the porch and stored corn and apples in bins, covering them with pine straw and dry leaves. At his mother's direction, Ned gathered twigs for kindling in a bushel basket. He stacked some near the hearth and put the rest, covered with a piece of canvas, beside the logs on the porch.

One morning, after Ned had been gone from the cabin for several hours, Pearl stepped out into the sunshine and called for him.

"Ned. Come on back. I need ya to help me."

From a distance, she heard him answer. Shortly, he appeared through the trees.

"Mama, come see!" he said.

"Whadya say?" She cupped her hand to her ear.

"I made something." With a broad stroke of his arm, he motioned for his mother to come.

Pearl stepped off the porch and followed him to the edge of the river.

Ned was holding a rope with a bucket tied on the end.

"Watch this," he said. He leaned over the riverbank and threw the bucket across a large branch that overhung the river. Holding the rope, he lowered the bucket into the river and then pulled it up full of water. Walking back several feet, holding the rope, he hooked the other end of the rope where he had made a loop over a small stump.

"Now watch," he said, beaming. Taking a crooked stick, he snagged the rope above the bucket and pulled it back until he could reach it. "This winter if we need extra water—if the barrel runs dry or freezes—we won't need to go all the way down to the shallow part. And we won't have to worry with pullin' in gritty water."

"What if the river's frozen?"

"Thought of that," he said. "Look over there." He pointed to a large pile of river rocks that he had hauled up from the river's edge. "I'll take one of them rocks and heave it over to break the ice. Might take two, but all I need's one hole, and I got water for us."

"That's downright clever, son."

They stood for a moment looking at Ned's invention. The sun was warm and sparkled across the river.

"He'd a been proud of me. I'm gonna take care of you, Mama."

Pearl teared up as she rubbed her son's shoulder.

# 1881

## THE WINTER IS BLEAK

# January

Winter came with a vengeance. Pearl knelt near the hearth washing clothes in a bucket of water warmed over the fire. She rubbed each garment against the washboard and hung it on a makeshift clothesline strung along the cabin wall. Small droplets of water stained the bare wood floor but evaporated almost as quickly as they appeared.

Dry, brittle cold had settled into the hollow, and for weeks on end the sky remained gray and overcast. Everything took on the look of hard slate, a devilish lack of color and an absence of movement that harmonized with Pearl's lingering pain. Winter had been waiting for her, baiting her, toying with her mood—a confusing brew of sadness and anger. It had been a half year since the Dunkard had left her, abandoned her, but she refused to blame him. She directed her anger elsewhere.

For weeks the Dunkard's Bible lay untouched on the table, collecting dust, until she had moved it to a high shelf and left it there. She had no need for it anymore, other than as reading lessons for Ned, who by now was wholly competent. She wished for other books, but there were none. The minister's wife who had been so generous with Pearl believed in the power of education to lift one up—a sentiment opposite to what Pearl's illiterate father thought. He had scoffed at education. But the minister's wife, duty bound, had never shunned an opportunity to do good, even to those of lesser means like Pearl and her mother. Education was a fundamental good, as fundamental as her theology.

Pearl learned to read with the borrowed books—careful to keep them out of sight from her father. The books had prompted dreams that lingered long enough to charm Pearl, but her dreams had gradually faded like desert caravans disappearing into the horizon. When her mother died, the books and the dreams had vanished altogether.

Pearl wrung out a shirt like she was strangling a chicken and then shook it out.

At the table, sitting hunched over, Ned examined the parts of a broken watch spread out on a piece of cloth: tiny clicks and barrels, miniature screws and jewels, elfin bridges, and stems. He had found the watch in a trash heap deep in the woods. Determined to understand how this time-piece worked, he pored over it the way an archeologist examines specimens. In another time, another place, Ned might have made a fine engineer.

In another time. In another place.

"Son, I need more water," Pearl said. Her bucket was nearly empty, and the tenor of her voice was the same.

The boy looked up. He was annoyed to be interrupted but stood without a word of complaint and collected a bucket near the door. He went out on the porch to the barrel and slid aside the wooden top. He reached down as far as he could, but instead of cold water, he hit thick ice. Pearl heard the clunk. She dried her hands. Grabbing the Dunkard's coat, she went to the porch.

"You stay here," she said, throwing the coat around her shoulders. "Go on back inside."

"I kin go, Mama."

"No, Ned. I'll go."

Pearl nearly ran from the cabin, heading to the river, taking deep breaths, and letting the gauntlet of cold assault her. As she passed by the shed, she stopped, put the coat on fully, and collected a second bucket.

She stood on the riverbank. Her breath materialized on the cold air. The sky, backlit by a dull sun, was striped with lines of bunched clouds. *Snow clouds.* The words were the Dunkard's. They echoed out of her memory and jarred her. *Snow clouds.* He had understood the signs of the heavens the way he had understood the continuation of life after death.

"Snow clouds," Pearl said with equal measures of confidence and fear. She looked across the glassy river that mirrored the striated sky. From a distance, it looked like a still pond, not a mighty river, but the closer she stepped, the louder its familiar rush grew.

She dropped the buckets and walked along the riverbank to the place she had last seen the Dunkard. Little had changed except the season. She stood where she had watched his body submerge. For Pearl this was the same as visiting his grave. Beyond this spot, she could only speculate on the fate of his remains.

A sudden wind gusted and interrupted her meditation. She felt the cold anew and remembered why she had come. Stepping away from the bank, she walked back and picked up the buckets. She grabbed the rope on Ned's invention and quickly filled both buckets with water. As she left the river, Pearl spotted an owl asleep in a sycamore. His gray silhouette was sharp against the white-mottled bark and against the snow sky. Her heart stirred.

That evening snow came. The calm of the day was replaced with wind and blinding snow that blew through the hollow, rattled the windows, shook the door, and felt to Pearl as though it were threatening to take the roof. She and Ned huddled near the hearth. The cabin was smoky from the horizontal wind that sheered across the chimney and prevented it from drafting properly. She felt Ned quiver.

"Ned, you'll be warm in his bed. Go on. You go on and go to sleep."

Ned looked at her incredulously, remembering her earlier scolding. He didn't think he had heard right.

"It's all right, Ned." For the first time in months, Pearl's heart began to thaw. She smiled at her son. "He'd want you to be warm. I'll tend the fire. You go on."

Ned jumped up, and soon he was sound asleep in the place where the Dunkard had lived and died. Pearl sat up late into the night, stoking the fire every hour. She and Ned had brought in plenty of wood so they would not have to open the door. This is what the Dunkard would have done, and this small act brought Pearl a sense of fulfillment. He would have approved. Hadn't he said for her to go on, to live here, to raise Ned? Yes, he would approve. Maybe he was looking down on her now. The thought comforted her, encouraged her to continue the fight that was life. *This is what he wanted—for us to go on.* The thought gave her hope. And on this hope she had prepared for the coming storm. She focused on it, this immediate need, and in a kind of blessing, she did not think much beyond the night that held them.

While Ned slept that night and snow fell, life began to flow once again into Pearl as surely as the warmth of the fire seeped into her pores. The cabin felt cocoon-like as she listened to her son's even, rhythmic breathing in the same way she had listened to the Dunkard's breathing that first night she had come to the cabin. Pearl was re-emerging, finally shedding her grief. She knew she must for Ned's sake.

She lifted the poker—formed by the hands of the one she had loved, who had loved her. She wrapped her fingers around the grooves that his hands had gripped, that those strong hands had made. Thrusting the poker into the fire, she turned a log. Sparks crackled, and one fresh log spewed and sputtered against the grate. The smell of the burning wood was comforting. As she watched the sparks dance and fly, her eyes lost focus as she stared into the fire.

By the time the storm subsided, and the wind died away, it was near dawn. The cabin was newly insulated with snowdrifts, making it warm, even cozy. Pearl finally lay down to sleep. She dreamed of the night Ned was born and how the Dunkard had helped her.

# March

A sweet breeze perfumed with emerging leaves caught Pearl as the sun rose above the ridge. The sun's heat on her cheek warmed her winter-weary bones. Standing on the stoop, she pulled her shawl around her shoulders. She had repaired the shawl in places, but washed and worn hundreds of times, it was wearing thin. Throughout the woods, redbuds blushed, and the stark white blossoms of wild cherry trees punctuated the perpetual greens of scrub cedars and white pines. Along the riverbank, pale grasses and nascent leaves half-submerged in tangled brambles begged to erase the brown winter landscape. The greening was early this year—and more welcome than in any year Pearl had spent there. Together, she and Ned had fended off the winter that threatened to snatch them, the same way the summer had stolen the Dunkard. She had survived the blue winter, although she had hovered on the edge of despair through much of it. Now, these first hints of a curative spring cheered her.

While Ned slept, Pearl drank in the sun. Her breath hovered in the air before it evaporated, as if it also realized that winter was retreating, giving way to the coming raucous spring. Nourished in part by the stores that she, Ned, and the Dunkard had put away during the Dunkard's final season, she had conquered the long, dark winter—and as the pain of childbirth had disappeared, the drear winter felt far away this morning. Pearl felt strangely happy. She glanced back inside the quiet cabin. She would go for a walk while Ned slept. She tied her shawl around her shoulders and slipped away from the cabin.

Winter had ravaged their garden, stripped it of every ounce of nutrient the Dunkard had grown. She noticed this as she passed by the neat but empty rows she and Ned had picked clean. Strangely, however, Pearl had little memory of doing so. It was as if the bitter winter with its cleansing cold had erased the memories. Only occasionally now did the pain of the Dunkard's death sting her. But when it did, it was unexpected, a sudden piercing pain—interrupting the chronic ache, now a permanent part of her life.

Beneath the collapsed limbs of bean plants and corn stalks, Pearl spotted tiny green sprouts. They were a curiosity—and a sudden, unexpected inspiration: she would need new seeds. This must be one of her first duties. It must be. For the first time in months, she felt a twinge of purpose beyond the quotidian. But how could she find seeds? Instinctively, she turned and looked toward the shed where she—as the Dunkard before her—had spread out some seeds to dry, collected them, and stored them away in the cellar. But they wouldn't be enough. She would need new seeds, too.

Pearl had not left the Dunkard's homestead since finding it a decade before. It had always been the Dunkard, not her, who ventured into town on the rare occasions when they needed something other than what they could produce for themselves. Carrying a few coins that he kept in a wooden box, the Dunkard had walked to town early every spring and returned with new seeds for the garden, a few onion sets, some seed potatoes. At his suggestion, Pearl had always stayed behind.

"It is wise," he had told her when she finally and tearfully confessed to him some of what she had suffered at her father's hand. His reaction had been visceral, and then protective.

Pearl looked down at the garden's tiny sprigs of green. What would she need? *Corn. And beans. Potatoes and onion sets. Turnips and parsnips. How can I get 'em?* She considered this dilemma for a moment but decided she would think about it later. For now, she would enjoy a walk. She noted the sun and calculated how far she could venture before Ned awoke.

The forest, still harboring the winter's cold grudge, was brilliantly crisp and clean in the early light—almost iridescent. Washed by snows and winds and chill antiseptic rains, it felt new, renewed. The birds had returned with their full-throated songs. Above her, Pearl heard them trill and chirp.

Wandering aimlessly without a destination, she found herself near the gristmill, walking the same path the Dunkard had walked. She climbed to the top of a small rise that overlooked it. The mill sat near a millpond along the edge of a narrow stretch of the river where the current was strong. The sight of it made her sad, a sudden intrusion of heartache and longing. Pearl had hardly thought of the place during the intervening winter, while she had marshaled all her strength to survive both winter and grief. She had never wondered about the gristmill's fate. The Dunkard had never mentioned its future, and Ned was too young to take it over.

From her vantage, she saw two men working. The runner stone on the mill was turning with small clouds of dust hovering around it. The mill-race was full and running freely. The men's voices curled above the sound of the mill and through the forest's half-bare branches, but she could not distinguish their words—an absence that made her yearn for conversation, for human connection. She strained to hear, but she only caught a few disembodied words and a few bursts of laughter. In that moment, the loneliness of the winter and her isolation captured her, and her desperate ache for the Dunkard overwhelmed her. She was torn between worlds; her secret world of survival and the enticing but painful world she had once known—that world she had fled. It had been almost nine years. She was curious about the world she had traded for life with the Dunkard, and she was struck with a desire—a strange and conflicting yearning—to climb down the knoll, to go to the gristmill, to enter the human assembly. But she didn't dare.

Rightly she feared what reaction these men might have if they were to see a woman alone in the woods. She looked down at her worn dress. She ran her hands across her cheeks and through her unruly tangle of hair.

As she watched them, something awakened in Pearl—an unexpected and potent desire for companionship. It lured her. The ripening spring no longer soothed her. She was arrested by an illicit thought—one she had not felt throughout all the years and months and days that she had been with the Dunkard. A desire for human contact overpowered her, excited her. Frightened her.

Pearl ran back to the cabin. As she returned and passed back by the garden, she knew. Seeds. She must have new seeds, and she must have them soon.

# April

Pearl slipped through the door of Pulaski's Hardware, avoiding the customers who were gathered around the front counter. It had taken her half a morning to walk out of the hollow, to retrace the path she had taken nine years before. But for this trip, the sky was clear and inviting, the trek invigorating. With her hair tied back and a handful of coins in her skirt pocket, coins left by the Dunkard, she felt daring.

The hardware was more crowded than she had remembered. Her hands were clammy and a deep thudding in her chest kept every sense alert, cautious, on guard. Her mind bounced between fear and excitement. She moved toward the rear of the store, pretending to be absorbed in the pursuit of some ware to avoid casual conversation. How brave—how brazen—to be here, to have returned to the town she had fled. She lifted a contraption that she had never seen before. It had beaters and gears and a small green handle. She turned the handle. The beaters turned. She was curious, but curiosity could wait. Today she had a different purpose.

Standing with her back toward the other shoppers, she kept her head covered with her shawl. Her plan was to bolt if anyone recognized her. She struggled to stifle her greatest fear—that her father should appear.

But the risk was worth taking. Pearl was weary of her solitary life, and she had decided that her needs—and Ned's—required breaching her isolation. Increasingly, she had relived conversations with the Dunkard, as if he were still with her, but they no longer satisfied her. The memory of the Dunkard's voice was fading, and she had grown tired of imagining, tired of living in her mind and not in her body. She craved more. She craved something real that would touch her ear, perhaps her cheek. The encounter near the gristmill had triggered this craving, and though fear had initially stopped her, desire and loneliness had finally pushed her to take this chance.

Now she had done it. She had left the hollow.

"Hep ya, ma'am?" A man's voice startled her. Mr. Pulaski had slipped up behind her.

"Oh, no," she said, reacting more fearfully than she intended. "No, but thank ya," she said, smoother this time.

"Well, you jus' holler if you need 'nything, ma'am," he said. "I'm right here to hep ya."

As she pretended to inspect a set of nested measuring spoons tied together with a piece of red cord, Mr. Pulaski examined her closely. She felt his gaze on her back. To her relief, though, he displayed no hint of recognition, only the curiosity any stranger evokes in a small town.

"Yoo hoo. Mr. Pulaski." A woman's voice chimed along with a little bell on a flange above the door as she entered.

"Be right with ya, Mizz Horton," he answered, heading back toward the front counter.

Pearl picked up a maple rolling pin and rubbed her hand along its smooth surface. She remembered coming here as a girl with her brothers. Little had changed. Chatty, friendly customers still swarmed the counter in front of shelves bowed with stacks of sundries. A sooty potbelly stove, smelling of damp coal, was still anchored at the center of the room with its stovepipe that angled off toward a sidewall. Voices drifted through the store like melodies. Pearl listened.

"You got any new silk thread?"

"Right over there, Mizz Horton. Down there beside that row of liniment. Ya see it?"

"Whatcha got for gout?" A man's voice.

"Try this, Mr. Cole. Rub this on your foot. It oughta cure you in no time."

"I'm gonna hold you to that, Mr. Pulaski. I gotta get this cleared up and get back out to my fields. All this settin' around don't get my fields plowed. I gotta get to work."

A simple truth began to dawn on Pearl as she looked over a line of bins filled with seeds. *No one knows me anymore*. No one seemed to recognize the shy and disregarded daughter of the livery owner. She was no longer the child who had been left behind by circumstance to care for a father who treated her with less respect than the horses he housed—and with less interest than the cronies he drank and gambled with in the back of the livery.

As she passed a shelf lined with shiny metal boxes, she caught a glimpse of her own face. Shocked at first, she stared at her appearance. Even in the distorted view, she saw looking back at her a thin, gaunt woman with uncut hair tied at her neck like a horse's tail, its color, dull brown. It was no longer the shiny auburn mane that had cascaded across her shoulders a decade ago. In a split second, she blew threw a book of emotions: shock, sadness, fear, despair, disappointment, wonderment, disbelief. She looked away and closed her eyes briefly. But in that moment, a sudden freedom washed over her; surprise turned to revelation. In the intervening years, Pearl had born a son and grown thin from work and a limited diet. Sun and work had lightened her hair and darkened her skin. When she opened her eyes again, she was settled. She could use this change to her full advantage—move around the town—invent whatever story she fancied to explain her life.

She could leave her past behind.

But in the same split second, an unwanted afterthought intruded like a bully's taunt. She wondered if the mistakes and misfortunes that had driven her into the forest long ago would eventually catch her again. Pearl raised her chin and stared back at her changed face. She would not let it! She had come for seeds.

Only seeds.

She swallowed hard, avowing her resolve. Only seeds.

She lifted several small paper sacks. Choosing bean, squash, and corn seeds, and a half dozen potato and onion sets, she filled the bags and carried them to the counter.

"That'll be forty-two cents, ma'am," Mr. Pulaski said, after he lifted the bags off the scale on the counter. She counted out the amount from the handful of coins she had taken from the box. Privately, she blessed the

Dunkard. He was still taking care of her.

"You new to town?" Mr. Pulaski asked.

She kept her face lowered. "Yes, sir. New." Had she looked up at the man full faced, she would have seen a friendly smile.

Pearl took her purchase and hurried out of the store, leaving with a sudden exhale and a nearly imperceptible smile. Emboldened by this success, she was struck with a curiosity to touch the past, the way a child is tempted to touch a candle flame.

She turned toward the center of town, toward the livery, her father's livery. She stayed close to the buildings and huddled into herself whenever a stranger passed. Rounding the corner at the Presbyterian Church, she looked down the street toward the building that had housed her father's livelihood. Her pulse quickened as her curiosity pushed her like a dare. *Would he know me?* She wanted neither contact nor confrontation. She only wanted to peek into her past, to see if it had changed as much as she had changed.

The livery doors were shut, and as she stole closer, she could see that a two-by-four was nailed across the heavy doors. *Strange*, she thought.

She slipped into the alley that ran next to the building and peered in through a broken window. The livery was empty. Cold flowed out of the broken pane on dank, sour air. Pearl shuddered. She went around to the back of the building and noticed the rear door gaped open on rusted hinges. Her father had always kept it closed with a wooden latch thrown from inside, but the latch, rotted through, hung useless. As if drawn unwittingly by her past, Pearl stepped inside.

The cavernous livery was dark and cooler than the alley. It smelled of dirt and horses, of hay and manure. Sunlight pierced through cracks in the weathered boards and played off empty stalls. The livery had been stripped of every carriage and wagon that her father had lent or repaired, and no horses waited to be harnessed. Only some broken wheels, and a few broken leads and hanes lay about, discarded. No whole carriages stood, and no saddles or bridles hung where they once had. She expected to hear a snort or the padding of hooves, but everything was quiet, except for swallows darting back and forth overhead in the rafters.

"You lookin' for somebody?" A stocky man with a saddle slung over his shoulder had stepped to the door. "I seen you go in."

Pearl was rattled. Forgetting her newfound confidence, she didn't answer.

"If you're lookin' for somebody, you're out of luck, ma'am," he said politely.

"Where's the owner?" she asked in a tremulous voice.

"Ol' man Goff?"

Pearl held her breath, determined not to react.

"Oh, he's long gone. They hung him after he kilt that boy."

*Killed. Killed a boy.* Pearl's mind reeled. She battled to hold onto her composure. "That so," she said, her voice as controlled as she could manage. "When was that?"

"Some time ago. I 'spect it's been more'n a half-dozen years. Yep, they strung him up right out there in front," he said, pointing toward the street.

Pearl's insides went dead cold. Images from her past hit her like shards of a broken mirror. She knotted her fists and paused before she managed to speak again. "That so."

"Yessum. Buildin's been vacant ever since. Ain't nobody—not even his son's—got the want to open it no more. Too much bad went on in here. Ol' man Goff was a mean man."

He shifted the saddle to his other shoulder. "Well, ma'am, if you be needin' you a horse or a wagon, you go see Mr. Pulaski over at the hardware," he said as he left. "He knows a man. He'll hep you."

"Thank ya."

"Good day, ma'am." He tipped his hat and was gone.

Pearl stood frozen for a long time, letting the cool air and the sudden knowledge sink into her. The news threatened to suffocate her as she tried to piece it all together. She wanted to run back to the Dunkard's cabin, to be safe, to not know.

Bright moonlight slid along the cabin floor. Pearl, sleepless, tossed and turned in her bed. Finally, she gave up and slipped out of the cabin. It was a warm night, the kind that bathed her in rising dew. It felt good on her skin, as did the ground, cool beneath her bare feet. She walked to the river and sat down, pulling her nightgown over her knees. She rested her chin on her crossed arms.

"He's dead. Dead," she whispered to the night in an effort to understand. "They're both dead." She could not reconcile her immense sadness with her sense of relief. It made no sense. She was finally free of her father's threat. But she also knew—she knew as surely as she knew the Dunkard was gone—that the boy her father had killed was her dark-eyed boy. But why? Had he had some affection for her, after all? Or had he been so angry at her that he—her dark-eyed boy—became the focus of his rage?

She thought she should weep, but she had no emotion left for the boy or for her father.

The dark-eyed boy had promised to take her away, away from her cruel father.

"But you cain't tell nobody," he had said, as he stroked her body. "You understand? Nobody."

She had promised. And he had promised to take her away. It was their secret pledge.

But her dark-eyed boy had not rescued her. Instead, when he learned she was carrying his child, he disappeared. She remembered the shock and fear in his eyes when she told him. Still, she convinced herself that he would come around, gather his senses, and take her away. Of course, he would—because he loved her. Hadn't he told her so over and over? Hadn't he promised? She had hung on that hope and honored her promise to him not to tell anyone about him. In the weeks that followed, though, as she waited for the dark-eyed boy to return, she grew despondent.

Sitting by the river, her body went cold as she remembered. Wondering why he had abandoned her when all she had wanted was to love him and be loved. He had confessed love, but it was animal love. She knew this now because she had found genuine and selfless love with the Dunkard, love never consummated but pure. Maybe it was best that it had not been tainted in that way.

In time, no promise could conceal what the dark-eyed boy had done to her. Her father, enraged, had tied her hands to the side of a horse stall and beat her with a wooden stirrup and whipped her with a bridle. Even tonight, far away in time and space, she flinched.

Pearl had been a fool. She had pleaded for mercy, but instead of mercy, she had condemned the dark-eyed boy. She had never meant to say his name, but it was beaten out of her. Now he was dead. They were all dead. The dark-eyed boy. Her father. Her mother. The Dunkard.

Only she and Ned were left.

Pearl stood up and brushed grass from her nightgown. For the first time in her life, she was free. She could finally let go of her past, all its fears and hurts. She could live again.

Pearl decided. She would not be Pearl any longer. She would be someone new.

# May

Pearl walked into Pulaski's. This time her face and her head were uncovered, daring anyone to recognize her—and confident they would not. She strode toward the back of the store. Her pocket was heavy with coins, and she began to look around for items she needed. On her tongue was her new name, well-rehearsed: Nadine Sill. It sounded real to her—honest, authentic—but ordinary enough to avoid undue attention. She had considered her choice carefully, running through names of characters she had read in books. She had thought about Annalee and Sally and Lydia—she liked them all—but she had settled on Nadine. It felt right—and it had to be exactly right—for this was her mask, her protection, her new self, the one to erase Pitiful Pearl forever. Ready to become someone new, she had practiced speaking it aloud as she walked alone in the forest. Her new name. Her new past. *Nadine Sill. I come from North Carolina.*

Masquerading as someone else was childish, but Pearl remained a child in many ways. She had never had enough of the stuff that turns children into full-fledged adults. Years did not mature one automatically. Neither did hardship; Pearl had seen plenty. If it were true that hardship alone made one adult and wise, she would have arrived a long time ago— the year her mother died, the year she turned eleven.

Pearl collected a few items, some she needed and some she wanted, including the curious contraption she had seen earlier. She chose heavy thread, two new needles, a crochet needle, a skein of yellow yarn, a pair of sturdy shears, and a new thimble. Nadine Sill needed new clothes. Gathering these items in a splint basket, she also picked up a bolt of muslin and another of a rose-colored calico. She walked to the counter and laid down her purchases.

"I need three yards of each," she said.

"You'll like this," Mr. Pulaski said, lifting the strange object with the green handle out of her basket, and twirling the handle to make the blades rotate. "My lady customers, they tell me it mixes jus' 'bout anything—whips up cream faster'n a boy can find a mud puddle. And eggs—scrambles 'em in a flash."

Pearl smiled, glad to know what the contraption was used for, and immediately wondered where she could buy a couple of chickens. The thought of eating eggs made her mouth water.

"That's good to know," she said, and handed him her money. It was a large purchase, but Pearl had found ample funds the Dunkard had left behind.

Over the next few weeks, Pearl made clothes for herself and some for Ned, who was fast outgrowing the few he had. Most were left over by the Dunkard. Pearl had put them away, knowing that Ned could use them eventually. She also took the opportunity to show her son how to make a garment. She would not always be there to sew for him.

From a farmer in town, she bought two hens and a rooster and managed to drag them home alive in a burlap sack. She locked them into the loft of the shed and set Ned to building a small chicken house, a task he relished. The Dunkard had taught the boy well. And all the Dunkard's tools, the rasps and chisels, the saws, and axes, still lined the wall of the shed. Like most things, Ned had absorbed this knowledge the way parched soil takes in a long and gentle rain.

Pearl crocheted herself a new shawl with the yellow yarn and finally dispensed her original one to the rags, but not before she cut off one strand and knotted the old into the new. Letting go of the past was hard, even if the past held bad memories. Making her new shawl, though, invoked some of Pearl's few sweet memories. She could no longer remember her grandmother's face, but she remembered her hands, gnarled but nimble, teaching her to crochet and to sew. Her grandmother, like her mother, had cared for Pearl, but both women had died too early to be a comfort when Pearl needed them most, when her father's darker moods overtook him, and Pearl became the object of his fury. Her father had always managed to persuade outsiders of his joviality, but not Pearl. She knew, all too well, the malevolence behind his drunken laughter.

Pearl took on all these new tasks with enthusiasm. She was buoyed by her new freedom. Moving forward again, she was no longer hemmed in by her fears or inabilities. She was reinventing herself and, in doing so, she was seeking some worth. Sometimes, she let herself imagine she was Miss Louisa Cross, mistress of a fine house—a fine, white house with lacy tambour curtains, floors spread with carpets and walls filled with books. It was only a dream, of course, but her imagination had been rekindled, a tenuous hope restored by her new identity.

With each chain stitch she pulled, each knot she tied, she blessed the Dunkard for his kindness. In the shadow of their past together, she understood, at least in part, how much he had loved her and how much she had loved him. Theirs had been a sustaining kind of love—a provocative and transformative kind of love—that would never disappear. As she sewed, she occasionally set her work aside and took up the Dunkard's Bible to hear his voice again. In this new spring, his words had a fresh and healing resonance.

# June

Pearl stood again in the empty livery, listening to the wind whistle through the broken boards. She had bound up her hair in the manner she had observed on other women in town, pulling it back and tacking it up with stiff bits of reed. She wore a dress she had made that was becoming of her figure.

A strange hunger had driven her back to town again, a hunger she could not satisfy with anything she grew in her garden. It was a social kind of appetite, a physical starvation that had only one satiation. She had lived with this hunger for too long—it gnawed in her—and it dulled the memory of her earlier mistakes.

She walked to the center of the large building, running her feet along the ruts the carriages and carts had made long ago. They were still deep, cut into the bare dirt floor and now hardened to a solid, rippling surface. Whispering, she rehearsed another trip to Pulaski's.

"Good morning, Mr. Pulaski."

"Good morning, Mizz Nadine. Fine weather we're havin'."

"Fine weather, indeed, Mr. Pulaski."

The abandoned livery had become her staging area where she summoned her courage, rehearsed her new name. Visits there were a strange reminder that her past was gone. Her father could hurt her no more. And the outside world would never know what had become of his sad daughter—if they had ever been vaguely curious.

She smoothed out wrinkles in her skirt, readying to walk to Pulaski's. She carried a list of items to buy. She was picking a few brambles off her sleeve when one high window clanked against its frame. Behind her, the back door whined opened. Startled, Pearl whipped around. A man walked into the livery. Quickly, she gathered herself into her new identity.

"Afternoon, ma'am," he said, tossing down a bridle he had slung over his shoulder like a fourragere. "You lost?"

"Oh. No. I jus' stepped in here to get out of the heat," she said, and she fanned her face using a gesture she thought Nadine might use. "Mighty hot today."

"Got no argument from me on that count. Hot for June." Standing near the door, he eyed her head to toe. "Always nicer in the shade, outta the sun."

"Yes. I was lookin' for a bit a shade," she said, fanning again fast, but now out of discomfort, not heat. She peered out the window, feeling the man's gaze sweep her again. She wondered if he had seen her come before. Had he watched for her? Followed her? A bead of perspiration wriggled down the small of her back. She fanned more.

The man stepped closer and leaned against a post. He dug the heel of one boot into the dirt floor. He was not tall but had strong, angular features and was clean-shaven except for a light-colored mustache that overwhelmed his mouth. He pushed back his wide-brimmed straw hat, revealing eyes that roved independently of the rest of a tanned face. "Too hot for June, if you ask me. This heavy heat, it feels more like the middle of August," he said. He took off his hat to fan his face.

"Yes, it does," she said, drawing some confidence from her new dress and purposely not looking in his direction. "But it's a mite cooler in here, out of the sun, don't you think?"

"You need you a fancy parasol," he said, gesturing like he was holding one. "Keep that purty face protected."

*Pretty face.* His description thrilled Pearl, and she looked down, more self-conscious than ever.

"I wonder where a lady might buy a parasol?" she asked, trying to be coy, thinking of Miss Louisa.

"Cain't say, ma'am. Never bought one myself."

"They have them in Paris," she blurted out, summoning the courage to look at him directly. "I've always wanted to visit Paris."

He laughed, and she felt suddenly foolish. *Why did I say that? Paris! A million miles away.* She deflected. "I've never been to Paris myself."

"Well, I have," he said, puffing out his chest. Strands of thick yellow hair fell across his face, and he flung them away with the toss of his head.

His expression, so far as she could ascertain, was one of amusement and curiosity. *He's teasing me.* "Now you're tellin' tales," she said. "Paris."

"Well, now, I am not," he said, feigning insult. "I'm tellin' you the gospel truth. I surely have been to Paris. Paris, Kentucky. I done lots of business there. Lots of business."

"Oh." She turned away, embarrassed to have been taken in by his little joke. She swept her skirt toward the door. "I should go," she said.

Pearl expected him to follow her lead, to turn and leave, but instead he stepped closer to her, blocking her path to the door. He slung one foot onto an upended wooden box and put a hand on his knee. He leaned forward.

"You're new 'round here, ain't ya?"

"Yes," she said.

"Well, you got a name?"

"Nadine." The words slid out of her mouth as if she had said them a thousand times. "Nadine Sill."

"Nadine. That's a right purty name. Where you hail from, Mizz Nadine Sill?"

"I'm from North Carolina." And to her delight, words bubbled up from inside her: "I'm from where asking too many questions is rude," she said coyly.

Amused, he pulled his foot off the box.

"Ask me no questions and I'll tell you no lies. That it?" he said.

It was clever repartee—and she was enjoying it now—to her great surprise. "How can I tell you lies when I don't even know your name?" she said.

"Excuse me, Mizz Nadine. O'course! You're absolutely right. I ain't mindin' my manners a bit. Shame on me. So, let me introduce myself proper." He bowed low until his hat swept the ground. "My name is Cutler. Argus Cutler. Pleased to make your acquaintance, Miss Nadine Sill."

Nadine laughed out loud. The tension had broken.

# July

Pearl untied her apron, hung it over a chair and threw her new yellow shawl across her arm in case the night air was cool. She stepped out to the porch. By this time, she had made more trips to the hardware, bought more seeds, and planted her garden, which was beginning to produce. She had purchased more cloth and made more clothes, some in bright colors that defined her newfound identity. Her travels to town had emboldened her. With renewed vigor, Pearl was reclaiming her life. She wondered if she and Ned could move back to town in time or to another place altogether and settle down where she could have friends and maybe even find good schooling for the boy.

Pearl stepped off the porch and yelled to Ned who was in the side yard. "I'll be back this evening. Late. Get your chores done. And go to bed with the sun."

He acknowledged her with a nod. His arms were full, carrying the hoe, a bushel basket, four long stakes, and a jar.

Ned dumped the basket and hoe beside the garden and knelt in the dirt to pick off bean beetles. Before finishing his tasks for the day, he would hoe the corn, pick some small squashes, hammer in stakes to trellis the pole beans, and weed between the garden rows.

Pearl watched him. Her son was strong and lean and capable. Ned could take care of himself. On this comforting thought, Pearl headed toward the forest.

Ned looked up when his mother passed by the garden. He had grown curious about her frequent absences from the cabin—and about the new buoyancy in her spirit. These trips made her happy. But he did not know how to frame a question. Whenever he tried, she was evasive.

Ned set the jar for beetles close to his knee. He watched his mother disappear down the forest path. He would not see her again until the next day.

Dusk. The streets were mostly deserted, and Pearl wandered into town unnoticed, blending into the evaporating light. She slipped into the back door of the livery and waited. She untied her hair, fluffed it, and pulled it around her face. Her hair, now the color of copper, was tinged with early gray and in the livery's shaded light, it was almost smoky.

She walked to a front window and peered out. A persistent caution whispered in the back of her mind, but she dismissed it, the way one can ignore distant thunder. She had no desire—or power—to listen to it this evening. Instead, she thought of Miss Louisa. More than anything, Pearl wanted to be Miss Louisa—living forward with an absence of sorrow and struggle and pain. This was her chance. Perhaps, her last chance. Pearl was designing a new future, a new hope. Nadine Sill was emerging as flesh and bone, stepping out of the person who was once Pitiful Pearl.

When she saw him coming, she walked to the back to meet him as he came through the door. He took her hand and led her out of the livery.

A narrow exterior staircase mostly hidden by wisteria accessed the high room above a garage at the back of a local hotel. The room was small and hot, the windows, closed. The only air circulating that night came from the fanning sheets. Pearl surrendered to him once again and satisfied her own hunger for love. Argus Cutler was patient and attentive. He had treated her like a lady, inviting her to his room so they could "get acquainted."

Pearl did not recognize that Argus Cutler was the dark-eyed boy in another form. He had sensed her need the way animals smell prey, in the same way the dark-eyed boy once had sensed her hunger. He spoke love. And with such a feast offered, she was deaf to the past, blind to her earlier mistake. She had always longed for a love that would embrace and keep her, that would make her safe and happy and secure. Argus seemed genuine, gentle, and caring. Pearl fell under his spell. He became the betrothal of her dreams. How could she not have eventually relinquished her body to his hands, her soul to his pleasure? Wasn't this love?

By the summer's moonlight, he caressed her body and swore his love, as she gave herself completely. But each of these nights with him flew by on broken wings, the kind that no longing can mend, the kind that only masquerades as real love.

Pearl disappeared before dawn, as Argus always insisted. It left her puzzled but unable to question, her hunger so great. As she ran back through the forest carrying with her the dirty rags of perceived love—the sackcloth she hoped would turn to silk—how could she understand that her own heart, injured so young, was wounded beyond repair?

# August

Pearl stood over the rain barrel and splashed water on her face. The stultifying air clung to the cabin windows, dampened the porch, and hung in the trees like soured laundry. Even the persistent leaves of a morning glory vine drooped on the post beside her. Pearl sipped a handful of water, but her nausea persisted. Her eyes burned. Finding little relief, she ran to the woods where she vomited until her hair was wet with sweat and soaked strands stuck to her cheeks. She pushed her hair out of her face and sat down in the leaves, leaning back, seeking any kind of relief.

Pearl missed the Dunkard, desperately now. She delighted in her son and found his companionship pleasant, but loneliness and the deepest human hunger had chased her, driven her to find another kind of company. She should have known how foolish she had been. Now she knew with tardy clarity.

Once again, she had fallen prey to desire, succumbing to an undeniable need to salve the deepest of human wounds, to satisfy her hunger, and once again she would pay a price. She had let her body have its way, ignoring what her mind knew. Sometimes, when she had lain with Argus, she had thought of the Dunkard.

But who would save her this time? There was no one, except herself. She resolved not to compound her misfortune by repeating her earlier mistake—this time she would hide. She would disappear for a season, a winter of birthing, and return only when she could do so without the burden of child. He would wait, wouldn't he? Because he loved her. Didn't he?

Pearl lay down in the cool, damp leaves. She longed for the Dunkard with an anguish even she didn't understand. She missed his prayers, now fading memories. Once they had reassured her, protected her—or maybe it had been the perfect calm of his voice. But he had left her, too, hadn't he? In dying, he had left—and without him, she had felt wild and loose, as if she were clinging to a windy peak, fluttering precariously.

And now she had let go and plummeted. Or would the Dunkard have said she had jumped? No. Never. He had never condemned her.

The Dunkard had given her life worth by his attention. He had given her soul strength. Though he and she were opposites, he had completed her in ways she would never fully understand. Pearl had come from a harsh world that had left her soul tattered and weak. He had come through the cloistered Dunkard fellowship. Both of their lives were hard, tried, and tested. Both required sacrifices. Unlike Pearl's father, though, the Dunkard had recognized her worth. He had nurtured her, valued her. Even now, she missed their hard fought but civil arguments about scripture, their discussions about life. These had sustained her, satisfied her, held her to some standard—but now she was lost. Without his voice, without the restraint and comfort of his presence, without his protection, she was alone and lost once again.

Although Pearl missed the Dunkard, a part of her was glad he was not there today to stand beside her as she vomited, as confusion, loss, hurt, and despair assaulted her. Once she had stood at his door, ashamed in his presence; now she stood ashamed in his absence. Pearl understood guilt. She had done this to herself. Now she faced the consequence of her communing summer.

As she sat on the cooling forest floor, Pearl felt her skin crawl. She wondered if the Dunkard would have forgiven this second transgression as completely as he had forgiven the first. She also wondered if eventually he might have fallen prey to her desire. It had consumed her. Would it have eventually consumed him as well? The thought made her cry, as more vomit splashed in the dirt and mixed with bitter tears.

Pearl stood up and walked farther into the woods. She knelt in the leaves to wash her face with water standing in the crook of a tree. Her nausea subsided, but she knew it was only temporary relief. Tired, drained, and dirty, Pearl glanced back toward the cabin where Ned was busy working. She stood up again and walked farther into the woods toward the river until she found a secluded cove hidden by low hanging trees that filtered the hot sun. She stripped off her clothes and lowered her body into the water. As she lay naked in the shallows along the shadowed river, she watched the hot sky while the cool river water encased her. She wondered what would happen if she sank beneath the water and out into the deep. Ned was old enough to take care of himself. He was old enough—but would he be as hopelessly naïve as she? She closed her eyes and felt the water soaking into her pores, into the curves and crevices of her body. Her hand found her belly. Already, she felt the small bulge. Pearl wept.

# 1882

## BLUE AS THE SKY

# May

It was barely May when Pearl was jolted from sleep by pain like a millstone crushing her. Beneath her, the bed was warm and wet. No moon graced the sky to allow her the luxury of seeing. Although she knew what she faced, she found it strangely comforting that she faced it in utter darkness. For hours, she struggled with waves of pain. She stifled her moans, breathing panicky short breaths, her eyes wide, searching for some miraculous deliverance from the ordeal. When it became more than she could control, she called out to her son, her voice strident.

"The baby, Ned. You gotta help me."

The boy awoke and ran to his mother's side. Seeing her face distorted in pain, the boy was alarmed. His hands shook as he lit a candle and set it near his mother's bed.

"Ned," she cried. She grabbed his arm.

"Right here, Mama," he said, kneeling beside her.

As the Dunkard had labored nearly a dozen years before, Ned worked, directed by the few feverish words his mother managed in between moans of agony. Light from the candle flickered against the cabin walls and into the hollows of the mother's contorted face. When Pearl's pain grew unbearable and her screams filled the night, Ned felt as if he and his mother were sealed in a tomb. He glanced toward the black window. Would the sun never rise?

At last Pearl's body signaled her to push, and she bore down with all her might, but the effort was fruitless. The baby wouldn't come. She wept, defeated. She knew she would die without making this delivery. With her last bit of strength, Pearl raised her head, held her breath and pushed with all her might. Her flesh ripped, and the baby emerged partway but lodged on a bone. Exhausted, drenched in sweat, blood, and mucous, Pearl lay helpless, sobbing, no strength left in her to finish the job. Her work, diffused by tears and screams, was incomplete.

Ned did not know what to do. In the pale candlelight, the blood that covered his mother's bed looked black.

"Pull," Pearl cried with a shred of breath. "Help me, Ned." Her words were desperate. "Pull!"

Ned knelt on the bed between his mother's knees and grasped the swollen, bloody body, partially emerged. His hands trembled. He stanched the revulsion that threatened to overtake him. Remembering how the Dunkard had gripped the calf, he tried to copy the old man's clinical calm. His mother lay helpless, groaning, delirious with pain. Ned gripped the small body and pulled as one last involuntary and merciful lunge of muscle thrust the child out of the mother onto the bed.

The baby lay blue and lifeless.

"Rub. Rub, Ned." Pearl's voice sounded strange and ghostly, as if she were traveling down a long tunnel.

Bewildered, the boy looked up at his mother's face. He thought she was dying. "Mama!" Tears streamed down his face.

"Rub." He heard her raspy whisper. "Rub hard."

Ned unwrapped the cord wound tightly around the child's chest and neck and began to massage the baby. After what seemed an interminable length of time, the infant finally gasped, and a weak cry emerged from the tiny lips. Pink flooded the wrinkled arms and legs, and after a few minutes of crying, the newborn fell into a deep sleep. Ned looked up at his mother. The color was gone from her face, and she slept, her task complete.

Not knowing what else to do, Ned wrapped the tiny baby in his mother's yellow shawl and held her. He listened to the child's rattled breathing, as he waited out the long night. Finally, mercifully, dawn came soft as a bird's breast.

Pearl awoke to her newborn's tiny wail. Ned, unable to quiet the infant, was exhausted from the night's ordeal.

"Mama?"

"Give it here, Ned," Pearl said. "You go on—go sleep a while."

Ned complied, gladly. Pearl watched the boy curl up on his bed, close his eyes, and fall effortlessly into sleep.

Pearl examined her baby. A girl. This surprised her, and a part of her ached for her own mother. The tiny, pinched face stirred a strange mixture of tenderness and fear. What fate awaited this girl child? Had her own mother once had the same misgivings?

The baby's mouth was small and perfectly formed, but Pearl found it difficult to get her to suckle; her throat and muscles seemed weak. Ned had been strong and aggressive, but this passive child would not survive if Pearl could not get her to eat. With difficulty, Pearl managed to get some small measure of nourishment to pass to her daughter. Soon, both the mother and her children slept.

When Pearl awoke again it was not to her daughter's cries but to the cramping of her own belly. She tensed as her womb contracted again, flushing the last of the birth from her body. She lay still as the afterbirth passed. She was desperately hungry, but her own hunger would have to wait, at least for a little while.

She listened to Ned's steady breathing. Rising quietly, she attended to herself, first fashioning an undergarment suitable for the next weeks while she recovered from the birth. Next, she rolled the bedclothes together and replaced them with a coarse blanket, all that she had, and secured the sleeping infant there. While Ned and the baby slept, she slipped out the door carrying the soiled bundle and walked to the edge of the river. She tied the bedding to a low-hanging branch and left it there, dangling in the water for the river to flush. She washed her bloodied and tired body with the river's cold water before she returned to the cabin.

Pearl's milk came in on Sunday, but even though Pearl's breasts had swelled and dripped of the thick, yellow life-giving fluid and then of rich milk, the baby did not suckle well enough to be nourished. As hard as mother and child tried, the infant grew hungry and irritable. Pearl resorted to position-ing the baby under her leaking nipple, the way one might feed a baby bird.

It was a temporary solution that relieved somewhat the pain and pressure in her breasts, but she knew this would not do for long.

The next morning, Pearl rose early. While Ned and her newborn slept, she pressed her engorged breasts, one and then the other, into the open mouth of a Mason jar, creating a slight vacuum. When the jar was partially full, Pearl's relief was great. When the baby woke next, screaming, Pearl dipped a clean cloth into the milk and let the child suck from the cloth. Soon the baby was satisfied and slept peacefully.

Pearl whispered to Ned, shaking the boy's shoulder to roust him. "Ned, come with me."

With her son's help, Pearl pulled the cradle out of the loft of the shed—the same cradle the Dunkard had retrieved for Ned. Pearl had never thought to ask the Dunkard why he had a cradle. Perhaps it had been his own. "Put these in the cradle and help me," she said, handing Ned a bundle of rags.

They dragged the cradle from the shed and set it next to Pearl's bed. Pearl took rags the Dunkard had wisely saved and lined the cradle. On top, she spread an unfinished quilt piece she had found in an old, flat-top trunk in the shed loft. When it was ready, she laid her daughter in the cradle.

The baby's large searching eyes were a luminous blue, prompting Ned to call her Sky. Exhausted from the ordeal and the assumption of another child to care for, Pearl let it go. Sky would do for now. Pearl would think about a name later. She had always favored the name Annalee; she had once read it in a poem. This child was different, though, strange even, and didn't seem worthy of such a name. Pearl dismissed any worry—surely her daughter would grow strong as Ned had. Half-heartedly Pearl searched for a more suitable name, but in the end she never decided. Her daughter would be Sky, and a part of her liked it.

*Blue as the sky, my darling.*

# October

In midafternoon, Pearl was leaving Ned to tend the baby while she escaped into the woods. She needed air. Summer had been short this year, and now autumn was deepening, fading toward winter. All the living colors were decaying to a dull brown, and with them, Pearl was slipping into melancholy. Her baby was slow and less responsive than Ned had been. It was a disappointment and a worry for Pearl. Ned didn't notice. He doted on his sister, whose temperament was so quiet it was almost otherworldly.

"You keep her warm. Out of drafts," Pearl told the boy as she dispensed with her apron and slipped on a well-worn coat. "Wind's chilly today."

"I will," Ned said. This reassured his mother, but for Ned it was a natural response. He took care of Sky because the child needed him. He looked down into her tiny face, white as dough. Sky rarely cried and her blue eyes were luminous, often staring off as if she saw things that neither Ned nor his mother could ever see. Ned scooted his chair closer to Sky's cradle and leaned over. He tried to engage her, to get her to smile, but she didn't respond. Still, he tried. He tucked a wrap around his sister who lay as still as a sleeping calf.

"Can I feed her a little mush?" Ned asked. "When she wakes up?" He knew she liked a little honey on his finger. He would give her some. Maybe he could get her to smile.

"If she'll take it. Jus' a little, but not too much. You don't want her chokin'."

"Yessum."

"I'll be back afterwhile," Pearl said. "Wrap her up if it gets too cold in here." She tossed her shawl on the back of Ned's chair. "I'll work up the fire when I get back." She left the cabin.

As soon as his mother was out of sight, Ned picked Sky up and carried her around the cabin. He was determined to make her smile.

Pearl hunched forward, stepping carefully as she ascended the hill up the west ridge of the hollow. The ground was scattered with loose rocks. She found an outcropping of shale and sat down. The heavy autumn sun streamed, warming the layered rocks that were mostly barren except for little maps of lichen and a few stubborn grasses. Once again, Pearl was drowning in despair. The coming winter felt like a kind of death, an end to thriving.

She had come here for a purpose—to let the full sunlight enliven her, give her the strength to face the coming cold. She knew it would be difficult. No longer was she immune to the slow process of dying that steals the soul, then the body. Summer labors, the weight of another child, her new self-imposed isolation and the strain of her life had worn her down. Would they all starve? Or would they die from the coming cold? She picked up a stone and hurled it, dispensing a kind of resigned frustration.

Pearl knew winters and hardship, and thus far she had surmounted them all, but now death felt close—too close. With the Dunkard, hardships had been passable, even pleasant, but his absence had left her wanting and vulnerable, as if a protective cover had been lifted from her. Now, alone with two children to care for, she wondered. Could she hold up the tent of life for another winter? Did she have the same fortitude? Did she have the conviction?

The same despondency that Pearl felt the first frozen night at the Dunkard's door weighed on her like a drowning wave. Her strength was almost gone. She could take her children to town and leave them at the church door. Surely some good people would take in two orphans. *They would be better off. Wouldn't they?*

She looked heavenward in a vain hope, a formless prayer, that the Dunkard would advise her, tell what she should do. *Where is your voice? What can I do?*

When the sun dipped and flickered through the trees, Pearl rose reluctantly and started back toward the cabin. Halfway there, she came upon a plump, young rabbit caught up in a thick bramble of wild roses. The creature's silky brown fur was tangled and matted from struggling, and it was covered with burrs and bits of blood, the result of a fruitless struggle against the thorny bush. Trying to free itself, the creature had strangled. She stooped down to touch the rabbit; it was still warm. Pearl was painfully torn. Should she take this as an omen, a sign, a gift from heaven to promote their survival? Or was this a test? Or an answer? Again, she looked heavenward. Would the Dunkard be watching if she chose to take this animal and cook it for her son and herself? Would it be an act of betrayal to the man whom she was so indebted to—whom she had loved? She weighed her choices. Pearl had not killed the rabbit. It was already dead, wasn't it? Surely some creature would consume it. Why not her? It was the act of killing he had objected to, wasn't it? Without looking up again, Pearl untangled the rabbit from the bramble and lifted it out of the thicket. Wrapping it in her apron, she carried it back to the cabin.

The rabbit lay on the table inside the cabin, while Pearl worked in the garden. In her mind raged the battle between guilt and desire. As she hoed, she replayed the good-natured arguments with the Dunkard. He had reasoned. She had reasoned. But more importantly, he had listened to her, listened as if what she said had value.

She and the Dunkard had never agreed on the construal of the sixth commandment, the prohibition against killing. His view was theological; hers was practical. His concern was survival in heaven; hers was survival on earth. Pearl needed to believe he was wrong—on this point at least. Someday, he had told her, he would know for certain. But now she believed her son needed the sustenance—and she wanted it, wanted the strength and vitality she knew it would give them both.

All these coalescing thoughts were sweet memories. She mulled them as she hoed the rich soil until she reached the end of a row. Her garden had been good this year. Her seeds had come up thick and her harvest was rich. Even this late, the garden was still producing, though the tender crops were gone. She had grown tired of the repetitive fare of vegetable stews. Her hunger for meat had never left her.

Pearl stopped hoeing and looked heavenward. "Do you know now?" she said. "Did you know about the rabbit?" She smiled, the first genuine smile in a long time.

Ned wandered along. She heard him leap up the steps, go into the cabin, and step out again, coming toward her.

"Mama! There's a rabbit in here," he said in a half-whisper, half-shout, so as not to disturb his sleeping sister. "There's a rabbit."

"I know, Ned." She stood up and brushed her hands off. "I know, son. I put it there."

Ned, walking toward her, looked perplexed. He didn't know how to formulate the question that occurred to him.

"Come on in with me, son." She draped her arm around Ned's shoulders, now nearly as high as her own, and steered him toward the cabin. "I'm gonna teach you something."

She looked at the sky and judged the sunlight left in the day, as they walked toward the cabin. Perhaps finding the rabbit was heavenly direction? She hoped so. As she had done as a girl years ago, she would skin this rabbit the way her mother had taught her, and she would boil it to make a stew.

Pearl smiled again. She could already taste it. With this rabbit had come a kind of permission in absentia and a profound sense of hope. Now she would trap and hunt, as her brothers had. And she would survive. She would teach Ned, and they would build a trap together.

They mounted the steps.

"Ned, go find the whetstone."

Her knife would need sharpening.

# December

Pearl sat beside Sky's cradle. The child was wrapped tight to ward off the cold. She watched the baby's breath collect in the winter air, watched the almost imperceptible rise and fall of her small chest. Pearl had sent Ned into the forest to collect sticks so they would be ready for the next snow. He had returned with an armful.

"Stack them with the rest," she said when he entered the cabin. "Would you like to go catch us some fish?"

Ned beamed. "Right now?"

His mother nodded. "Take your pole."

"Do you think I would forget it?" he teased.

A trip to the river to fish was a task Ned relished not only for the freedom to be outside but also for the opportunity to provide food. He had been born with a strong sense of responsibility—or had it been shaped by the Dunkard's example? Either way, Ned was eager to comply.

Pearl watched him collect his equipment: a partially broken basket he had lined with a piece of a feed sack to make a creel, a tin filled with night crawlers he raised in a bucket in the root cellar, and a newish fishing pole—hand-fashioned from a willow branch and equipped with sewing needles bent around the hot poker over the fire.

*What would I do without Ned? He would be so pleased with the boy.* Thoughts of the Dunkard were never far from her mind.

While Ned went to the river, a pot of rabbit stew simmered in an iron pot over the fire. In spite of the burden of two children—or perhaps because of it—Pearl with Ned's help had managed to fill the cellar with food, a considerable accomplishment that buoyed her spirits as much as the satiation of their new meals. She had started teaching Ned to trap—a gift her own family had given her—and now she braced for the onslaught of winter with a newfound hope, one that surprised even her.

In time, she resolved to put aside her grief over the Dunkard's death, but she would never stop missing him. In his absence, though, she was beginning to understand—in the way that understanding can creep into the mind uninvited—that her daughter and her son were the result of a profound and permanent wound, one she would never outgrow, one she need not bother to address, one too deep to understand—or to escape. She knew this somehow, but it was a thought she rarely dwelt on. To do so was to suffer again the callous disregard with which her father had treated his own daughter. She also began to wonder if she could ever control her own destiny. Would this wound find her again, trick her again—even ambush her the way her father had ambushed her and often punished her to within an inch of her life?

Sky stirred, opened her eyes, and then fell back to sleep. Pearl covered her daughter with an extra blanket and went to stir the stew. The rich aroma filled the cabin.

This winter Pearl was determined to survive, an instinct embedded in her spirit. Her resolve was emboldened by some deep but unspoken obligation to the Dunkard. She wanted to survive now more than ever before. She had to. Her gratitude to him demanded it.

She glanced out the window to look for Ned. He regularly brought home crappie or bass and occasionally a catfish. Momentarily, she heard him mount the steps and stomp his feet on the porch.

"Look what I got," he said, as he came through the door.

"Shhhhh," she said, raising a finger to her lips and motioning toward the cradle.

Ned lowered his voice. "I got a catfish."

Pearl whispered to her son, "Hang it out on the porch."

Ned stepped out and tossed a line over a nail hammered high into the side of the cabin beneath the porch ceiling. He strung up the large fish high, out of the reach of scavengers.

"We'll cook it in the morning," his mother said, when he came back in. "You set out the plates."

From the shelf, Ned lifted two plates. They were delicate with an elegant blue and white pattern. The dishes had been a curiosity to Pearl until the Dunkard explained that they had belonged to his mother. The plates had been part of her trousseau—stored long ago in the trunk in the shed loft and long forgotten.

Atop two thick pieces of coarse bread, Pearl ladled the stew. Ned pulled up a chair and bowed his head. "Bless this food," he said, "Amen." And he began to eat. Pearl watched him. He was either very hungry or efficient to offer such a brief prayer.

Outside a cold mist began to fall. It would turn to snow and continue for two days. Another long winter was setting in.

Pearl was ready.

# 1883

## MERCY RESERVED

# April

Carrying two jars, Pearl emerged from the cellar into the morning's sunshine and stood to let the light soak into her body. Warmth oozed into her pores as a morning salve. Sky was sleeping in the cabin. Ned was already out in the forest checking traps he had built. After a winter of confinement with his mother and sister, the boy had jumped at any task that let him roam the forest. Perhaps he would bring back some quarry they could feast on. Pearl set the jars on the ground beside the step and sat down, pulling her skirt around her knees.

In the year that followed Sky's birth, Pearl had been troubled by a premonition. It came to her in her dreams. It haunted her waking and denied her the night's quietude with a hint of dread she could not shake. It was not a thought she pondered, though. She was too busy for that. Yet the strange sensation lingered with her—a vague and unsettled feeling that nagged at the edges of her consciousness. Did it come from her part in burying the Dunkard the way she had? She wondered this on the nights when the dream woke her in a panic. Or was it the inevitable progression of life? Someday, she would die. She knew it, accepted this—though never as obediently as the Dunkard had. Why did this dream haunt her? Why did it interrupt her sleep?

She picked up one jar—peaches—and rocked it back and forth, watching the light brown syrup ebb and flow. She had taught Ned how to keep them, to boil them in a water bath, to store them out of the light. They had worked together in the same way she and the Dunkard had worked together to fill the root cellar. She had taught Ned how to mine the forest and the river for food. He knew the duties and the necessities. It was comforting to know how much Ned had learned.

Pearl held the jar up to the sun and admired the color of the fruit. The Dunkard had loved peaches. Still rocking the jar back and forth, she watched the sunlight fill the glass, as if a piece of the sun had been captured within. She stood up, shaking off her skirt, and carried the jar into the cabin.

Pearl was hungry.

# June

As the sun descended toward the ridge and the evening gray prepared to absorb the forest, Pearl quickened her pace. By the time she reached town, it would be dusk, when the glow on the ridges would be backlights, a time of day when Pearl would be least recognizable and most presentable.

Tonight, she had estimated her travel time well. In the distance, she saw the man at the garage slide his establishment's door closed. She hung back along a fence line overgrown with stubborn mulberry shoots that fanned out and twined through the broken and neglected barrier. At her feet, she noticed asparagus shoots coming up, too. She would break some off and take them when she returned to the cabin.

She watched another merchant close his door and walk away. When he was gone from sight and the street had emptied, she proceeded. She spotted the wisteria that hung along the narrow stairs at the back of the local hotel. At the top, beside a rickety landing, a light shown behind a curtained window. Her pulse quickened. Would Argus still know her? Had it been too long? Would he? Had he missed her as she had missed him?

Or was it something else that had spurred her to come? She had run through the coins left by the Dunkard to buy seeds and canning jars and lids. This trip to town—a confusing collision of needs—was necessary, she told herself. Surely, Argus would help her.

Pearl had tried to be wise, but deep inside her remained the young girl wanting. As she struggled under the responsibility of the family she had borne, she could not shake the need to satisfy her lifelong poverty— the lack of love haunting her since girlhood. She tried to endure it, as one would endure hunger or thirst, but her need was insatiable. And Pearl loved her children. For them, she would do what she must to ensure their survival. Her deep hunger, thus, had fused with her instinct to protect her children. It became a dangerous amalgam. Perhaps that is why her fear of dying troubled her so—or why her instincts were so tangled with her desires, one dependent on the other, one justifying the other. Love was a powerful, intoxicating need, as fundamental as breath but as perilous as acid handled carelessly. Need affirmed desire.

Checking the street once more and remaining in the evening's shadows, she stole toward the steps. Pearl slipped her shawl from her shoulders. She cinched up her bodice to make herself more desirable. She looked out across the town's shadowed buildings where a swollen moon was rising. She crept up the stairs and tapped on his door.

"Argus?" she whispered. "Argus?" She heard the clink of a glass and a shuffling of unsteady footsteps. The latch moved. "Argus, it's me. Nadine."

The door opened. He peered out to see who was there. He coughed and stared at her fiercely through bloodshot eyes.

"Damn, Nadine," he said, the smell of whiskey strong on his breath. "That you? Damn if it ain't." He grabbed her wrist and pulled her into the room. The door shut. The latch fell. The light in the room went out.

But this was not the reception Pearl had hoped for.

The hot room spun around as Pearl opened her swollen eyes. Struggling to become fully conscious, she lay on a cot in the back room of local doctor's office. The smell of medicinal compounds stung her nose. Her mouth felt full and pasty. Every part of her body ached. She touched her face. A long crescent of stitches stretched across her right cheek from the crease of her nose to the end of her brow. Once again, love had betrayed her.

Argus had used her and then, angered by her long absence, he had beaten her brutally and dumped her in an alley near Main Street. A local merchant found her midmorning and carried her to the local doctor.

"Pity" was the word the doctor had used as he stitched closed the gashes in Pearl's face with black catgut sutures while she lay unconscious on his examining table. "Right pretty girl. She's going to have a bad scar. Can't do much about that."

"Pathetic," the nurse said with nostrils slightly flared. "Brought this on herself," she added, assuming understanding. Her mercy was reserved for the deserving.

After the doctor finished and he and the nurse had moved Pearl to a cot, he left to go home for his noon meal. "I've got calls to make this afternoon. I'll check back on her later if I have time. When she wakes up, give her some water."

The nurse looked at the clock. "I need to leave by two o'clock."

"That's fine. Let the poor girl sleep."

Hours later, Pearl sat up and opened her eyes wide, wincing as the stitches pulled. She was alone. By the color of the sky, she judged it to be late afternoon. Her brain was foggy. Her consciousness was broken into jagged pieces. She trembled as memory came back in painful visions. Always before, Argus had been kind. She had loved him, met whatever demands he made, but her absence had angered him. After wringing from her whatever pleasure he could, he had turned on her, a vicious dog.

Through her dizziness, she tried to fill her mind with something other than the image of his brute hands and snarling mouth. She began to shake. She clutched her bruised breasts to stanch the pain, pulled her torn garment around her. And she sobbed as she had never sobbed before, emptying herself of years of regret and pain and loss. Salty tears stung her face as they flowed across her fresh wounds. Now more than ever she wished for the Dunkard's embrace—an embrace she had known only in her dreams, but a heart embrace that would have been as real as any man's arms.

The office was quiet. With difficulty, Pearl rose from the cot and peeked into the anteroom. She stole in. Through the front window, she saw the tapered shadow of the church steeple falling across the town like a compass point telling her where she was. Up and down the hardpan street, storekeepers were closing their doors for the day. Occasional footfalls passed along the wooden walkways lining the street. The sun sagged in the sky.

Pearl waited until the sun had set and it was fully dark before she slipped out a back door and started for home.

Ned was relieved to see his mother. He ran to her, but she rebuffed his affection, and he, alarmed at her wounded and disheveled appearance, withdrew.

"What happened, Mama?"

"Where's Sky?"

"Asleep. I gave her some milk and a little mush."

"Good, son."

Pearl was spent, and even though the walk to the cabin had stretched and relaxed her tense body, her spirit was broken as it had never been broken before. Within her was a complete and utter absence of hope.

"What happened?" Ned asked her again.

With a faint gesture, she brushed aside his question. "I met some trouble. You don't worry about me. I'm gonna lie down."

"I made some supper."

"Thank ya." Pearl whispered, genuinely grateful and relieved at the boy's initiative. "You're a good son. You eat. I'm not hungry." She tried to smile at him, to reassure him, but stitches pulled at her mouth, and she hurried inside the cabin ahead of him.

Pearl curled up on her bed. A couch of roses could not have felt any better to her pummeled body. Soon sleep embraced her. Even in her dreams, though, she found no peace. *The wages of sin is death*. She awoke with a start at the words reverberating in a voice that was achingly familiar. Was the Dunkard here with her again? She looked around for him but saw only shadows, and none resembled her kind Dunkard, the one who had loved her. Sometime after midnight, when the moon was high and the night sounds intense, she fell back into a tortuous sleep.

Ned sat on the porch steps and watched the moon rise over the ridge. He had eaten alone, fed his sister once more, cleared the table, swept the floor, and covered up his sleeping mother's shoulders. Her appearance frightened him.

From his spot on the stoop, he listened as his mother tossed and turned.

Intermittently, she cried out. He would jump up each time, listen, and then sit back down as she resettled.

Tonight, the moon overwhelmed a clear black sky. It made the atmosphere so bright that Ned could see deep into the woods where moonlight pierced through with ethereal lances. But even the bright night was of little comfort. Ned felt alone. Beside him on the porch lay the Dunkard's Bible. He had already read his daily verses, holding the open book toward the fall of the generous moon to read the way his mother had taught him—and the way the Dunkard had encouraged him.

Inside the cabin, his mother stirred.

"Ned?" she called.

He hurried to her.

"Get me some water." Her words were garbled, the saliva on her lips, white and dry, her mouth badly swollen.

Ned dipped water from the rain barrel and brought her a cup, holding it up to her mouth. Heat radiated from her face. Her upper lip was beaded with droplets of sweat that clung to tiny white hairs on her skin, catching the moonlight. Pearl tried to sip, but water dribbled from her swollen lips. Only then did he notice several of her teeth were missing.

"Thank ya, son." Pearl tried to smile at him, but once again the tight stitches twisted. Her smile became a wince. She closed her eyes to sleep again, hoping dreams would ferry her away from her pain—and her shame. Once again, she wished she could disappear, as she had so many years ago in the cold forest before the Dunkard had taken her in. She fell asleep wondering why she hadn't let go of life when she had had the chance.

Ned returned to the porch. Eventually he went to bed, but he did not sleep. He lay on his bed all night, wakeful, listening to the night and to his mother's shallow breathing.

A few days passed. Ned watched the stitches across his mother's cheek turn an angry red, and then, too quickly, the stitches bulged and broke. The wound oozed.

Around noon on the third day, Pearl became delirious. Feverish and not wholly conscious, she thrashed about and talked nonsensically. And Sky began wailing. Though tired and overwhelmed, Ned managed to feed and quiet his sister, while he tried to subdue his own fears. Finally, at the end of a long afternoon, as the sun began its descent, his mother fell into a deep sleep that reassured the son. Perhaps the worst was over. He hoped it was.

The next evening, however, Pearl's face was more swollen and felt hotter to Ned's touch. Ned worried anew. Mercifully, Sky had been content all day—as she often was—in the yard where Ned confined her in an empty dog run. The child was more than a year old but not yet walking, hardly crawling. She would sit hour after hour staring at shadows of flut-tering leaves or examining a flower as if she were learning its most intimate details.

After Ned fed Sky some supper and put her to bed, he sat beside his sleeping mother. Her breathing was labored. She seemed to be struggling as little gasps of air came between long gaps of frightful stillness.

Once again, the moon rose full and bold in the night sky, a solitary and strangely reassuring companion for Ned.

In a sudden moment of lucidity, Pearl called out. "Ned?"

"I'm here."

"I don't want to leave," she said.

"You're not."

"No, Ned. When I die. I don't want to leave."

"You ain't dyin'."

"I want to stay here, near the cabin. Bury me, here. Please, Ned."

"No!" he said, though he was denying her death rather than her wish.

"Please, son. Please." Pearl's voice cracked. "Let me stay here. Don't put me in the river."

Ned suddenly understood and could do nothing but acquiesce. "All right, Mama," he said, hoping it would put her mind at ease and let her rest.

Reassured, Pearl sank back. "Get the Bible. Read to me."

Ned stood up, found the Bible, and opened it, randomly choosing a chapter.

"Feather," she whispered. He barely heard her. Her mouth was swollen and her words, unclear. He leaned in close.

"Feather," she repeated.

Ned noticed a large feather, a hawk's feather, marking a page. He opened to the place and read the passages that had been underlined.

"And they will all come and settle in the steep ravines, and in the clefts of the rocks, and on all the thorn bushes, and on all the pastures…"

A strange and welcome peace began to descend over Pearl.

Ned turned to other passages, ones he knew well, passages the Dunkard had often read, passages about mercy and redemption and eternity. With a kind of desperation, he read by the light of a flickering oil lamp. He read and he read and he read, as if this unbroken act would heal his mother.

The longer he read, the more his mother relaxed, as if a salve had been applied to her spirit. When he looked up once, he saw that she was forming a word. "Mercy." He stopped, listened to her quiet invocation—until her words disappeared altogether.

# July

Ned kicked at the grass alongside the river as it ebbed and flowed rhythmically beside him. Out of the corner of his eye, he caught the glint of gray light flickering among the river rocks and weeds. The thin edge of a large, translucent flint rock, frost heaved over winter, was poking up out of the ground. Kneeling, he separated the grass and dug around it with his hands, unearthing the rock from among the duller limestone and shale embedded in the sandy riverside dirt. The smooth, glass-like rock was the size of his two young hands outstretched. Lifting it, he brushed it off and rubbed it clean with his shirt. He held the thinnest edge up to the sky to let the light of the sun become a backlight. Gazing through the smoky rock, he knew what it was for.

Ned walked back to the cabin, carrying the flint rock to the higher ground near the edge of the woods where he had buried his mother, just as he and the Dunkard had buried the cow, just as his mother had asked him to do. The mound of dirt, covered with large field stones that Ned had hauled from the river's edge, was still fresh, and the aroma of turned earth and summer growth suffused the air as he laid the flint rock at the head of the grave. It was fitting, this marker. The rock's translucence was a symbol of his mother's understanding of heaven—and its solidness, a symbol of Ned's understanding of his own future. As he stood, looking at the flint rock, a voice long silent, echoed through his memory: *For now we see through a glass, darkly; but then face to face: now I know in part; but then shall I know even as also I am known.*

Ned paused, listening to his memory, straining to capture the Dunkard's every word. Then he returned to the cabin where his infant sister slept. Sky was his now, his alone, to care for, to raise, to protect, to love.

# August, September, October ...

The sun rose and the sun set two thousand times. Hot summers faded into mild autumns that hardened into harsh winters that melted away into curative springs—and began again. Year after year. Through all these seasons, Ned lived in the Dunkard's cabin in the hollow and watched over Sky, the strange and delicate flower he loved and cherished. She was the purpose for his life. He was devoted to her wholly, and he cared for her as a tender protector, a beneficent parent, a faithful brother, a friend and companion. Their life together was simple and good, long, and pure.

And perfectly balanced.

# Part Two

## NED AND SKY

*The days of our years are threescore years and ten; and if by reason of strength they be fourscore years, yet is their strength labour and sorrow; for it is soon cut off, and we fly away.*

*Psalm 90:10*

# 1938

## A GOOD AND DEVOTED BROTHER

# June

A n acorn fell from a branch, bounced, and rolled up and down each side of a hardened rut that had been carved out by the tires of Ned's truck. The acorn shuffled like a roulette ball until it came to a stop. Sky watched it and then looked up smiling at the munificent tree, whose branches extended toward her as open arms. Beneath the trees, she was sheltered from the blunt noon sun that would be brutal come midsummer. What pieces of heaven that were visible through the dense canopy above her were perfectly blue, uninterrupted by even a single cloud. A blue summer sky with no end.

She knelt to pick up the acorn and dropped it into her apron pocket where it clinked against the others she had collected. She shook her pocket and listened. Together, they made their own natural tympani. She found four flat pieces of shale and two of birch bark, which she examined closely before she slipped them into a burlap bag, the same one she used to gather chinquapins in the fall. The bag was little more than a piece of burlap with a hank of rope threaded along the edges. Drawn up, it formed a bag.

Today was a long day, the kind Sky liked best, with still air that coaxed creatures out of trees and burrows and holes. She paused to listen as they raced along the spines of half-buried roots. Even when she couldn't see them, she knew they were there.

Sky jangled her pocketful of acorns while she looked for more. Stopping along the rutted path that snaked through the deep forest and eventually led out of it, she took several acorns from her pocket. She drew back her arm and threw the acorns, one by one, back into the woods, listening as each one landed in the forest's lush carpet. With each toss she waited for the small but distinct thud. It was important for her to hear each one, to make sure it landed. She imagined a gray squirrel gathering this manna for his winter larder, the same way she gathered black walnuts and chinquapins for her own. She listened intently; she thought she heard his footfalls.

Sky loved the hollow—this huge earthen bathhouse that stored water in the heavens for October to temper, December to chill, and January to freeze into flakes and sprinkle back onto the ground. Here was home—as much a womb to her as her mother's had been more than five decades before. She had never been out of the hollow and had never wanted to leave it. She loved it in the same way an ordinary child finds comfort in a welcoming lap, a cherished blanket, a favorite corner. But Sky was neither ordinary—nor a child any longer, in body at least.

As sunlight fell across her eyes, she raised her rumpled face to receive the sun's anointing and its gentle stroke. This delicate kiss of summer glistened on her hands, her forearms, and her face. But along with the sun's warm touch, she felt the cool breath of winter lingering in the summer forest. It was like the breath of an animal waiting to pounce, and it stirred a strange, foreboding sorrow in her, reminding her that summer was only temporary, a transient part of the longer cycle she knew by heart. She lived by the forest's give and take, the coming and going of the seasons, the cycles of life and death. This was her rhythm, her measure of time.

Sky shuddered. Sooner than she wished, she would have to hunker in the cabin near the river. For the long winter months, she would huddle with Ned, as she always had. Every year it was like this when she bade farewell to the summer. It was like dying. Sky knew that after summer, the cold would come again. She could already sense autumn's foreshadow, even today, as the hollow sizzled with cicadas, moaned with bullfrogs, and flit with flying things. These sounds were as soothing to her as a mother's voice—and were, in fact, the only such voice she knew. But summer never lasted, so she relished the days of heat and the warm nights, like sodden sheets that dampened the hollow. Eventually summer would fade away, shrink ahead of north winds, the way wind scatters leaves before a storm. All too soon the cicadas would not buzz, the bullfrogs would not plunk and moan. The crickets, the night drummers, would fall silent. Too soon for Sky.

In the distance, Sky heard Collier, Ned's coonhound, baying. She turned toward the sound. Though she was too far to hear with her ears, she reckoned the other sounds—the screened door slapping shut, Ned tromping toward the old dog run to feed Collier. Ned expected to be fed as Collier did. Sky started back to the cabin, back in the direction of the river, back to Ned, skipping in a kind of joy dance, a pirouette almost, humming to herself.

"I pulled a ham down outta the smokehouse this mornin'. It's hangin' by the door," Ned said when he saw Sky. He was stacking wood. Sweat dripped from his chin into the folds of his stubbly neck. He wiped it away with the back of his hand and left the porch to bring up another load of logs. Sky nodded as she stepped through the door of the cabin. She smoothed out the blanket on her bed and dumped the rocks and bark onto it.

Sky stoked the firebox in the iron stove with kindling and lit it with shakes of discarded cardboard that Ned had collected in a dented can next to the hearth. With her apron she fanned the flames before shutting the door with a thud and turning the handle to latch it. The room soon smelled of burning wood as tiny flags of smoke escaped the stove. Decades ago, Ned had hauled it out to the cabin after pulling it from the charred remains of a house that had burned to the ground. Water droplets began to sizzle on its black iron surface, dancing the same way light sparkled across the river in the early mornings. Sky wanted to reach down and touch the bouncing droplets, but long ago she had learned that the stove would burn her. Still, she wanted to—a childlike curiosity that had never faded.

Sky lifted a large copper kettle and carried it out to the barrel that still collected rainwater running off the roof and down through a handmade gutter and pipe. The first sheets of rain were always turned out, redirected by a moveable flange in the pipe so that the spring pollens and summer dusts were washed off before the barrel filled. This turning out of the first water ensured that their water supply, soft and good as it was, was also clean. The flange had been Ned's invention, one of many he had created to shore up their independence.

Sky slid off the lid. Balancing the kettle on the edge, she fished out an errant leaf and ladled water with a cup that hung on a nail above the barrel. She re-covered the barrel and carried the kettle back inside. Some water sloshed on the floor and ran along grooves in the wood floor, slipping through cracks. But it didn't matter. The summer heat and the heat from the stove would soon erase it.

With a grunt, Sky set the heavy kettle on top of the stove. Once she would have hoisted it with ease, but her joints were stiffer now, her strength less than it had been, and for a year or so, her endurance had been waning. She lifted the ham onto the table and unbundled it from its canvas sheath. With the half-sharpened blade of a broken knife, she scraped off the mold. It took her longer to clean the ham than it took the water to heat, so the water was roiling when she dumped the meat into the pot. Droplets splashed onto the stovetop and hissed.

Their homestead was this: the Dunkard's cabin with its stone hearth and chimney, a rusty tin roof and a root cellar dug out by hand long ago. Close by was a chicken house Ned had built and kept in good enough repair to keep out foxes. Off to the side was the oft-repaired dog run where Collier stayed when he wasn't hunting with Ned. There was a pigsty and the lofted shed where Ned kept a cow or two, along with all the tools he needed to live. Many had belonged to the Dunkard, but many more Ned had collected for the work to support himself and Sky.

The cabin's furnishings were sparse. Two beds constructed from saplings and rope with tick mattresses stuffed with straw and feathers were spread with linen coverlets. In the winter, heavy fur skins from Ned's hunting kept them warm in the frigid nights. Pushed up against a window was a heavy pedestal table with claw feet. Made from oak, it was another throwaway rescued by Ned. One side of it was charred, but that side faced the window unnoticed. The table and the cookstove were the only exotic furnishings in the cabin. Everything else was handmade, fashioned from the forest. Under the high side of the cabin, accessed by a heavy door angled to dispel weather, was the root cellar where Ned stored canned goods, summer vegetables, and salted meats. Every few years, he plastered the cellar's walls with lime and patched the door to keep the cellar dry.

Ned made his living hauling things. At age thirteen, he had bartered for a horse and wagon and later for a broken-down Dodge Brothers truck, which he rebuilt with parts scavenged and knowledge acquired as naturally as scratching an itch. Ned was reliable, a trait not spoiled by any shiftless tendencies. And his labor was cheap as he was unaware of the full value of his service.

Ned had always been clever. He could observe any task, any action, and by virtue of this, he could duplicate any job. This is how he had acquired many of the skills and understanding to care for himself and his sister in the cabin by the river. Formal education would have done Ned a lot of good, but he managed well without its benefit. Sky lived by her brother's hard work, his ingenuity, and by his unfailing devotion.

With what he earned hauling, Ned bought from Fowlkes' Mercantile the few things he could not grow or produce himself—oil, gas, and belts for his truck, flour and salt, writing paper and an occasional treat for Sky. The mercantile stood at a crossroad where the hollow met the road into town. Ned had an account there, as did most of the hollow's sparse citizenry. But more often than not, Ned paid for his goods on every trip. He also picked up jobs there. Mr. Fowlkes kept a stack of requests for Ned. Everyone knew to summon Ned through the mercantile for work they needed done. The arrangement benefitted both men and the community. It was a service Ned offered to pay for. "No need," Mr. Fowlkes would tell him. "You git people in the door for me. I call that a fair trade."

Ned had always appreciated how Mr. Fowlkes treated people.

Though the current season marked the beginning of Ned's fifty-third year in business, he had no inkling of the concept of retirement. With his truck, built and rebuilt a half dozen times, he worked whenever people needed somebody to haul for them. He hauled livestock, furniture, farm supplies, barrels of kerosene, eggs, corn, hay, machinery—anything anyone needed to be picked up from one place and taken to another. He had moved growing families from one end of the hollow into larger houses at the other end. On a few occasions, he had moved folks out of the hollow altogether. But that was rare. He took cash for his work, and sometimes a bag of potatoes, a chicken, or anything else of equivalent value. A barter was just as valuable to him as money, sometimes more so. Once, when he was starting his business, he accepted a pony as payment, but the animal had died before he got it back to his place. He couldn't fix the pony like he could fix his truck.

While Sky cooked, Ned sat down at the table with a peach. He'd taken a bushel from a man for hauling five lambs to market. With his pocket-knife, he split the peach in half and hollowed out the pit, setting it aside. He peeled the peach and fuzzy peel fell onto a rag he'd spread out, its folds and ragged edges pressed flat.

Ned took one thick slice of the succulent peach and held it up. "Here," he said to Sky.

She bent down and took the peach with her mouth, nodding her thanks to her brother. She wiped peach juice off her chin with the back of her hand and went back to the stove. The pungent smell of ham broth soon saturated the cabin. The sun rolled through the open door.

Ned finished eating the peach and dumped the remains, except the pit, into a covered can that overflowed with vegetable peelings. He set the pit on the windowsill to dry and wiped his hands before he emptied his pocket of a handful of crumpled dollar bills. He flattened them, rolled them up without counting them and stuffed them into a jar on a shelf by the window. "I'll dump this," he said, picking up the can of scraps as he stepped out of the cabin. He headed in the direction of the garden.

While Ned scattered the vegetable scraps between the garden rows, Sky set two places at the table. With her apron wrapped around her hand, she pulled a meat pie out of the cook stove and set it on the table along with squash, applesauce, and spoon bread and butter. Ned came back through the door and set the empty can next to the stove.

Their meal began as it always began with a prayer that Ned recited, followed by verses he read from the dog-eared Bible opened on the table, a ritual he had learned as a young boy. They ate in silence. Neither Sky nor her brother was much of a talker. Their understanding of each other was hewn from decades of living together. Conversation was unnecessary for they were of like mind.

After their meal, Sky collected their few dishes and washed them in a tub filled with more water from the barrel that she heated on the stove. Ned settled on the front steps for a smoke. Shortly, his sister joined him and together they watched the sun flicker through the trees and sink into the horizon, the same way a hearth fire flames up and diminishes until eventually only the glow from the embers is left.

"I got to go up to Christiansburg tomorrow. You need 'nything?"

"Sugar. Cornmeal." Her voice was the purr of summer rain. Ned often thought he could probably count the number of words his sister had said in her fifty-six years. She raised her hands and formed a square in the air between them. She was asking for paper.

Ned nodded and smiled. "I'll see what Mr. Fowlkes is got."

When the sun was gone, Ned rose and went to his bed where he slept soundly. Sky stayed on the porch after the last light faded, and she listened for a long time after that. She listened to the quail and pheasant running, to the beavers gnawing and felling trees, to the raccoons scavenging and fussing. Under the black canopy, hawks sailed—she heard their wings thrash the air. Owls conversed. Rodents scurried along the forest floor. Sky knew each sound the same way a conductor hears each instrument, each single note in a symphony. The moon in the last stage of waning gave faint light, and deep in the hollow there was only ambient light, leftover vestiges of the day. When a cloudbank closed the heavens, Sky sat comfortably in the darkness, leaning up against the porch rail, distinguishing the night's sounds.

Sky needed little to make her happy, but she needed Ned. He had taken care of her all her life. Long ago, on the night flagged in the brother's memory with fear and pain, he had brought Sky into the world. Ned remembered their mother, but Sky had no recollection. To her, there was only Ned. For Ned, there was only Sky.

As Sky sat in the darkness, she felt the summer currents stir, sweeping the clouds to the east and uncurtaining the moon's half-light. Across the river's inky water there appeared a band of gilded moonlight, so thick and distinct she might have walked across the river on it.

Sky was plain as muddy water. Born with difficulty, she lived with certain oddities and limitations, but she had learned by rote all the duties she needed. Ned had taught her what he could. She took care of the cabin and cooked. Purpose had graced both brother and sister. Sky was happy in a way that only simple people know. Her temperament belied her age, but her body did not. Her hands were knotted and calloused, and her face was a parched white leather that covered a gossamer soul. She was a mist that wanders through the forest after a storm or gathers with the quiet sounds of early morning.

Sky looked up. Above her, a lone hawk—a red-tailed—squealed, soared across the river, and perched high in a tree. Transfixed, she watched the bird's silhouette against the moon until it took to the air again, once more squealing. She listened to the trail of the bird's wings and voice bounce across the meandering river.

Sky had always wished she could fly.

# July

Ernie Fowlkes flipped on the lights in his storeroom at the back of the mercantile and found the bucket of nails to refill the bin in the hardware section. The bell attached to the double-screened front door tinkled as a customer came through.

"Ernie? Where you at?" a man called.

"Back over here, Dudley. How're you this mornin'?"

"Good. Good, except for my rheumatism."

"That's what comes with being older'n dirt."

"You oughta know, Ernie."

Both men chuckled. Ernie had an easy rolling kind of laugh. Dudley's was more of a snort, but they harmonized nicely, the way the laughter of old friends always does.

"What can I do you for?" Ernie said, as he dumped nails into the empty bin. He wiped his hands on his leather apron and then leaned on the counter.

Ernie Fowlkes had run the mercantile ever since his father died in a farming accident. He had been young, just back from the Great War. The community depended on the mercantile, so Ernie took it over. He hadn't really wanted to. He'd had bigger dreams. But what else could he do? The rambling, white frame building with a full, overhanging porch and double doors that stayed open more than they stayed closed was important to the community. His late father had opened the business at the turn of the century when optimism was high, and it had sustained a whole lot of folks during the hard times that followed. Ernie had come back from the war—escaping only with nightmares that would plague him for years, but whenever they appeared, the lure of the mountains, the comfort of the land, and the embrace of family and friends had sustained him, kept him happy. If nothing else, he was safe here, safe in the hollow. After all these years, in spite of his bigger dreams, he thought things had worked out as they should. The mercantile was part of him now.

A visit to the mercantile made a trip all the way into town unnecessary. Most folks appreciated that. The store sat near Jasper's Gap at the north end of the hollow and southeast of the town along the only road that ran straight through the gap to Galilee, a small community of plain and independent-minded people.

Galilee had grown up slowly. It had a tanner who kept a harness shop, a miller, a lumberyard and a cabinet shop, all commerce to support the farming community that tended the land as carefully and faithfully as mothers tended their children. It had once had a livery, but that had closed years ago, and when automobiles arrived, it was an industry left behind. Generations of families scattered throughout the hollow all held to the same code of hard work and self-sufficiency, a code as solid as the mountains.

"I need me a couple cans of oil. You got 'ny Pennzoil?" Dudley asked Ernie.

"You ain't takin' up racing, are ya?"

"Hull Free up at the Esso station told me it was good. Told me if I'd run this stuff in my engine, I'd get more life out of my truck. Thought I'd try it."

Ernie set two cans of oil on the counter. "Here ya go. Thirty cents."

"Whew! That's mighty expensive. It'd better be good—or I'm gonna want my money back."

"Take it up with Roy." Roy Turpin came every third Monday to stock the mercantile's shelves. He worked out of Roanoke and supplied all the stores scattered throughout the highlands, as far south as Bristol.

Dudley dug in his pocket and produced a handful of coins.

"Give me some Red Man, too."

Ernie handed him a pouch.

Out in front of the mercantile, Ned pulled his truck up to the building and parked. As he stepped into the store, he took his list out of his pocket.

"Mornin', Ned," Ernie said.

"Mornin', Mr. Fowlkes," Ned replied. He handed his list to the proprietor and greeted Dudley with a nod.

"I'll fix you right up, Ned."

Ned stepped aside to wait for Ernie to collect the items on the list: sugar, cornmeal, peppermint.

"You're in luck, Ned." He shook the list. "I got me a new stock of peppermints in yesterday afternoon. How many you want?"

"I b'lieve I'll take four."

Ernie opened the bin for cornmeal and realized it was almost empty.

"Lemme get you some new meal, Ned. Be right back." He headed back to his storeroom.

More customers arrived. Sunshine McCleary needed a bolt of calico to make dresses for her daughter and shirts for her sons and a can of alum for her cucumber pickles. Janie Philpot had come for a bag of flour so she could bake the next afternoon. As the women stepped up to the door, a tall, smiling man, the color of a buckeye, opened it for them.

"Good mornin' to you fine ladies," Estes Adams said. He tipped his hat, a brown fedora, well-worn but stylish. Estes was Mrs. Louisa Cross Leaberry's handyman. He helped around her place, ensuring that the widow could live by herself and not be dependent on her children. "Mizz Louisa," as everyone knew her, couldn't do without Estes. Estes and his wife, Parthenia, couldn't do without Miss Louisa either. Theirs was a kind of friendship that benefitted them all—a kind of balance common in the hollow.

"How'r you this mornin', Estes?" Sunshine McCleary said.

"I'm doin' all right, Mizz McCleary. How be all your young'uns?"

"Fine, Estes, but I used up a whole bottle of Tonsilline gettin' through the spring. They're all healthy now, though. How's Mizz Louisa gettin' on?"

"Jus' like she always do. Stubborn as a swelled-up door." He chuckled and winked. "Mizz Louisa's a spry one. She keeps me hoppin'. Heps me stay outta trouble."

"Well, you tell her we said 'hey,' and tell her I made her recipe for rhubarb pie. Turned out right nice."

"I'll do that. She'll appreciate hearing that, Mizz McCleary."

Ernie returned to the counter with a sack balanced on his shoulder. He plopped it down on the counter, sliced it open with his pocketknife and poured the contents into the bin. A cloud of dust settled across the counter. He batted at it and then grabbed a rag to wipe it off the counter after he had scooped out enough to fill Ned's order.

"Mizz McCleary," he called to his customer. "Will you tell your good husband that I'm gonna need more cornmeal? Jus' broke open my last bag."

"Surely will, Mr. Fowlkes," she said, while she perused the bolts of fabric stacked up on a broad table once used to slaughter hogs. Mr. Fowlkes had commandeered it and covered it with red-checked oilcloth to hold bolts of fabrics and other sewing notions.

"You want Shep to bring it on down to you when he goes out next?" Sunshine McCleary said. "I b'lieve he's got a load comin' off this afternoon."

"That'd be fine. Tell him I'd appreciate that."

Mr. Fowlkes turned to Ned.

"Here ya go, Ned. I put your peppermints in this little bag. That be all for you today?"

"Would ya add these?" Ned said, laying a pad of linen writing paper and two lead pencils on the counter. Ned pulled money out of his pocket while Ernie rang up his purchase. The cash drawer rolled open with a ding.

"Thank ya, Ned. See you next time."

"Yes, sir, Mr. Fowlkes. I be seein' ya," Ned said, and he headed out to his truck.

Estes stepped up to the counter.

"Mornin', Estes. You got Mizz Louisa's list?"

"Right here, Mr. Fowlkes." Estes handed him a list written carefully in Miss Louisa's familiar hand.

"Anything for your good wife today?"

"No, sir. I'm jus' carryin' fer Mizz Louisa today. I'll bring Parthenia in on Tuesday. She likes to come. Gets her out a bit."

# August

Ned sat on the stoop of the cabin, his elbows resting on his knees. He inhaled a long draft on his cigarette. Soon he would head off to another job. *Gonna be a hot one*, he thought, blowing a puff of smoke. With his thumb, he mindlessly rubbed the back of his hand. He took another drag.

Sky was inside the cabin. The barest of breezes stirred the air, and the smoke from Ned's cigarette wafted inside. Sky didn't notice. She was busy.

Sky was Ned's responsibility, and he cared for her with a solitary devotion that rivaled the Dunkard's devotion to God. It was a fidelity born of need and of love, a potent mixture that life had never diluted. Ned's contact with the world beyond their hollow was infrequent, only necessary interjections into the community that spun around the mercantile where Ned was known principally for his hauling services. No one knew of Sky. The brother and sister lived apart, like quail nesting, buried into the mountain's curves and crevices, season after season, undisturbed, safe in solitude, content in isolation.

Ned's focus never left the simple life he and Sky shared, except for the occasional times he hauled a load beyond, to Christiansburg or other towns outside of the hollow. Together, Ned and Sky's life formed a kind of bird song, sweet and harmonious, one they did not fully understand.

Sky got up from the table and came out to the porch. Hearing the rustle of paper, Ned turned. His sister handed him a drawing.

"See," she said quietly.

He took the drawing, and smiling up at her, patted the porch beside him. She sat down, and hugging her knees, waited. It was a regular ritual.

Ned examined her drawing—three fawns gathered near a pond. Sunlight glinting off the water illumined the fawns and broadcast it across the trees. The light was just right for early morning when deer grazed. Heavy grasses and stands of cattails ringed the water. Patches of watercress covered the far bank, a marshy area where a spring bubbled up and fed the pond.

*All this needs is color*, Ned thought, *and it'd be like being there.*

"Pwetty?" Sky asked.

"Yes. Pretty," Ned said. He smiled. "It's real pretty, Sky."

Satisfied, Sky stood up and returned to the table.

Ned listened to her roll her pencils across the table, turning them under her hand like small fulcrums, back and forth, a repetitive action that founded her thoughts as another picture formed in her mind—at least that was what Ned had presumed she was doing whenever she began to draw. He stretched his shoulders and then leaned back on his arms, thinking back to the day he had first discovered Sky's drawings.

She had been only seven or eight, thin as a cattail and quiet as a rabbit. No matter how hard he had pressed his sister, her words always came sparingly. Single and simple declarations. Gradually, he realized her aphasia was more than stubbornness or simple mindedness. He couldn't say what made her that way or why. He only knew this was how she was.

But what Sky couldn't put into words, she could put on paper or bark or stone.

That long ago morning, after Sky had gone into the woods—a habit as perpetual for her as breathing—Ned had looked for the scrap of bark that he had seen her tuck furtively into a chink in the cabin wall. He wondered why his sister would hide something from him because the rest of her was as transparent as glass. She had no capacity for secrets. Ned had leaned over her bed and found a crevice where the daubing had fallen out. He pulled out a piece of bark with a picture drawn on it. He marveled at the detail—tiny, delicate lines that looked like they had been made with a piece of charred wood or the edge of a soapstone. He ran his finger along the picture of a tree with branches filled with leaves. It was a perfect rendering of the wild dogwood in their side yard. Puzzled, he had pulled her bed away from the wall and found more drawings. Some were on pieces of bark. Some had been scratched on flat stones.

Ned was spellbound. Were these Sky's?

On the floor, he saw a dust-covered arrowhead. Sky had used it to scrape away some of the cabin's chinking to make more hiding places. The more he looked, the more drawings he found, and the more astonished he became. Some were drawn on pieces of slate. Others were scratched onto laurel leaves. Any surface vaguely flat would do, it seemed. Had she drawn these? He wondered fleetingly if his mother or the Dunkard had left them behind. Had he simply not noticed them before? But how could that be? They must be Sky's—but where was the clue? How could she have a talent so rare, and he not know?

Gathering a dozen or so, Ned spread them out on the table, and one by one, examined the drawings. They were perfect. Perfect. He had never used that word for his sister. He had always thought of her as imperfect, even broken. She spoke so little—yet she could spend hours watching a spider weave a web or a bird build a nest. He had thought her reluctance to speak was an indication of her limits. But was it the opposite? Perhaps her lack of words made room for something else—a profound talent.

A gift from God?

Carefully, Ned had started to replace the drawings, but before he could finish Sky walked back into the cabin. Upset by what she saw, she opened her mouth.

"No!" she said. "Mine!" Panic overtook her, and she became wild. She lunged at him, yelling, "Mine! Mine! Mine!" She thrashed wildly, pounding her fists on her brother's chest, and crying hysterically.

"Sky! I ain't takin' them jus' lookin' at 'em. You settle down." He grabbed her in a bear hug and held her tight until she calmed.

"I'm not taking them. I like 'em, Sky. They're pretty."

"Pretty?" she said. Pretty meant something to Sky. Pretty. Even if she didn't understand much of anything else, Sky understood beauty. Slowly, Ned let go of her. She remained still as her gaze settled on the window. The trees outside were moving gently on a breeze. "Pretty?" she repeated. "Pretty?"

"Did you make 'em? Did you draw these?" He had to ask, if only to confirm what he already knew to be true.

Her expression swayed between pleasure and pain, excitement and fear—but eventually it settled on trust. He watched a smile emerge, a delicate, almost invisible shy smile.

He took her hand and led her to the table. "Show me," Ned said, gently.

That was the day Ned had decided he would buy his sister some paper and pencils, and he had done so ever since. He believed, as the Dunkard had taught him, that all good things came from God. Even the gift He'd given to Sky.

Sky was drawing contentedly when Ned finished his cigarette and tossed the butt out into the yard. He looked over at his truck and made a mental note of what he needed to do for the day. He would make a trip to the mercantile to pick up any jobs Mr. Fowlkes had collected for him. He would buy some cigarettes, more paper, and he'd see if Mr. Fowlkes had any peppermint sticks. He liked keeping a supply on hand. *Better get moving.* He stood up and rubbed his lower back with his knuckles.

"I'll be back this evening," he yelled at Sky.

He headed toward his truck.

⌍⌏⌎

When Ned got home that evening, Sky was waiting for him on the front porch. Beside her was a small stack of new drawings. She watched him pull his truck into the side yard, and climb out, carrying a paper sack. She looked eager.

"Pppper...."

"Of course," Ned said, handing her a bundle of peppermint sticks. "Got you something else, too." He handed her a paper bag, which she dumped out onto the porch. Two yellow pencils and a pad of paper fell out.

"Sharp?" She fingered a pencil's blunt end.

"Give 'em here," he said and took the pencils from her.

She followed him inside.

On the stove, a pot simmered. Ned's stomach growled. He sat down at the kitchen table, pulled out his pocketknife and whittled a sharp point onto each pencil. Raking the shavings off the table, he tossed them into the fireplace as Sky popped a peppermint stick in her mouth and began to draw. This was a special kind of delight for his sister and seeing her happy made Ned smile.

Their cabin walls were filled with pictures: birds drawn in excruciating detail with every feather, every claw, every eye as real and accurate as if they had been photographed with an expensive Leica and burned onto silver-laced film. There were studies of mosses, twigs and trees, stones and grasses, small things and large things, and pictures of the mountains from every angle, in every light, every time of day and season.

Ned understood that God had blessed Sky after all.

# September

The sun was shining as Ned carried in a basket full of October beans and set them down beside the stove. The crisp green hulls snugged together. Some that were overripe had split open, so the large pinkish-gray beans peeked through. He straightened up and mopped his face with a handkerchief. It was going to be another hot day.

"I 'spect I'll be back a good piece before supper this evenin'," he told Sky. He dumped a handful of coins out of the jar and dropped them into his pocket before he went to his truck.

Sky heard the engine start to chug, and Ned's truck roll out of the yard. She got a fire going, scooted the basket over to the table, and sat down to hull the beans. By midafternoon, she would have them canned and cooling. After the beans, she washed what few clothes they had, hung them up to dry, ran a hoe through the corn, and swept out the cabin.

Ned's job was close by, but a coming thunderstorm cut it short. He arrived back ahead of the rain. Sky was standing on the porch watching the thunderhead lumber over the mountain like a great black bear.

"You get the beans done?"

Sky nodded.

"I'll carry 'em to the cellar after it rains. Give 'em a chance to get good and cool."

A streak of lightning sliced the heavens. Silently Ned counted: one, two, three, four, five. As he got to six, the first thunder rumbled.

"Six miles," Ned said. "I'm gonna shut Collier up in the cellar, so the storm don't spook him."

Mesmerized, Sky watched the heavens. Another bolt split the sky, this one brighter and straighter. With the hard pads of her fingertips, Sky tapped her cheek: one, two, three. Thunder clapped. The trees began to rustle like tall, skirted dancers. Sky stood still as the storm approached. She heard Ned lead Collier out of the side yard to the cellar. She listened to the dog's nails click on the cellar's stone steps, listened as Ned reassured the hound.

"You stay here, 'ol boy. Get back up under the table. Storm won't last long."

When the thunder and lightning came closer, Ned said: "Come on in. You bes' watch from inside." Ned understood the power of the heavens. He took Sky's arm and led her into the cabin. She went to the window to watch. In a matter of minutes, the storm blew up. Trees bent low and leaves danced in eddies of wet wind as rain whipped the cabin, washed the forest, ran down the mountainsides and through the hollow where it flooded holes and gullies, filled up decayed logs, and turned runnels into small transient streams.

When the storm passed and the sun returned, the forest shimmered. As the clouds departed over the ridge, a rainbow hung in the heavens that drew both Sky and Ned back out to the porch. Side by side, they watched until it melted back into the fresh-washed sky.

"I'll get Collier," Ned said.

Sky watched him step out into the muddy yard. Ned was small and wiry but strong as men twice his size. His back was bent from years of hauling and his hands were crooked and calloused, his fingers stretched, but he walked solidly.

The latch squeaked and rainwater rushed off the heavy door as Ned opened the cellar and called to Collier.

"Come on up, boy," he said, clapping his hands. The dog shook and ambled up the steps into the light. Ned squatted down and grabbed the hound's dewlap, rubbing him affectionately. "Storm's over." Ned felt a bump on the dog's neck, separated his fur and pulled off a swollen tick before leading Collier back to the run.

Soon the cicadas sizzled again, and steam rose off the river like a lady lifting her skirt. The surface of the water was smooth and silent, but Ned knew the current was strong and powerful.

"River's way up, Sky. You stay up here now. Ya hear?"

Sky acknowledged him with her customary nod.

Ned took a long pole and creel and walked down to the river. Sky sat down on the edge of the porch. She watched her brother cast his line a dozen or more times and bring in three fish: two crappie and a nice small-mouth bass. When he started back toward the cabin, Sky stood up to get the fish knife and the fry pan.

# Late September

The forest looked as if buckets of Indian corn had been tossed into the trees. A light ground fog lingered, muting the scene to a lovely watercolor. Sky walked through the woods absorbing every varied color, every shadow, every sound. She was searching for the circle of black-barked trees that she visited every year about this time—the stand of black walnut trees surrounding a wet weather pond that emerged every spring, disappeared reliably by midsummer, and reappeared with autumn rains that could come with the force of a hurricane or settle in gently for days. Either way, the pond was renewed and today, as she approached it, the pond was brimming.

Clouds of caddisflies hovered above its surface and sunlight sparkled randomly across the water. Under her feet, brittle leaves and sticks crackled. Off her narrow shoulders hung an oft-patched cloth coat, and she carried her burlap sack. Today, Sky would collect walnuts. After they dried and she pried them open, her hands would be stained black from the stubborn shells, but her larder would be fuller.

She collected the hard, green pods in her apron and poured them into her sack. When her bag was full, she walked around the periphery of the water. The pond, bottom-lined with oak leaves whose half-life was the longest of any others in the forest, was bronzed and reflected the surrounding trees. The sight intrigued Sky who looked at the sky, then at the pond, back and forth, comparing and memorizing the images. She stepped slowly around the bank to watch the kaleidoscope of light shift and change.

Above her, a heron flew across the pond. She looked up as it alighted on the opposite bank. Sky stood motionless because she knew that any sudden movement would scare away the bird. Slowly, almost impercep-tibly, she raised her head and straightened her back to get a better look. She watched the bird turn its head from side to side, preening its feathers. Captivated, Sky watched until it flew again, sailing low across the pond before veering upward and out of sight.

"Bird!" Sky called, as if to bring it back. She closed her eyes and raised her arms in imaginary flight. "Fly."

❦

Sky stood at the center of the cabin with her hand extended. In her open palm, a gold necklace pooled. Attached to it was a small locket. Ned had forgotten all about it. He had forgotten that he had put it away. It had been so long ago.

"Where'd ya find that?" Ned asked.

Sky turned and pointed to the corner of the room where a small chest stood, one rarely opened because the drawers stuck, especially in humid weather.

"What?" Sky repeated.

"It was Mama's."

Sky looked puzzled. The siblings had rarely spoken of their mother.

"You can keep it," he said, preempting the question he saw on his sister's face. She put it in her pocket.

"No. It goes around your neck. Here, lemme show you. Give it to me."

Sky retrieved the necklace and poured it into Ned's palm. He held it, remembering the night he had taken it off their mother's lifeless neck. He wanted to open it to see the faces inside that he barely remembered, that had looked only vaguely familiar. He only presumed who they might be. But he didn't open the locket. Maybe he would, sometime, perhaps when Sky was sleeping.

"Turn around," he said.

Ned encircled her throat with the delicate links and fixed the clasp at the nape of her neck. Sky touched the locket.

"Pretty?" Sky said.

"Yes," Ned said. "She was."

Sky raised her shoulders and rubbed her neck where the chain fell. She pulled at it—the unfamiliar sensation agitated her. "Off!" she said.

"All right, Sky. Hold still." Ned unclasped the locket and handed it to her. She dropped it back into her apron pocket.

Ned knelt in the garden, weeding, as Sky came out of the cabin. He always planted a late crop of kale, onions, and red runner beans, banking on the benevolence of an Indian summer. Most years he got it, and an extra measure of food to put away.

He looked up as Sky passed by. Her apron was off, and her smoky hair hung across her shoulders. She pointed toward the forest, a gesture that Ned understood to mean she would be gone for several hours and return to prepare their supper when the sun got low.

"Be careful," Ned said, as he always said.

He watched her heading toward the woods. Occasionally, she stopped in midstride, put her hand to her chest and winced—a gesture that worried Ned—but it never stopped her from going into the forest or him from stopping her. Lately, he had noticed her ankles swelling and she suffered a cough that never seem to go away. A vague and distant memory, a memory of the Dunkard's last months, unsettled him.

Sky chose the path that ran up along the edge of the ridge, a course of natural switchbacks made by deer and elk. The lower, more protected side fumed with honeysuckle. On the upper side, thick stands of evergreens and mountain laurels filtered the sun. Although it was cool where she walked, autumn had not yet tempered all the summer heat, and when she reached each upper path, the air grew increasingly hot and windy. Everywhere was sound: buzzes, chirps, whirls, clicks. On her way, she disturbed a covey of quails that flew out of a thicket. She stopped to listen to squirrels chattering in a high nest. Beyond the dark green fortress, she emerged onto a rugged path of loose shale. She stepped carefully. Ned had warned her to watch for snakes. The hollow was full of copperheads, especially in the fall.

She reached her destination, a rocky outcropping on the eastern ridge that overlooked the hollow. High above her, clouds sailed through an endless blue sky. Sporadic gusts of wind upset the crisp shells of leaves, sending them skittering over the rocks. The wind was blowing north to south, shoveling out some of the lingering humidity, and she felt the cool of fall on the breeze. Autumn was a collision of temperatures, a time when hot and cold competed.

She lay down on a flat surface, pillowing her head with her hands and falling asleep. When she awoke, she saw that a black snake, a creature she knew to be harmless, had coiled near her side. Like Sky, the snake was drawn to the warming sun that reflected on his shiny scales; his lighter underbelly was only partially visible. She wanted to touch him, hold him, but knew she would frighten him, so she was content to lie still and watch this friendly serpent.

High above, buzzards flew in concentric circles soaring and swooping down below Sky's rocky perch to another ledge below her. They rode the swirling winds that drafted up through the hollow on a natural convection. She wanted to see what the buzzards saw. Slowly, she sat up. If she could remove herself with little vibration, she could slip off the rock without disturbing the snake. She got up quietly, stealth-like, and soon found the path winding back down the mountainside.

In a small clearing, she spotted the carcass of a huge groundhog. The buzzards circled and glided on their long black wings. Landing, they tore at the bloated carcass with their strong hooked beaks. Sky pressed her fingers against her cheek. One. Two. Three. Four. Five. She looked at her fingers so she could remember to show Ned how many buzzards she had seen.

The sun began angling down and soon she was back on the path toward home, crossing through the pines. Near the wood's edge, she slowed down. The cabin was in sight, but Sky was not ready to go back. She would extend her day as long as she could. She checked the sun. Seeing a small patch of sunlight in a circle of oaks, she sat down and, without thinking, thrust her hands into the dry leaves. All of a sudden, she felt a sting and jerked her hands back, uncovering a copperhead. Two drops of blood and two small fang marks dotted the back of her hand. Sky let out a wordless cry.

"Sky!" Even from a distance, Ned could tell his sister was upset. He stood up as his sister ran toward him. "Sky! What's wrong?"

She could not find words. Instead, she thrust her hand toward him.

"Calm down," he said, as adrenaline shot through him. "Rattler?"

She shook her head.

"C...C....C....Cc...." was all she could manage to get out.

"Copperhead?"

"CCC cop-head," she stuttered. Her head bobbed in affirmation. Ned took her hand and led her to the cabin where he made her lie down. He let her hand hang below the edge of the cot.

"Does it hurt?"

Sky shook her head, but Ned could see fear in her eyes. She knew what could happen from this kind of snakebite. He answered her fear with a reassuring pat on her arm.

"Close your eyes, Sky. You jus' go on to sleep," he said with intentional calm, even though his own heart was racing. "If you can't sleep, you lie real still," he told her. "I'll watch your hand."

Sky lay motionless, as Ned prepared a poultice of snakeroot and white oak bark to draw out any poison. He knelt beside her, examined her hand before he applied the poultice. *No swelling yet—a good sign*, he thought. Ned noted the sun.

"If it don't swell by sundown, you pro'bly jus' got you a dry bite. I 'spect that's all it is," he said. He smiled at her, trying to allay her fears.

She looked up at him. Sky remembered their first hound, how he died after a rattler bit him. His leg had swollen and stiffened. Unable to walk, he had flopped on the porch whimpering, his tongue swelling as the poison moved from his leg through his body. Sky had stayed with the dog and slept out on the porch to give him what comfort she could. She had watched him writhe and die.

"Nothing I can do," Ned had told Sky, who had petitioned him with a look he wished he could erase. "Nothing to do 'cept get us a new dog."

Sky had rarely cried in her life. There had never been a reason. But that night she cried as if she were made of tears. She had been consoled only when Ned reminded her that the hound's suffering had finally ended.

Ned looked at Sky. A single tear slipped down her cheek. With the side of his thumb, he wiped it away.

"It'll be okay, Sky. I'll take care of you."

Sky believed Ned. She closed her eyes and fell asleep.

Night came with no swelling. Still Ned kept her hand below her heart and never left her side. By morning, the two small marks were almost gone.

# Early October

The mercantile was abuzz after a visit by company men. Month after month, suspicions had followed these newcomers like wakes, breaking hard, then smaller, but ever wider. Early on, locals hadn't believed it. The company men called it progress. Inevitable progress. Locals didn't think so. In the beginning, it had all sounded impossible, but now, when the wind blew just right, the murmur of distant and ominous industrial thunder thrummed through the hollow.

It had come after all.

"Sometime next summer," said Ernie Fowlkes, standing behind the counter. His fingers drummed the worn numbers on his cash register. "That's what Shep McCleary told me. He's talked to 'em." As his voice trailed off, his eye found the window. He was searching for some reprieve, some miracle deliverance.

"I heard late next spring," said a tall, boney man named Cecil, who loitered near the counter. Next to him, a third and a fourth man shook their heads. In their eyes, a sad acquiescence lingered. They had the look of men on death row.

Daily they gathered at the mercantile. Sometimes there were three men, sometimes as many as a half dozen—distant neighbors tied together by community. It was their ritual. Ernie loved the constant parade of customers who walked through his front door every day of the week except Sundays, when the mercantile was closed. He took care of them. He kept a jar of deer jerky sitting next to the register for them. He dried it in a shed behind the store and sold it, four sticks for a penny. He made sure his stock of tobacco was always ample. On hot summer days, regulars would pony up for a cold coke, bottled down the road in Marion, so they could stand around a little longer and discuss the local news, the state of affairs, and the world in general. What direct knowledge they had of the outside world came from their military service or the *Roanoke Times*. On wintry days they would gather around the potbellied stove in the center of the store to smoke and talk. When they weren't there, they were working hard—tilling, growing, fishing, hunting, building, chopping, plowing, planting, harvesting—anything that put bread on their tables and kept roofs over their families.

"Shoulda seed this comin'," said Ernie. He leaned on the counter.

"Wouldn't a done us no good," said Cecil. He slid his purchase across the counter—an iron hook, a paintbrush, and a bag of tomato dust. "Not a tinker's dam. The fix was in long 'afore we got any inklin' of it. That's how them people do. Make all their fancy plans 'afore they tell people like us. Cain't be upfront and honest. Not a one of 'em."

Ernie rang up the sale.

"Twenty-eight cents," he said as he pushed the keys on his cash register. The drawer of the old National rolled open.

"Can't stop progress. That's what one fellow tried tellin' me," said a man named Grover. He was heavy-set man, wrapped in overalls and a faded red flannel shirt. He raised his jaw and set it, as he dipped his hand into his pocket, withdrew some coins and laid them beside the register.

"Thank ya," Ernie said.

Ernie scooped up the coins, dropped them into the cash drawer and made change.

"Progress, my ass." It was a scoff more than a statement and came from Cecil. "I'd like to haul off 'n flatten their progress. Can't stop them is more like it. Somebody's makin'a killin'. It's got more to do with greed than progress if you ask me."

"Nobody asked you, Cecil. That's the whole trouble. Didn't nobody get asked," said Buford, standing beside him.

"Greed's gonna be the end of us all. They're all speculating. Gettin' rich off our land. They slid this under our noses like a polecat under a church," said Ernie.

Then came a moment of silence that wandered self-consciously through the mercantile as if a ghost had appeared and every eye, surprised, took a moment to absorb it. One by one their faces dropped. Each man pondered his life; they had good and decent lives.

"Damn," Buford said. The expletive of choice might have come from any of the men—a two-fisted curse that held a sad irony.

"Amen," said Grover. He handed Ernie a nickel. "Gimme a co-cola." He walked over and opened the red cooler. Frosty air pooled as he fished around the collection of cold bottles. He made his choice, closed the lid, and popped the top off on the opener fastened to the cooler's edge.

The men at the mercantile knew no one in high places, only low places, where smoke rose from lonesome chimneys and whole families lived cradle to grave in the deep cleft of the mountains without ever knowing the back side of their own views. Deep in their hollow they burrowed like animals and suckled on the river. Here they knew safety and comfort. They knew their place and understood their surroundings.

"Next spring, you say?" said Buford. He took a deep draft on his cigarette and looked out the window at the voluminous autumn sky through dark, heavy eyes. Slowly he exhaled a thin line of smoke. "Damn," he said again, followed by a deep cough.

Cecil pulled a plug of tobacco from a pouch and stuffed it in his cheek.

"That's what I hear," Ernie said, as he shut his cash drawer again. "Late next summer."

# Late October

Early in the morning, bloated storm clouds beat back the sun before they extinguished it altogether with a heavy, doleful rain. Those who lived in the hollow were accustomed to hard rains in the fall. Mostly, they welcomed them to nourish their soils dried out by the summer's heat. Sweeping in from the southwest, rain sometimes lasted for days, bringing more water than they needed into the steep hollow. It was a perpetual battle of feast or famine, part of the year-to-year cycle they rode, a cycle that brought life, death, and life again.

By nightfall, the heavy rain had not relented, continuing overnight and throughout the next day as a torrent.

Ned paced the porch as he kept tabs on the rising river. Sky, inside the cabin, was occupied with pencil and paper. Any sense of urgency she might have felt would come from a subtle change in Ned's mood, not from her own observation.

Near dusk, when the water had risen as far as the yard, Ned alerted Sky. She came out to the porch. Cued by the tenor of Ned's voice, she sat stiff and tense in a rocker fashioned out of bent dogwood. She rocked back and forth, listening to the rain, a sound she liked, a sound she did not usually associate with danger. The rain's cool mist blew across the porch. Sky shivered. Ned stepped back into the cabin, picked up a throw and wrapped it around his sister's narrow shoulders.

"You get ready, Sky. Any time now, we best be moving to higher ground."

As they waited—Ned for the water's rise and Sky for Ned's signal—Sky chewed on her thumb. Collier paced in and out of the cabin's doorway.

Like Sky, Collier was waiting for Ned to lead.

The river was growling now. In the darkness, Ned heard it flowing close to the cabin, too close, raising his anxiety. Without the moon, he could only speculate on its exact path through the hollow, which could become a funnel for water and debris, not unlike the water rushing through the sluice at the gristmill. As the river crept closer, Sky sensed Ned's concern, but she remained calm, sure of Ned. Neither knew that upstream the river had already torn out a footbridge.

A huge lightning bolt, brilliant and lingering, lit up the sky. In the split-second flash, Ned saw a huge, uprooted tree racing toward them.

"Sky!" he shouted. Ned rushed toward his sister, grabbed her and in one motion pulled her from the chair and into the cabin as the massive tree struck the porch, ripping half of it away. Water thundered past the cabin.

"Hold on to me, Sky," Ned yelled over the rushing water. He pulled his sister out the door, his arm tight around her, and together they felt their way along the broken edge of the porch.

"Collier! Come!" The hound followed Ned's voice.

At the corner of the cabin, Ned pushed Sky off onto the waterlogged ground and jumped after her. Grabbing her hand, he pulled her toward the woods behind the cabin. Their feet sank in the saturated earth, but they went as fast as they could in the driving rain. Collier ran ahead. Sky stiffened and stopped.

"No, Sky, don't stop," Ned yelled.

"Where go?" she shouted, her voice nearly drowned out by the roar of the rain and the river.

"Come on!" Ned pulled her.

"No!" she said, with a rare declaration.

In another lightning flash, Ned saw that Sky was pointing.

"There," she said. "Go."

He felt his sister tug on his arm. Ned allowed himself to be pulled along. These were Sky's woods. She took them in the direction of a rocky crag, a useless part of the hollow, too rocky to grow anything and too steep to hunt. Ned had always avoided it. But tonight, Sky led them straight for the rocks. The weight of the rain, its heavy scent and constant pounding all but overwhelmed them. They were soaked to the bone, shivering, but neither let go of the other's hand. In the dark, they struggled through the rain, the mud, and the thick forest, climbing away from the cabin and the angry river.

They reached a bank swarming with mountain laurel. To Ned, it felt impenetrable, but Sky knew her way and led as if she had all the advantage of daylight. She pulled him down underneath the thick canopy of dark leaves. The din of rain was deafening, but once they were beneath the canopy, it changed to a higher-pitched patter as rain splattered across the thick, broad laurel leaves.

Sky was searching for something. Ned felt her bend forward. He followed, holding tight to her hand. They entered a small cave, carved into the middle of the hillside. In the darkness, Sky felt her way easily to a side-wall. She sat down and pulled Ned down with her into a pile of bone-dry leaves. They leaned back against the cave's rock wall. Collier shook himself dry and then curled up at their feet. Neither brother nor sister spoke as they rested. All night, outside the cave, the deluge continued to flush the hollow.

When morning came, the sky was brilliant and clear, as blue as a robin's egg.

# November

Ned hammered the last nail into the last board of the new porch and stood up to straighten his back. He had wasted no time repairing the flood's damage to the cabin. Winter was coming, and he knew he would be foolish to delay. It had taken him a good week to finish after he bartered with Mr. McCleary at the sawmill for new boards and bought nails from the mercantile. Ned had always lived frugally, so the expense was easy for him to cover. His only extravagances were cigarettes for himself and peppermints, paper, and pencils for Sky. All his other purchases from the mercantile were basic. The real cost was the time and exertion to rebuild.

The river had ravaged the hollow, taken out several cabins wholesale and a few lives. All in all, Ned was thankful the cabin had survived, even though the porch and steps had been lost. These he replaced. Once the river receded, the full extent of the damage was apparent. Ned had lost his late crops, and much of the good dirt he had cultivated was scraped clean by fallen trees and washed downstream in the floodwaters. These were more difficult to replace. Their larder, though, stocked and tucked into the root cellar on the high side of the cabin, had been spared.

Ned tossed his hammer aside and stood back to survey his work. He paused and wiped his brow. Looking toward the river, he thought how soothing it would feel to his tired body. Sheets of light reflected off the water. Its surface was calm today. During storms, though, whitecaps would pepper the water, and he had watched strong currents strip trees from the riverbank. Whenever the river was angry, Ned was always stunned by its power. He saw it as the good with the bad; the weak with the powerful;

the life-giving with the life-taking. Everything has an opposite, he thought. Safety and risk. Obedience and disobedience. Beauty and ugliness. Life and death. The river was proof.

Ned heard Sky humming from inside the cabin. He listened. For Ned, work and purpose were not opposites. They were perfectly aligned. He collected his tools and returned them to the shed.

The mercantile's screened doors slapped shut behind Ned. The bright sun, even this late in the year, was heating up the building. The potbellied stove near the center stood ready for the cold winter days coming, but today, a dry wind, blowing west to east through the screens, freshened the large, welcoming store.

"How're you, Ned?" Ernie said.

"Jus' fine, Mr. Fowlkes." Ned acknowledged the proprietor and the cadre of regulars scattered around the center of the store.

"What can I do you for today?"

Ned handed him a list.

"And gimme some Lucky Strikes," he added.

Ernie tapped Ned's list. "How much flour you want?"

"Gimme five pounds. And I'll take me a few peppermint sticks. If you got'ny."

"Got plenty. How many you want?"

"I'll take five."

"You and Sunshine McCleary's the only one's buys 'em mostly. All them young'uns she's got. Don't care for them myself."

"Yes, sir," Ned said. He saw a pad of linen paper. He lifted it up and laid it on the counter. "This, too."

The proprietor pulled open the bin behind the counter and scooped flour into a paper sack, weighing it on an ancient scale poised on the counter. Sitting beside it were a jar of pickled eggs and a tin filled with small American flags that he had set out earlier for Armistice Day. He collected Ned's supplies, tallied them, and wrapped the peppermint sticks in brown paper.

"Luckys, you said?"

"Yes, sir."

"Eight cents, Ned."

Ned dug into his pocket for coins.

"You get your porch put back together?" Ernie asked as he opened his cash drawer.

"Yes, sir."

From the gaggle of men clustered to Ned's right came a "hmmmph" from Grover, and under his breath, he said, "What's the point?"

Ernie frowned at Grover, and then he turned back to Ned. "Here ya go. We was jus' talking about the dam, Ned. They was in here again this week."

Grover, Cecil, and Buford listened, ready to offer their opinions.

"Who's that?" Ned asked.

"Power company. All them college boys," Grover piped up. "Wet behind the ears. Know everything. They think so at least."

"Don't know much about it," Ned said. His statement was an honest one. Ned rarely lingered at the mercantile for conversation. He always had work to do.

"Why anybody'd wanna do that to the river's beyond my understandin'," Cecil said as he leaned over the open cooler and fished out a coke. A wind whistled through a window, knocking over a cardboard display advertising Red Man tobacco. Ernie set it back straight.

"They keep trying to tell me how much we need the power," Grover said, his thumbs hooked in the straps of his overalls, his abundant midsection puffed out. He was gazing out the window as the sun shone across fertile fields cradled by the hollow. "I lived here 64 years without their power. My Delco plant's done real good for me. I got no complaints."

"Progress," Ernie said, with a tone of voice tinged with disdain. "You been up t'wards Roanoke? Who'd wanna live in that mess, I got no idea."

Ned listened but made no comment.

"What kind of progress destroys people's homes? That ain't progress," Grover said. "Progress oughta make people better. If you ask me, I believe it jus' makes people greedy. More you get, the more you want. That's what I think."

"My boy's gone up to Washington to live," said Buford, who farmed along the river's eastern bank. "Don't see it's made him any happier. He comes back home once a year to see his mama for Christmas. Then he cain't get away soon enough. Complains the whole time about what all we don't got. Sometimes, I think it'd be best if he jus' stayed away. He thinks his ol' man's backward."

The wind shifted direction and now sucked out through the window. The screened door at the front of the store rattled. Ned listened to the conversation, but he offered no thoughts of his own. In truth, he had none. He stood long enough to be polite. When his obligation was fulfilled, he said goodbye, picked up his sacks and left.

But what Ned had heard troubled him.

When Ned's truck rumbled to life and the men of the mercantile heard gravel crunching as Ned pulled out onto the road, Ernie Fowlkes turned to his gathered neighbors.

"This gonna be tough on ol' Ned," Ernie said.

"Gonna be tough on all of us," Cecil said. He was shaking clods of dirt out of the cuff of his pants. "Least Ned ain't got no family to look out for like the rest of us got."

# December

The river's shimmer caught Ned's eye, but he put the image aside and continued walking across the yard and around the back of the cabin to the root cellar. After a heavy frost overnight, the scattered weeds that held the ground together crackled under his shoes.

Ned pulled back the heavy cellar door and crouched to climb under the rough head beam and down the few stone steps. Smoke from the burning twist of an oil-soaked rag he was carrying blew in his face. He shoved the small torch ahead of him so that he could assess the condition of his winter stores. The shelves were mostly full even though Ned had lost his late crop to the flood. For his sister's sake, he would not gamble. He had bought extra supplies at the mercantile. Rows of store-bought cans looked odd next to his home-canned goods. Satisfied, he extinguished the flame and climbed back out of the cellar.

Ned stood for a moment in the yard and examined the sky. Just as the Dunkard had done. The moon, already visible, was ringed. Snow was coming. He knew these signs well and devised his days and weeks and months by them. He always measured his stores and stacked his wood accordingly, some for the shed, some for the porch, some for the hearth.

Tonight, though, he was distracted, mulling the unsettling conversation he had heard at the mercantile. He closed the cellar and walked back around to the front of the cabin. He could see Sky inside, preparing their dinner. The light from the hearth silhouetted his sister through the door that she left open perpetually, as if the cold or heat, rain or shine connected her to the forest like an umbilical cord. Keeping the door closed, except in the most extreme weather, had become a discussion abandoned long ago.

Ned pulled his splitting maul from the shed. After his dinner, he would chop more wood.

That night snow came, and winter was upon them once again.

Ned had wanted to get an early start so he could get back before dark. The days had grown short. He stopped by the mercantile to get a new fan belt for his truck. His belt had squeaked intermittently, and he worried it would break, leaving him stranded far from home. He was Ernie's first customer of the morning.

"And gimme some Lucky Strikes," he said, paying Ernie for the belt and the cigarettes. As an afterthought, he added: "I'll take some of them peppermint sticks, too, if you got 'em."

"Sure do. Where you off to today?"

"Christiansburg."

"Ah. That big job."

"Yes, sir. Up at the college."

A scowl crossed the proprietor's face. He shook his head. "I had jus' about enough of them college boys. Arrogant. Think they know everything there is to know."

Ned had not intended to pick at the sore. He only listened. He was a man of peace.

"That's where they get 'em, ya know," Ernie said, in a tone laced with acrimony. "You seen the dam yet?"

"No, sir. No, I ain't."

"You ought to, Ned. It'll chill your bones. You oughta go up and look when you come back by there today."

"I might could. Thank you, Mr. Fowlkes." He took up the fan belt, the peppermint, and the cigarettes, which he stuffed in his pocket.

"You know how to get there?"

"Don't know that I do."

"You go in on Chestnut Ridge Road. You take you a right turn—at that little ol' gravel road—jus' 'fore you get to Mizz Lizzie Hutton's place. You know where I mean?"

"I b'lieve so."

"Then you go down an ol' loggin' road. You can see it all from there. You go look, Ned. You oughta see it."

"Yes, sir. I 'spect I oughta."

Ned didn't linger. As he left, Ernie called after him. Ned made a quarter turn halfway to the door and looked back at the merchant.

"You made your plans yet?" Ernie said.

"No, sir."

"Well, you oughta be thinkin'."

"Yes, sir, Mr. Fowlkes," Ned said, and he left.

⁂

Ned pulled his truck up in front of the administration building and shut off the engine. He stepped out of his truck and made his way through the throngs of students, most of them unmindful of the small, wiry man climbing the steps. Passing through the lobby, he walked along the right-hand corridor to the second office. He opened the door, took his cap from his head, smoothed back strands of his thin hair, and stood politely until the secretary looked up.

"Well, good mornin', Ned, you're right on time. I wish I could get these professors to be as prompt as you."

One corner of Ned's mouth lifted in a half smile. He nodded.

"You know where Knox Hall is?"

Ned cleared his throat. "Behind the library?"

"That's right. Dr. Lacey wants you to pull up there. There's a loadin' dock out back. If you go on over, I'll give him a ring and tell him to look out for you."

"Yes ma'am."

"Thank you, Ned. Don't quite know what we'd do without you."

As the secretary picked up the receiver, Ned slipped out as unnoticed as he had entered.

By midafternoon, Ned had hauled most of the English department to the other side of the campus, loading boxes of books and furniture onto the back of his truck without uttering a dozen words. Most loads he carried on his back, anchoring each as he leaned forward and supporting them with nothing more than his fingers turned up behind him. After so many years of hauling, his hands were stretched and strong. The heaviest pieces he attached to a small cart with wheels that pivoted—one more invention of Ned's own making.

Ned was headed back to the hollow with a crisp new ten-dollar bill, a small fortune, crumpled in his pocket when he decided to make a detour. He was tired and hungry, but he needed to do this. Mr. Fowlkes' words echoed in his head. *You ought to, Ned. It'll chill your bones.*

He took the gravel road past Miss Lizzie Hutton's place toward a ridge overlooking the river. He found the logging road and drove northward up it. Parking near the entrance of a trail where a heavy chain had been strung across and secured with a padlock, he stepped over the chain and hiked a path through a small shinnery.

Ned stopped at the edge of the ridge. Far below, bulldozers ran up and down the scarred sides of the riverbank, and huge cranes stretched out like praying mantises. Tiny men crawled over the lacerated earth that had been scraped clean of vegetation and laid open like a butchered hog. From his vantage, Ned could look upriver and see the whole hollow. Throughout, columns of chimney smoke rose as temporal signposts for significant lives.

Seeing all this with his own eyes, Ned cursed.

Sky brushed leaves off the cover of the rain barrel. She dipped out enough water to wash the garden dirt off the root vegetables that Ned had carried up from the cellar where he had stored them in straw-filled wooden bins after harvesting. Then she set about making their meal.

Ned was late. When he didn't return by suppertime, Sky ate alone and then went outside to the front porch to watch for him. Before the moon rose above the treeline, she heard Ned's truck and saw headlights bounce along through the forest as her brother made his way along the rutted path. Sky went to set out the supper she had kept warm on the stove.

While he ate, Ned looked especially tired. His shoulders drooped as if he still carried the day's haul. The lines in his brow were deeper.

"This is good, Sky," he said, trying to lift his own troubled spirit with an encouraging word.

Sky looked at him and touched her cheek in slight response. He smiled at her and watched her a little longer than usual. He had always been astonished at the color of her eyes. He had never seen another human with eyes so blue. Only in birds—in the feathers of an indigo bunting—had he ever seen such pure color.

After Ned ate, Sky washed the few dishes before she took up a bucket of milk and skimmed off the layer of yellow fat, ladling it into a glass churn. She thought she had enough to make butter. Tomorrow she would rise early to churn. Ned loved the buttermilk that the clotting cream would release.

Before the rooster crowed and as a thin line of light outlined the ridge, Sky awakened. As she did every morning, she took her locket from her apron where she kept it each night and slipped it around her neck. After many tries and Ned's patient instruction, she had learned how to close the tiny gold clasp by herself, and she had grown used to the feeling of the chain around her neck. It was a kind of artificial beauty for Sky, one she could hold and keep. Often, as she drew, her idle hand would grasp the locket.

Still in her nightgown, she lifted the churn out onto the porch where she could work without disturbing Ned. When his workdays were long, as yesterday had been, he sometimes slept late—not often—but as Ned had gotten older his nights had become longer.

Wrapping herself in a coat to ward off the morning cold, Sky sat down on the steps facing west and tucked the churn between her thighs. She brushed her hair back from her face. It fell down her back like snow.

A slight breeze blew cold with a hint of wood smoke and drying leaves. Sky turned the paddles. They made a rhythmic thud like the downbeat of a song. Ned had bought the churn for Sky at the mercantile to replace the old wooden one that had been their mother's. This modern one was easier for her to use by herself. At first, the handle turned freely, stirring the raw cream with wooden paddles. As she had aged, the strength of her youth had diminished. Ever so often, she stopped, out of breath, to rest her arms.

While Sky worked, the morning awoke. Burgeoning light crept over the east ridge. As sunlight began to amend the sky, turning it from blue-black to pink, streaks of butter began to coagulate in the churn. Light began to pool in the gap, flickering behind the tree line, before spilling out like poured diamonds, showering her with a glimmering raiment. Sky closed her eyes and lifted her face to gather the light. Backlit by the sun, trees shimmered, and as the sun warmed the cold morning, it stirred currents, rustling the withered leaves—an ostinato beneath the rich opus of morning sounds.

When the handle of the churn began to turn hard against large clumps of butter, Sky carried the churn back into the cabin where she unscrewed the top and lifted out the paddles before pouring off the buttermilk and turning out the butter. After scraping the paddles, she salted the butter and shaped it into a loaf. When it was formed to her satisfaction, she covered it with a damp cloth and set it in a cool spot out of the sunlight.

Next Sky picked up a basket and went to gather fresh eggs. As she did, Ned began to stir.

# Late December

Ned sat on the bottom step of the porch cleaning the spark plugs for his truck. His hands were black, and the rag was black, and the spark plugs were so clean they shone. Still, he rubbed and rubbed, as if he couldn't get them clean enough. He looked up as Sky stepped down the stairs and pointed toward the woods. She had prepared Ned's breakfast and cleaned up, swept the kitchen and porch—as she always did before she went to the woods. Today, the air made her shiver.

"Sky," he said. "Wait."

She turned back to look at him. He stopped rubbing and looked her square in the face.

"Why don't you come with me this afternoon? I got a job up at Galilee."

Sky looked puzzled at this strange request, one she had never heard before. She shook her head.

"Come on. It's not too far. Won't take long." Ned pressed her, but she only shook her head with more resolve. He watched a strange apprehension cloud Sky's face, but as soon as her gaze shifted to the woods, she relaxed.

"You might enjoy it. There's a whole world out there you never seen." He smiled at her, trying to wedge some confidence into his sister. "They got lots of peppermint and paper. More'n you'd ever think."

"No," she said, drifting away from her brother toward the forest. She shook her head again, this time with finality, and then turned and hurried into the woods.

Ned sighed. He watched her until she disappeared past a thicket. He went back to his task as a wave of concern washed over him.

Sky reached the pond and sat down. The air was dry today, cooler, and the wind had picked up and was coming from the north. The pink heat lightning and hazy skies of summer had departed long ago, replaced by the crisp of early winter. From her pocket, she pulled a peppermint stick. She savored the pleasure of its sweetness on her tongue. She turned into the wind and let it caress her face the way the fingers of a blind child might. She felt winter lurking through the low dark places and in the unsettled currents of air. Sky could feel it pushing against her spirit like a lodestone.

Later, she would collect more acorns and hickory nuts to toss deep into the woods. For Ned, she had already collected chinquapins.

# The last day of December

Louisa Cross Leaberry stood by the window, tilting the letter toward the sun. She could barely bring herself to read it again. The letter infuriated and saddened her, but what was worse, it made her feel helpless, almost as if she were being widowed all over again.

*The Office of The Honorable Lemuel Q. Hillbert, Esquire*
*Richmond, Virginia*

Mrs. Robert Leaberry
Rural Delivery
Dunkard's Hollow, Virginia

My dear Mrs. Leaberry,

It was wonderful to hear from you after all these years. I hope this letter finds you well and prepared for another Virginia winter with vim and vigor.

I remember your late husband with great fondness. He was quite kind to me years ago when I sought to begin my career. Although I was just a young whippersnapper, he took me under his wing. In fact—and I am not sure you are aware of this—he wrote two letters of introduction for me. As a result, I was employed quite advantageously after my studies, and this led me into public service and my current position in the legislature. I appreciate your letter. I always welcome correspondence from friends and constituents such as yourself.

You are quite correct when you say that your late husband would certainly have had a few things to say about our new project. I hope he would have believed that such progress is inevitable and moves our region forward. Given your geographic location, which I am sorry to hear places you in the path of this important project, I am most aggrieved to learn that you are to be relocated. I am afraid, however, that I cannot provide you with encouraging news in this regard. I sincerely wish I could tell you something different, but I must report that a project of this magnitude, which is already well underway, precludes any changes in course. There is nothing I would be able to do to stop or to alter it.

While we all acknowledge the inconvenience this creates for some people, and you are perhaps the most notable of this citizenry, it is a step toward the future that we must take to ensure that our community grows and thrives.

If I can be of service to you in any way as you make this transition, please do not hesitate to contact me again.

With kind and sincere regards, I am your public servant,

Lemuel Q. Hillbert,

*Delegate to the Ninth District*
*Commonwealth of Virginia*

"Inconvenience!" Miss Louisa tossed the letter on a table, muttering, "Inconvenience, indeed!" Despite her long-practiced self-control, she teared up. "How dare he presume my Robert would have supported this."

After fifty-three years alone, Louisa Cross Leaberry still missed her husband. They had been married only eighteen years before he died unexpectedly of a ruptured appendix. Her life had begun when she wed and would have ended with Robert's death had she not had their children to rear and a farm to run. How many times over the years had she turned to speak to him only to realize once again that he was gone?

During those early years, she thought she would break, but she had managed—and she had thrived. Robert Leaberry had left her with more than enough money and land to live on for the rest of her life, and Estes—*thank goodness for Estes*, she thought—she had always had Estes and his wife, Parthenia, to help her run the farm.

Gradually, Miss Louisa had come to understand that power such as Robert Leaberry once had was non-transferable—and neither was devotion. Except for a few faithful friends and her church family, all the people who had fawned over the living Robert Leaberry, a man of means and influence, and who had competed for his attention, paid his widow only obligatory attention after his death. Lem Hillbert's letter had proven that sad truth to her once again. She had written a most reasonable letter, and she had hoped for a reasonable accommodation. After all, there were other ways to route the river. She knew there must be. Miss Louisa was no engineer, but she had lived long enough to know that every problem has more than one solution.

Miss Louisa sat down on a small loveseat upholstered in light blue damask and picked up the small frame that held her favorite picture of her husband. "You could have stopped this, Robert. I know you could have. Why aren't you here? Why can't you be with me?" She pressed the picture to her cheek and closed her eyes. She didn't know which emotion to choose. She was angry. She was disappointed, bitterly so. And she was scared, but no one would ever know this. Of this, she would make sure, if for no other reason than to plan for whatever future awaited her. It would not, however, be in the lovely river home that Robert Leaberry had built for his bride so long ago.

Her tall clock moaned just before it struck eleven. Eleven deep tongs. Silently, she counted them. "The eleventh hour," she said to herself in the empty room. "How appropriate."

# 1939

## THE WATERS PREVAIL

# January

Ned straightened the tools that hung on long box nails hammered into a beam above a workbench in the shed. This was the place where he sharpened his hunting knives, cleaned his rifle, rebuilt parts of his truck, fashioned inventions to solve problems, mixed feed for his animals, planed boards, kept tools, and accomplished a multitude of tasks. Today, though, he found it difficult to concentrate on any job.

He picked up a new calendar and hung it on the wall. It was a gift from the Lucky Strike people to local merchants, including Mr. Fowlkes. Ernie had saved it for him. "I know you're a Lucky Strike man," Ernie had said. "The wife won't let me hang it in the house. I got me one from the Farm Bureau that's more to her liking. Got a nice scene on it. No girlies."

Ned stared at the calendar. 1939. The girl dressed in white with a wide brimmed hat held daisies. She reminded him of a girl he had been smitten with when he was young, when he first started hauling. The first time he had seen her, he was picking up a load of cracked corn—he remembered this clearly. She was standing in front of the feed store with her father. Her grace and beauty had captured him, and he recalled how his heart had beat faster. He had tried not to stare, but he couldn't help it—she was beautiful. For weeks, he had returned to town hoping for a glimpse of her. She had made his visits to town pleasant; otherwise, they were awkward and uncomfortable for a boy raised away from the ordinary interchange of life. The lovely girl, near his age, would have made a beautiful wife, but Ned did not have the acumen or the opportunity to pursue her—or any young lady. His life's path was already set. He could not figure how another person would fit into his life with Sky.

Eventually, the girl stopped coming. He presumed she had married and moved on, but he thought about her for a long time afterwards. He thought he would never forget her, but now, after all these years, even the memory of her face was disappearing.

Ned flipped through the calendar months. He used a calendar to mark his plantings, his harvestings. But this year would be different. His mind wandered to the image of the scarred riverbank. It should have been a beautiful sepia landscape of winterkilled grasses, bare-limbed trees, and faded groves of oaks, hickories, and tulip poplars, all lining the wide river that would shift color from blues to greens to blacks depending on the color of the sky. But the sight of the river and its beautiful banks autopsied for a different purpose haunted him. In the pit of his stomach, a knot formed. The world was changing, encroaching. He took down the old calendar and hung up the new one.

There was no future for Ned other than the next season, the next crop, the next hauling. He understood that all life would come to an end eventually, but the present or the very near future was always his focus. He would let the rest sort itself out. He had no power to add to his days or to change the passing of seasons, so he did not try. He took each day as its own portion and used it as best he knew how, squandering neither time nor energy. He had only one purpose—to take care of Sky.

He lifted an oilstone and a knife from its place on his bench. He ran his thumb across the blade, and with his oilstone secured in his palm, he sharpened the blade, drawing it against the stone at the proper angle, in the proper direction, listening to the sound, a sound like a mother quieting a child. As he drew it across the stone, he stared at the calendar. He thought about his life. It, too, had been sharpened, made smooth and useful and effective. He had done well by Sky, by his mother, and by the Dunkard. His mother was gone. The Dunkard was gone. Forgotten, as if they had never lived. Ned was probably the only one left who remembered them.

He set down the knife and the stone. He looked toward the cabin. How could he persuade Sky to go with him to the mercantile? Could he entice her with the promise of peppermint or a soda pop? Or perhaps colored pencils—he had seen some made of wax. He had to find a way—something, anything that would persuade her to leave the hollow. He had to find a way.

He had to.

Collier loped into the shed and lay down at Ned's feet.

"What'd ya think, Collier? You'd go ridin' with me, wouldn't you, 'ol boy?" The thought cheered Ned. He pulled his rifle off the shelf. The barrel was clean, the brass fittings polished. "I'm thinkin' it's about time we do us some huntin'. What ya think, boy? You'd go with me? You wanna go ridin' with me?"

The hound lifted his head. Ned thought he saw him nod as he replaced the rifle on the shelf.

"Come on. Let's go talk to her."

⸎

Ned slid into the cab of his truck and pulled it up to the cabin. Leaning across the seat, he pushed open the passenger door and called to Sky.

"Come on. I want you to come with me," Ned said. "We're gonna get you a whole bag of peppermints. Many as you want. Come on now. Mr. Fowlkes's got a whole box of 'em. Let's go."

Sky stood on the porch, unmoving, her face betraying a fear as endless as the river.

"No."

He watched a shadow pass over her face as she pressed a knotted hand to her chest and winced. She shook her head.

Ned grit his teeth. "Come on. You gotta go," he said firmly, yet kindly. He could not afford to weaken or let her see his own anxiety. "You come on and get in. It'll be all right. You know I'd never do nothing to hurt you. It'll be all right."

Sky took one tentative step. She did not know how to argue with Ned; she had never needed to. He had never forced his will on her—not so much as scolded her. Never. There had never been a need because her way had always fit with Ned's way, as naturally as rainwater fills up gullies.

This was different, a different request, a strange request. It was confusing for Sky—an unknown destination and untried transportation. She had never ridden in Ned's truck, never even climbed into it. Her feet always touched the earth. How could she live untethered from the soil, the dirt, the leaves? Sky did not want this, but she did not know how to refuse Ned. And she did not understand why Ned was insisting.

"Come on. It'll be all right," he said again, smiling kindly at his sister. "Come on."

Not knowing what else to do but obey Ned, Sky climbed into the truck slowly and warily, never taking her eyes off Ned. When she was seated, he leaned across her lap and pulled the door shut. She tensed at the sound of the door shutting. Ned cranked the starter. His banty rooster of a truck shook and vibrated. Sky grasped the dashboard. Her swollen knuckles turned white. Her face was as pale as the moon, and her breathing, fast and shallow.

"I'll buy you more peppermints—much as you want," he said over the engine's commotion. He gunned the motor a little to warm it up. "A whole 'nother bag if you like." Ned was almost giddy that he had gotten her this far.

But Sky hardly heard. Her anxiety was so immense that she heard only a soft whir in her ears.

Slowly, the truck rolled forward. Out of the corner of his eye, Ned watched her. Sky turned and looked back toward the cabin. She didn't like being caged in the truck. As they bumped along the rutted path, Sky watched the cabin recede. A sudden pain in her chest made her wince again. She pressed her fist against her chest.

Once they passed the garden and entered the woods, Sky's agitation grew, and a terror ramped up inside her. It was a mixture of fear with a sudden and a wholly unfamiliar distrust of Ned.

"Turn around, Sky. It'll be okay," Ned said, gently coaxing her. "You can't see where we're goin' if you don't turn around."

When they rounded a bend, the cabin disappeared. Sky turned to stare out the door's window. Ned couldn't see her face, but her back was board straight. Her hands clutched the door as the winter landscape rolled by. Ned was cautiously hopeful.

But less than a hundred yards into the woods, Sky panicked.

"B..!" she said. "Ba..!" She was forming the words in frantic stutters.

"Bac..! Back!"

"Sky, you'll be all right. You'll see. Look up there." He reached over and touched her shoulder, but she jerked away and began to thrash around. Her eyes were wild. She began to tremble. Her absolute trust in Ned was eroding as quickly as sand gives way to rain.

"Back! Back! Back!" she said over and over until tears came and her words came in great gulps of sobbing. She banged her hands on the door.

Ned clenched his jaw, steeled himself, and gripped the steering wheel. He had to keep going. He had to.

When they reached a clearing where the road bent sharply again, Sky saw the forest ahead of them thinning and beyond that, a tin roof flashing in the cold sunlight. A lonely vehicle sauntered along a road that snaked down a treeless hill in the distance. Sky cried out. It was an audible, desperate cry, like an animal's cry. She looked at Ned. Her eyes pleaded with him, but Ned, resolved, looked straight ahead. He could not look at his sister.

He slowed the truck to cross a particularly rough patch in the road. The truck hit hard and bounced. He brought it to a crawl. Sky pushed open the door and jumped from the truck, landing in the dirt on her hands and knees.

"Sky!" Ned yelled.

Sky scrambled to her feet, and before Ned could pull the brake and kill the engine, she was running back toward the cabin. He saw her disappear into the forest. He placed his hands on the steering wheel and dropped his head, defeated.

All Ned could do was turn around. He shoved the truck into gear.

"Sky!" Ned yelled when he arrived back at the cabin. He lumbered up the steps and across the porch. "Sky!"

Ned found her huddled on her bed, her back to the door. Her head was covered with a tattered yellow shawl, little more than a rag. She would not look at Ned or answer him when he spoke. He sat down beside her and stroked her shoulder. For more than an hour, he sat with her, waiting for her to look at him, even scold him—to respond to him in any way. But Sky had retreated into her silence so deeply this time that even Ned's pleading could not pull her out. In that hour, he understood, perhaps for the first time, the depth of his sister's soul. She was part of the hollow, and to force her out was cruel. He knew this now, but he also knew he had no choice. Sky had to leave. She had to. But he would have to find another way. This way hurt too much, and he had never, ever hurt Sky. She was too dear to him. She was his lifelong companion, as faithful to him in her own way as he was to her. He loved his sister with every fiber of his being. But now Ned wondered with a horrible sense of dread whether Sky could ever survive outside the hollow.

As Ned sat with Sky that cold January afternoon, he wondered what his life might have been if Sky had died the night of her birth. In all his years in the hollow, he had never considered this. The answer troubled him.

The early winter sun began to dip low. The sun's warmth, what little the winter sun lent, evaporated. Sky was calmer now but lay still like a stone. Ned gave up. He covered her with a blanket.

"I'm hungry," he said, exasperated and bitterly disappointed. He stood up and left the cabin.

Only then did Sky rise. She went to the cookstove.

# February

Smoke drifted from the chimney. The plume strafed the rooftop, hesitated at the cabin's eave before it spilled over the edge of the rooftop and meandered off into the woods at a level most men could reach. Ned stood beside the cabin watching the smoke, rubbing Collier's head. Overhead a low ceiling of clouds bunched like rumpled cotton batting.

"Gonna git snow, boy," Ned said. "I 'spect I oughta bring you up into the cabin tonight. That sky's awful full." He sat down on the stoop of the root cellar and pulled Collier up close. He gripped the dog's dewlap, shook him affectionately and talked low. "You're a good 'ol hound, Collier. Soon as this snow's all laid down, we'll go do us some tracking."

By dusk, a hush had settled over the hollow, an absence of sound both Ned and Sky recognized as the herald of snow. Every creature in the hollow waited. Sky stirred a pot on the stove before she slipped out onto the porch to watch the sun set. At the base of the snow-laden clouds, the sky was a flaming furnace, and against it, the forest stood in blackface, fencing the fire. Sky could feel weather coming. She soon returned to her duty at the stove, reluctantly though, for any change in the weather drew her attention like a great performance.

Ned pulled a shovel from the shed. He carried more wood onto the porch and covered it with a canvas tarpaulin he used whenever he hauled in bad weather. It would keep the wood dry. Before coming to supper, he wanted to pull his truck up under the boughs of a white pine.

Sky set two places at the table and ladled out two bowls of steaming rabbit stew before she went to the porch and motioned for Ned. Ned's last task was to empty water from the barrel into a bucket. Ice was already skimming the water, but so long as they got only snow, he doubted the barrel would freeze solid. He carried in the bucket and set it by the stove. Collier had ambled in behind him and stretched out near the hearth.

As Ned and Sky ate their supper in silence, each wondered what the night would bring. Sky glanced through the window at the last daggers of red light filtering through the woods, eager to gather each vision the way an artist collects muses. Ned listened for the telltale patter of snow—a sensation more than a sound.

When Ned noticed the first flakes, light as a dove's breath, he signaled to Sky. She jumped up from her chair and rushed out onto the porch where she thrust her hands, palms up, from underneath the protective roofline. She watched as snowflakes landed and melted on her warm hands. Soon they were covered with snow. She looked back over her shoulder at Ned. Her face was radiant.

Where moments before the forest had been full of flame, it was only shadows now that quickly faded behind the curtain of snow. Soon, the only light remaining was the light of the fire coming through the gaping door.

"Straight down and fine. No wind," Ned said. "We're gonna get plenty."

Ned led Sky back into the warm cabin. He welcomed a heavy snow because it stopped time. Ned wanted to stop time. Shadows gathered shoulder to shoulder throughout the hollow as Ned and Sky huddled safe within the four walls of their cabin.

⁂

Ned woke with a start. He had dreamed he was drowning. Beads of sweat gathered in the creases of his brow as milky winter light filtered through the windows. Nearby Sky snored, her breathing, jagged and rattly. Outside the woods were white; snow covered everything. Only the chimney smoke marred the colorless landscape.

Ned threw back the bearskin that kept him warm. He had taken two bears one winter, and he and Sky had scraped the skins clean. Ever since, the skins had kept them warm during the coldest winter nights. He swung his legs out of bed and stretched. The cabin was cool but not uncomfortable even though the fire in the hearth had dwindled. He stoked the fire, taking care not to disturb Sky. Soon the cabin was warm.

Ned pulled his Bible off the shelf and sat down to read his morning devotion, turning the words toward the fire's light. Ned was sure there was a God. He was a man who understood enough of nature to know it to be so. It was February, so he was reading the Gospels. He had numbered the chapters and read a handful every day from both testaments. By the end of the year, he would finish so that by the beginning of each New Year, he was reading Genesis again. Yearly, he read every verse except the few that had been struck out long ago, making them indecipherable: Exodus 20:13. Deuteronomy 5:17. Matthew 5:21. Ned did not know why these had been marked out.

Sky had never learned to read, so Ned read to her every evening. She had no aptitude or interest in learning, but she listened to Ned's voice with rapt attention, absorbing the poetry of the words as readily as she absorbed scenes throughout the hollow. To her, the words were not deep or profound, or even instructive—they were pretty the way fool's gold shimmers in sunlight. Sky did not need to know the meaning. She was satisfied with the sound. Some reminded her of the wind, some of the river, some of the shifting seasons, some of the hollow's exquisite beauty—all her favorite points of reference. Sound was her music, and Sky was a virtuoso even though her words were limited. She could imitate the sound of a chattering squirrel or a cardinal's crisp staccato. She had never come to any understanding of the concept of salvation the way Ned had, but her brother felt certain she had enough good book in her to give God reason to pardon her of whatever natural sin she was born.

Ned finished his daily reading and turned to another passage. This one was marked with a blue feather. This passage—the one Sky loved most—was soiled from constant touching. Ned read it silently:

*For, lo, the winter is past, the rain is over and gone; The flowers appear on the earth; the time of the singing of birds is come, and the voice of the turtle is heard in our land; The fig tree putteth forth her green figs, and the vines with the tender grape give a good smell. Arise, my love, my fair one, and come away. O my dove, that art in the clefts of the rock, in the secret places of the stars, let me see thy countenance, let me hear thy voice;*

*for sweet is thy voice, and thy countenance is comely. Take us the foxes, the little foxes, that spoil the vines: for our vines have tender grapes. My beloved is mine, and I am his: he feedeth among the lilies.*

Ned bowed his head and asked for wisdom and forgiveness, as his mother had taught him to do—as the Dunkard had taught his mother to do—and as the brotherhood had taught the Dunkard to do.

Ned replaced the feather and lifted the Bible back onto the shelf. *Forgiveness.* He stood up and stoked the fire. *Forgiveness.* He chewed some jerky as he watched the flames grow. *Forgiveness.*

# March

Ned rose early and stood by the window watching the first sunlight make its way across the high ridge and cast a bright glow around the cabin's frozen landscape. Although it was March, the hollow was covered with a bluish white where, once again, snow enveloped the cabin. It had swirled around the cabin for months, but Sky and Ned were safe and warm. Ned had secured the cabin and kept it in good repair, as he had always done. He'd split ample wood and stacked it on the porch for the cook stove and the hearth. Together, the brother and sister had filled the cellar with food, enough to last them well into spring, until planting could begin anew. What was lost in the October flood, Ned had replaced with goods he had bought from the mercantile.

Ned wiped condensation off the window, along with a few ice crystals, before he turned to begin his day's work.

For most of the winter, some parts of Ned's truck sat disassembled and spread out on rags along the cabin wall where they wouldn't rust, where he could clean and repair them without trekking to the shed. After months of work, they were ready to be used again.

As winter lingered, Sky paced and when she wasn't pacing, she drew, ever watchful of any hint of thaw. For her, winters were long and drear, broken only by the beauty of a new snowfall or the power of a blizzard. Like her brother Sky had tasks. She prepared their meals and mended their clothing. She swept the cabin clean and listened by lamplight as Ned read passages from the Bible each night. Often, she climbed down into the root cellar to count the jars lined up along shelves in the cellar. As their numbers diminished, Sky knew spring was coming. It was a fine and accurate calendar, never failing to alert her to the first inklings of spring. Sky never worried or thought about the future. It was Ned who took on that task.

Near the end of winter, as soon as enough snow had melted to make the forest passable, Sky would venture out. Wrapped in a coat, she would sit alongside a runnel, watching the ice loosen and break away. When she was very young, Ned had let her play in the runnels that rainwater carved through the woods, runnels that autumn leaves re-lined every year. Rains would come along and beat them down, creating pools. Ned had always cautioned Sky against going near the river. He had a healthy fear of its power. Once when he was young, a spring rain had swept him downstream, out of his mother's reach. Only the grace of God—this the Dunkard had told him unequivocally—and the mercy of a low-hanging branch had saved him. Thus Sky, heeding Ned's caution, never went near the river, though the waters that collected in gullies and runnels and in dry-weather ponds were safe, and they drew her.

Once the ice began to disappear along the riverbank and the neutral colors of winter gave way to the pastels of spring, Sky would reawaken with the earth. With each new growth of tree or root, she would emerge more, her own winter dormancy falling away.

Ned left the window, and while Sky slept, he pulled on his boots and coat. A good day for cleaning, he thought, noting the windless morning. For the last month, he had been forced to burn green wood. Winter had gone on longer than he had anticipated, and his four cords of split, dried firewood had not lasted. The moist green wood had snapped and crackled in the hearth and coated the chimney's throat with a thick tar.

He trudged through the snow to the shed for a bucket of dry kindling, which he had saved for this purpose, along with a burlap bag filled with dry cottonwood seeds and pods. Cottonwood itself was no good for burning, too porous, but the seeds made good fire starters. As he walked back to the cabin, he observed the foot-thick snow that covered the roof. By the time he returned, Sky had awakened. She was loading the stove to make their breakfast.

"I'll have this up in jus' a minute," he said, nodding at the hearth where only a few feeble embers remained.

Ned crouched down on one knee beside the hearth. He built a small teepee out of the dry kindling. Underneath it, he stuffed cottonwood seeds and feathery milkweed fibers, stacking them loosely so air could circulate. He pushed one hot ember into the structure. With a flash, tiny red flames leapt up with a small cloud of white smoke. Ned grabbed the bellows he'd fashioned out of deer hide and fanned the flames. Once the fire caught, he stoked it with more kindling and added some quick-burning cardboard that Ernie Fowlkes saved for him.

Next, he stacked his driest logs onto the iron grate above the fire. Soon the fire was robust. Ned watched it and listened carefully to it sear and pop. Flames licked the brow of the hearth and rose high into the chimney's throat. The fire turned from bright red to blue and then white, signs of rising temperature. Waves of heat billowed into the room. Ned's cheeks were flushed. Sky fanned her face as they watched the inferno grow. Ned listened for it to crackle, a signal that the flames had ignited the soot and tar inside the chimney.

Once the fire was roaring and he heard the crackling, Ned took Sky by the hand, and they went outside into the cold, leaving the cabin door open to aid drafting. They walked far enough into the snow-covered yard to see the top of the chimney where heavy white smoke billowed out. In a few moments, they heard a loud whoosh and watched as fire blew up and out of the chimney, spewing soot and ash and flaming cinders. They watched the embers and soot fall and fizzle, snuffed out by the roof's thick snow covering.

"That oughta do it," Ned said, matter-of-factly.

Sky went back inside to make their breakfast. Ned stayed in the yard a little longer to ensure no errant embers had penetrated too deep into his snow-covered roof, now pockmarked. As they ate together, the fire calmed down. The chimney was clean.

The last spring could come.

# Early April

Parthenia Adams stood with her arms akimbo, facing off with her husband of more than four decades. "You an ol' man, Estes."

"I know that, Parthenia, but ol' or not, I got to go, and you got to go wif me."

Beads of perspiration collected on her generous brown chest, which was wrapped in a cotton blouse with a lacy neckline she had sewn on herself. She stood up straight, challenging Estes.

"I'm too ol' to go," she said.

"Old ain't no excuse. Don't know where you git your ideas from, woman, but you're talkin' crazy."

"It ain't crazy to want a little rest. I'm tired, Estes. Look at my hands. I've 'bout worn the lines off 'em."

Estes took his wife's hands and examined them. Then he stroked them and spoke gently to turn away her wrath.

"Parthenia, we got to go somewhere. Cain't set here and get drowned. But I don't think we oughta go moving in with Cyrus or Henry, like Mizz Louisa be doin'."

"Why not, Estes? Them boys would take us. Otherwise, we gotta start over again."

"That wouldn't be right to the boys. We ain't gonna do that."

"Then where we goin' ta live?"

Estes was quiet. He looked around the modest cabin that he'd built for his bride so long ago. They'd been married in the spring, on one of those spring days a painter might want to capture. Then they'd gotten right to work making a family. Their boys came quickly, only thirteen months between them. They'd lost a little baby girl somewhere along the way, but they didn't talk about that much anymore. The cabin's walls were solid wood timbers chinked and daubed together with a mixture of lime, straw, and mud that came straight out of the river. For as long as Estes could remember, the cabin had kept the wind out and the heat of his hearth in. Two oil lamps—gifts from Miss Louisa when she found out they were still using beeswax candles—sat on two tables Estes had made from a chestnut tree that had come down in a windstorm. Underneath each lamp was a hand-tatted doily, which Parthenia had made. One for each lamp. Her lamps, along with her two living children, were Parthenia's pride and joy. She called them her "four joyous lights."

Estes looked around the room. It wasn't much, but they had raised their children here, scraped out a good living, even helped found the Free Methodist Church. Could he start over? Did he want to?

Parthenia was glaring at him, tapping her foot. "Well, where we gonna live, ol man? Where?"

Estes sighed. Parthenia kept tapping.

"Parthenia. I jus' keep on going. I jus' don't know how to stop. I cain't, ya see. I don't know how. I cain't jus' sit down, call it quits, and wait 'round till's time for me to head to glory. I couldn't do it even if I tried. And I don't think you could neither. Sometimes when I'm having to work so hard, I say to myself, I oughta should quit, but it ain't in me—quittin'. I don't know what else to do 'cept keep on going, keep on workin'."

"Well, I'm tired, Estes. God knows I'm tired."

He looked at her with a smile that was full of sympathy and understanding. Estes was the kind of man who did what he could do, whatever the Good Lord put in front of him. He looked down and stroked his chin.

"Tell ya what, honey. I'll ask Mizz Louisa if she thinks she might need us to hep her move on down ta Chilhowie. Maybe her daughter could use some hep."

"Chilhowie might not be so bad."

"All I kin do is ask."

"I wonder if Chilhowie's got itself a river?"

"I kin ask her that, too."

Parthenia laid her hand on Estes's arm. "You a good man, Estes."
Estes smiled.

# Late April

Once again Ned stood on the eastern ridge of the hollow overlooking Lowman's Ferry. Down below, the afternoon sun blazed off the river like a welder's torch. Ned shaded his eyes to better see the cliffs and scarred banks. The landscape was still gray and brown. Only a week before, the last ice had disappeared from the riverbank's coves and bends. In another week or so, the full flush of greening would begin.

The river ran north out of the Carolina mountains into the highlands, filling the valleys with vital water, undergirding commerce, and supplying food. The river primed life. It was as old as the Nile—so said the geologists. It ran free, they said, long before the Dunkards and Scots and Primitive Baptists, before the Cherokee and the Catawba, before the Africans and Czechs and French and Melungeons. Before them all. It was a haven for strong and independent people who settled along its banks. The Dunkards had come to find solitude. The Scots had come for commerce and freedom. All this they found along the river.

But the river was selfish, too, protected by treacherous rises and falls, by sheer gray-green cliffs that towered hundreds of feet above the rushing waters, by rapids strong enough to swallow a man and peaceful stretches calm enough to float a feather. Indians called it the River of Death. Explorers going westward made it a way station. A few—the hardiest souls—settled along its banks, homesteading in its coves and inlets, building communities, wresting life from the River of Death. The willful river crossed the mountains through deep, barely forgiving gaps, and the people did the same. Only the most adventurous came, and only the most determined stayed. For a thousand years, the river ran free. Any obstacles in its way, the river eventually overwhelmed. The river had always had its way.

Ned felt the sun warm on his chest. He struck a match and lit a cigarette. By birth and the Dunkard's kind bequest, Ned and Sky had inherited their home in the hollow. They had never thought of leaving. Why would they? Where else would they go? There was no other place on earth for them.

Ned watched a ferryman navigate upstream. The man knew where to thrust his pole, knew where the deep holes and strainers were—and knew to watch for them. He knew the river's dangers, as well as its gifts. From this vantage, Ned could not see his own homestead, hidden beneath the thick centuries-old blackjack oaks, hickories, tulip poplars, and cottonwoods, his hidden homestead, shielded and scented by pines and spruces and cedars. Hidden. Protected.

Ned took another cigarette out of his pocket, lit it, stood, and watched the river. A Psalm wandered into his head: *Rivers of waters run down mine eyes, because they keep not thy law.* Ned took a deep draw and held the smoke before exhaling slowly. His throat burned. More holy words came to mind. He stood up straight, and these he spoke out loud: "When thou passest through the waters, I will be with thee; and through the rivers, they shall not overflow thee: when thou walkest through the fire, thou shalt not be burned; neither shall the flame kindle upon thee." His voice was flat and tired. He looked heavenward.

Ned finished his cigarette, dropped the butt in the dirt and ground it out with the toe of his boot. He scratched his ear, brushed his cheek, and put his hand to his mouth, pressing it hard against his upper lip.

# May

The air was thick and damp as Ned wiped his brow with his faded hand-kerchief. Sky, beside him, fanned her flushed face with a piece of card-board. Standing together on the edge of the porch, they watched the morning bloom.

The sun was burning off an early fog that drifted lazily across the river in translucent clouds. Although the nights clung to winter's chill, the days foreshadowed the coming summer heat. The air held the peculiar mixture of hot and cold, the tepidness of seasons silently and effortlessly changing, like boats passing in a fog bank. Throughout the forest, wet leaves and trees fumed a pungent mixture of wood smoke and leaf decay and pollen and damp earth. Spring in the hollow had always been an eclectic blend of cold and warmth, joy and sorrow, life and death.

This year would be no different.

"I gotta haul up past Christiansburg today. You need 'nything? I'm planning on stoppin' by the mercantile."

Sky shook her head.

"Why don't you come go with me?" Although he knew the answer, he asked anyway. He had to. He had to try.

"No."

If Sky could have explained herself, she would have said she was rooted here. Always. She had never known enough of anything else to tempt her away. Her response was love and honesty bound up in a single declaration. Sky loved the forest the way a child craves a mother's embrace, a safe place where happiness is whole.

Ned knew all this, but he still hoped.

"I'll buy you a co-cola. Buy ya 'nything you like."

"Bring me." She pointed to Ned and then to herself, tapping her collarbone. Sky was wordless but not mindless. She was clever enough to know Ned would deliver what she asked for.

Ned stepped off the porch, discouraged. His knees cracked as he climbed into his truck. As soon as the truck disappeared, Sky hurried into the woods.

New life suffused the forest. Sky kept to the storm dampened leaves, avoiding the pools of rainwater that collected in bowls formed from tree roots and in the runnels that flowed down through the leaf-clogged channels.

With endless wonder and fascination, Sky roamed. She stopped to watch a garden spider weave a web between two saplings. Water droplets like tiny crystal birds clung to the web, and as if poised to fly away, they rocked on the warming air, stirred by the small shifts in the forest's temperature. Sky wanted to collect them in her pocket the way she collected acorns or chinquapins, but she knew not to disturb them. She left the web alone, ducked underneath, and walked deeper into the forest, which was alive with small animals scurrying and insects that floated all around her. Next to Ned, these were Sky's best friends.

Along the edge of the small wet-weather pond, she crouched down to look below the surface at a collection of frog eggs suspended in a jelly-like sack. She shoved a stick down into the mud to mark the spot so that she could find it again and come back to watch the tiny tadpoles emerge. She loved watching them free themselves and swim away. To make sure, she added another stick, and then a third. She knew from experience that it could take weeks. She would come back often to check.

When the sun hit its zenith and pierced the forest's canopy, Sky lay down on her back in the wet velvet leaves. She was unconcerned that the dampness would soak through her clothes. Around her neck, a faint white line was visible where her locket, out of its ordinary orbit, hung down limp. Sky fell asleep in the mottled sunlight and awakened when a small twig rustled loose by a breeze fell gently across her chest. She brushed the twig away and sat up. The locket fell into its place, and while she watched the sun descend from its high spot in the sky, she fingered the locket unconsciously. Inside were two small faces. She had asked Ned about the pictures once, but he had said he did not know who they were. That was all it had taken to blunt her curiosity.

She leaned back and propped herself on her bent arms. Nearby, a spring bubbled, sending ribbons of liquid crystal across a bed of smoothed stones. Sky was comfortable, safe—far beyond the call of any human and too deep in the forest to be interrupted.

⟳⟲

Ned pulled up to the mercantile as Ernie was propping open the doors with a couple of large flint rocks, each the size of a cantaloupe. Ned climbed the steps.

"Mornin', Ned."

"Mornin', Mr. Fowlkes."

Ned had readied his truck and gone back to work as soon as the redbuds blushed and the roads were passable. It would be a busy spring. Folks were moving, pulling up roots, so he had lots of work—plenty to keep him busy and to keep Sky's kitchen stocked with alum and flour and Tryme baking powder, the brand she favored because of the orange, decorated can. When she was a child, Ned had filled an empty can with stones and let her shake it as a rattle.

Inside, Ernie pulled a handful of paper slips off his counter. They were skewered on a miniature pitchfork that was stuck down in a miniature hay bale—a souvenir from last year's county fair. He handed Ned the slips.

"You're gonna be busier than a one-legged man in a butt-kicking contest. All this work comin' in." Ernie chuckled at his own joke. He was trying to be jolly. It was the least he could do for his customers.

Ned nodded with a thin smile. "Thank ya, Mr. Fowlkes."

Each slip had a name, a date, and a time—morning or afternoon—and two addresses, rural delivery numbers, and sometimes a hand-drawn map. Ned slipped them into his pocket. This much work felt heavy to Ned, who already shouldered a considerable burden.

"What else can I do you for today?" Ernie said as he straightened up his counter, moving the jar of deer jerky to within easy reach. He pulled out a feather duster and dusted the lids of the bins and a shelf behind the counter.

"I need some oil for my truck and some wheat flour and sugar."

"Oil's on the rack over there." With the duster he pointed and squinted. "Looks like I got a couple cans left." Then he set down the feather duster and pulled two paper sacks from under the counter. He snapped them open. "How much flour and sugar you need?"

"Pound each. And give me some Lucky Strikes."

"Sorry, Ned. I'm all out. Got no cigarettes left. First thing I sold out of. Guess I'm finally seeing the writin' on the wall."

In Ernie's eyes was an angry surrender. Still, he tried to smile, but Ned didn't see that. He was fishing money out of his pocket.

"You got'ny peppermint?"

"Yep. I do have some of them. Right here. Enjoy 'em, Ned. Last ones I got. No charge."

"Oh, no, Mr. Fowlkes, I cain't…."

"I insist, Ned. Consider it a little parting gift. You brought me lots of business over the years."

"Well. Thank you, Mr. Fowlkes. That's awful nice of you."

The small kindness buoyed Ned as much as the gesture felt good to Ernie. Ned turned to leave.

"You made your plans yet, Ned? It's nearly done."

Ned stopped. After a pause, he shook his head.

"No, sir," he said, "I'm still thinkin'."

And Ned was gone.

It was a dark moonless night. Sky shifted her weight on the porch steps, waiting. Supper was long over, and the tree frogs were singing as if a curtain had risen and their chorus had begun. Ned was deep in the forest hunting with Collier.

Sky could tell by the angle of the moon that Ned was late—too late to have been delayed by the pursuit of a raccoon or by temporarily losing his way. She pulled her shawl around her shoulders and stood up, pacing back and forth along the porch, the new boards squeaking under her feet. She watched the woods and the path that Ned always took toward the eastern ridge when he and Collier went coon hunting. The pair had left after supper and should have come back by now. Finally, Sky lay down on the porch, her head cushioned by her raised arm, and fell asleep.

By first light, Ned had not returned. Sky, still on the porch, woke abruptly. Realizing it was morning and Ned was not back, a mild panic overtook her. The nocturnal animals had retired, and the night mist had silvered a thousand webs throughout the woods—a sight that ordinarily would have enticed Sky. But not this morning. Instead, she strained to listen through the quiet for Ned. Why was Ned not here? Sky was confused and frightened. She stood up and paced again.

When the early sunlight began to amend the sky from black to indigo, she sat back down on the stoop and, hugging her knees, began to rock back and forth. Never before had she been separated from Ned for so long. Never in her lifetime. A wholly unfamiliar fear grasped her throat and from it came a low disturbed whisper, almost a moan. *Where Ned? Where you?*

She whispered into the quiet pre-dawn: "Ned?" Her voice began to rise with a childlike panic until she was shouting as loudly as her limited voice could yell. "Ned!" But Sky did not know what else to do but wait. She would have waited forever.

From a distance, she heard a sound. Finally. Leaves rustling, footsteps crackling through the understory that was vaguely visible in the morning's deep blue translucence. Relief flooded her. She jumped up, expecting to see Ned with Collier emerge from the forest with whatever quarry they had taken.

When she saw Collier, her relief came in tears, but it was short-lived. Ned was not there. Only Collier. The faithful hound loped toward her. She raced down the steps and dropped to her knees in the dirt to grip the hound's head. "Ned?" she whispered, her face inches from the dog's snout. She shook Collier's head. "Ned? Where Ned?"

Collier pulled away and turned back toward the forest as if to say "follow." Sky ran after him, keeping pace with the animal's quick clip.

The moon and the sun were now passing, the night returning to its place behind the hill, while the sun, waking, gilded the hollow's east rim. The morning light turned purplish, then pink, as Sky ran through the forest after Collier.

"Sky!" Ned yelled when he heard her coming. He knew it was his sister because her steps were like the footsteps of a doe. The hound bayed at his master's voice and led Sky toward a depression in the forest floor.

"Over here," Ned called out. He was on his back, wedged against a boulder, his hips pinned by a fallen tree. "This way. Come 'round behind that poplar. But watch out. There's a low place. You can't see it under the leaves."

Sky ran to him and tried to lift the log. Ned flinched.

"No, Sky. It's too heavy. You cain't move it." His voice was calm and reassuring for Sky's benefit. "Now listen to me. You run back to the shed and get me my rope. The long one. It's hanging in there."

"No." Sky didn't want to leave.

"Go on, Sky," Ned coaxed her gently, masking his pain. "I need the rope, the long one. You go get it for me. I'll be right here."

Agitated but helpless to refuse Ned, Sky ran back through the forest until she realized Collier had followed her.

"Go back. Git," she said to the hound. "You go Ned."

Collier turned and obeyed.

Ned watched her disappear through the woods. He tried to shift his weight; his legs were beginning to feel numb. The forest was all at once overwhelming and for the first time, felt dangerous. His plight scared him. Not for himself but for Sky. He could not help but wonder what would have happened to Sky if the tree had killed him. Lying helpless, the thought overwhelmed him, adding even more weight to the burden he carried.

Soon Sky returned. She had found the rope, and hiking it over her shoulder, ran as fast as she could in a lopsided gait back to her brother. She arrived gasping and pale, holding her chest. She coughed, and handing the rope to Ned, bent forward putting her hands on her knees to catch her breath.

"Sky, get me that stick over there. See it?"

Sky picked it up and took it to Ned. He tied the end of the rope around it and handed it back to Sky who was struggling to catch her breath.

"Now, look up there. See that branch?" Ned pointed. "You gotta take this stick and throw it over that branch. See it? Understand?"

Sky nodded and pulled the rope and stick as she climbed up on an outcropping above Ned. After several attempts, the rope landed across a hefty branch and dangled low enough for Sky to reach.

"Now grab it and pull it over to me," Ned instructed.

Sky climbed across the rocks and stretched to grab the stick with the tips of her fingers.

"That's it. Good, Sky. Now pull it over this a-way to me."

Ned looped the end of the rope around the tree pinning him, tying it tight. "Come down here, now. I need your help." Using the branch as a fulcrum, together they hoisted the tree enough for Ned to roll out from under it. When he was clear, they let go of the rope. The log thudded to the ground and rolled farther down into the depression. Slowly Ned got up, tested his legs. He was bruised and sore, but he could walk.

"Thank you, Sky," he said, as he brushed himself off. He looked up at Sky. She was crying.

Late that night, Ned was unable to sleep. He sat down beside his sister's bed and listened to her ragged breathing. He took his sister's small hand, the hand that had rescued him, and held it.

# Early June

Morning was dawning across the mountains, that moment when darkness and light co-mingle into a smoky yellow gray. The air was damp and quiet as Ernie Fowlkes flipped on the lights in the mercantile. They flickered before coming on fully. He made a note to check the water and acid levels in his Delco plant housed in the back of the store.

Just back from the war, he had installed the Delco plant himself after he persuaded his father that it was the wave of the future. Ernie had seen them in Chicago, and so the mercantile had been the first establishment in the hollow with electric lights. His plant had spurred a lot of interest, and most farmers soon shelled out the hefty sum of $450 to buy them for their homes. Ernie had thought about going on the road selling for Delco-Light himself. Traveling around the country, demonstrating the invention to farmers would be interesting for a young man. But then his father had died. That changed his plans, leaving Ernie, the only son, to take over the mercantile.

Ernie walked over to the counter and ran his hand along the worn surface as he looked around the store. In more than three decades, the mercantile had never had empty shelves. Now every shelf was empty. To him, the store looked naked. The cooler was unplugged and propped open with a broom handle so it could dry before the bottling company sent a truck from Marion to pick it up.

Ernie stopped for a moment and surveyed the scene: the counter oiled by commerce and human hands, the round potbellied stove, the long windows that rolled up and down on heavy cords, the wood floors cupped where his customers had lined up with their lists. He had sold his customers flour and tractor parts, dress fabrics off the bolt, yard rakes, eggs by the dozen, and nails by the pound. He had sold them pickled eggs and baking pans, newspapers and work boots, bushels of apples and skeins of yarn. He had sold them push brooms and flags, clotheslines, and pressure cookers. They had paid their bills across this counter. To many he had extended credit to help them through lean times. He felt good about that. It was good commerce that helped his neighbors.

He remembered the times when the mercantile was full of customers. He and his friends had solved all the world's problems standing right here. They had greeted soldiers returning from the Great War. They had shared the news of babies' births and elders' deaths. They had debated which tractors were best—and which oils and grains and seeds and fertilizers they favored. They had traded advice and passed around jars of moonshine— on the sly for a time. They had rehashed Sunday sermons and debated politics, never letting any disagreement sour a friendship. They had mourned the departed, helped the downtrodden, and fed the penniless. For as long as Ernie could remember, they shared their lives. The mercantile had been important to them, a gathering place, the most important establishment in the hollow.

It didn't seem right to see it so bare and empty. It didn't seem right at all.

But it was. Quiet. Empty. Abandoned. Ready to disappear.

Ernie rolled open the drawer of the National cash register. Only a few dollars and cents remained. He lifted them out and stuffed them in his pocket. The rest he had already taken to the Bank of Christiansburg and put in his savings account. Passbook savings. Compounded quarterly. Lord knew he would need his savings.

He stroked the top of the ancient register. The display read: "No sale." An antiques dealer from Abingdon had come in the week before and offered him an ungodly sum for the machine, but he wouldn't take it. It would be the same as selling one of his children, he told him. As the man left, Ernie heard him call him an "old fool."

"I am an ol' fool," he said to the register. Then he pulled open a drawer, took out a screwdriver, and started unbolting the register from the counter.

❦

Ernie sat next to the dining room table with his legs splayed to accommodate a large cardboard box pushed up against the front of his chair. For months he had been collecting boxes in the storeroom of the mercantile and had given them out to his customers. They had appreciated it. Everyone needed boxes these days.

He pulled a sheet of newspaper off a pile beside him to wrap another plate exactly as his wife, Ruth, had instructed. His hands were black from the ink of the *Roanoke Times*. He was tired, his back ached, and his disposition was cranky, but he kept that to himself, choosing instead to behave with faultless cooperation. It's what the situation called for. Ruth had finished unloading a collection of music boxes from a walnut bric-a-brac and stood facing the piano they were donating to the church.

"I got aholt of Ned and his truck," Ernie said to her. "You think you'll be ready by Saturday?" He looked at his wife. She had tears in her eyes. He noticed her hands. Her fingers stroked the keyboard of the upright piano without depressing the keys. It had been years since any of their children had played it, not since Clara had quit taking lessons from Miss Harman.

"Nobody should have this much stuff," she said, attempting to be practical, attempting to blunt her sadness.

"You gonna give some of this away?"

"I got some boxes settin' out in the kitchen full of things for the Associated Charities. I understand from Mizz Pennington they're needin' all sorts of things down in Wise County. She says they're collectin' things up next to the Pentecostal Church. Glad people can make use...." Her voice trailed off. He could read her mind. She depressed middle C. The resonance hung in the air and slowly dissipated. "Some people are awful needy. I guess I'm glad we can help—what we have can make a real difference to somebody."

Ernie wrapped the last plate.

"Can you take the boxes up there in the morning?" she asked her husband.

"Be glad to. I can swing by on my way to town."

It would be an inconvenient swing, Ernie knew, but he also knew it would ease Ruth's pain considerably. He would do about anything to make it easier on her. He was more ambivalent about moving—less sentimental. He had tried to convey that earlier, but she had interpreted it as callousness. So, today he was tacking on a different wind. The constant shimmer in her eyes bothered him. He hated her pain. He hated the whole situation. Everyone did, but Ernie was naturally hopeful, while Ruth fed off the past. Her whole life was here in the house—the children, their life together, memories—and now everything it represented was pulled out, packed up, and ready to give away or relocate.

"You go on and get you whatever you think you need for the new place," he said. "Ya hear me? Don't worry about how much it costs. Jus' go on and get it. Might be nice to get some new things." It was a generous offer and elicited a tiny smile from Ruth.

"You deserve it, Ruthie." He only called her Ruthie when he was trying to be especially solicitous.

She sat down at the piano and played the first bars of a favorite hymn. The familiar verse played in both their minds: *When peace like a river, attendeth my way. When sorrows like sea billows roll. Whatever my lot. Thou hast taught me to know. It is well, it is well, with my soul.* Neither voiced the words.

"It'd it strange?" she said, "how you wanna replace an ol' beat up sofa. That ol' brown sofa. Then when you finally get to, it jus' don't seem so important."

Ernie raised his eyebrows and looked across the room. Every stain on the slipcover had a story—every chink in the dining room table, every scuffmark on the woodwork, every odor and sound, every angle and view. It all meant something to Ernie and Ruth Fowlkes, especially Ruth. Nearly thirty years of marriage. Decades of memories corralled in a well-used white clapboard house with a mile-wide wraparound porch and a hundred windows—or so it seemed when they had to be washed.

"You 'member the time Rufus kicked up his shoe and broke out your kitchen window, broke it all over the pies you'd made for the church homecoming?" Ernie said.

Ruth almost laughed. "I was so mad at that boy, I couldn't see straight," she said. "Four peach pies all covered with glass. Nothing to do but throw 'em out."

"I b'lieve I musta fixed every last one of them windows back there," he chuckled. "Comes with having young'uns, I 'spose."

"We raised all five right here. Five. Don't seem right to be leavin' it all behind." She said this in a way that Ernie knew needed no comment. "I always did want me a new place, but now...well...seems I'm moving for the wrong reason. I don't know what we'll do come Christmas when all the children come home."

She looked around the room and saw it as it had always been decorated for Christmas. The tree, the papier mâché crèche that Evelyn had made in vacation Bible school. Clara's tin foil star that always graced the top of the tree. The few presents they could afford stacked under the tree, wrapped up in funnies from the Sunday papers. Ruth had always started collecting them in September to have plenty for wrapping presents at Christmas time. The carved manger scene her Uncle Virgil had sent her when he was serving in France during the war. Five little nail holes in the mantel to hold the stockings she'd knitted, one for each child, each with their name: Evelyn, Jake, Rufus, Clyde, Clara.

"I can see about us renting the Ruritan Hall up in town," Ernie said. "We could take our meals up there when the kids come. If need be, I'll jus' spring for a couple of rooms at Waddell's Motel up on the Springer Road for the children. Girls would pro'bly love to spend the night in a motel anyway. Be a real treat. The little boys could bunk with us. Bring sleepin' bags an' all."

Ernie knew this was another extravagant offer, but what else was there to do? And why shouldn't he? What did it matter, the cost? What money he had saved might as well be spent on his family. If it made his wife feel better, then it was worth it.

"We'll manage," she said. Ruth knew she had to put on a brave face, too. "Long as we got room for a Christmas tree, I 'spect we can manage."

Ernie set the last dinner plate in the box and started on the teacups.

"Be careful with those, Ernie. Those go to the girls." She got up from the piano. "I'm going to check upstairs, see what's left."

When Ruth opened the door to the front bedroom, she was struck by how bare the room looked. Boxes tied shut with bailing twine and ready for transport lined an empty wall where shadows marked where family pictures had come down. Her grandmother's high carved bed, the one all her little girls had slept in, was disassembled, leaning up against the far wall. Underneath the open window, the sun played off the cane of a small child's rocking chair, moving through the holes and sprinkling the floor with light. On the bare floor dust gathered like a shroud.

Through the open window, wind blew in and rustled the white curtains. She hadn't realized that the day was windy. She hoped a storm wasn't blowing in, but then she realized that a storm was indeed coming.

But not the kind that brought rain.

Sunshine McCleary pulled her bedsheets off the clothesline one by one and dropped them into her basket. Nearby, five children played on an old dray. The axle was broken, and one wheel was gone, so it listed at an angle that made it versatile and enticing. It was a horse, a boat, a castle, a sliding board.

"Ooo be fare-ful..." Sunshine pulled a clothespin from her mouth. "You be careful, ya hear me? I cain't afford no broken arms. Lucas McCleary! You quit pushing Emaline. Teddy and Vernon, you two get down off there. I got visions of you kids fallin' off and breakin' your necks. And I don't want to be pulling splinters out of your backsides neither." As she scolded her children, she smiled. Sunshine's duty was done; if they got hurt, it was their own fault. She had warned them.

The children waved at their mother and ran into the side yard to a tire swing hanging from the high branches of a skeletal tree, one of many killed by the blight that had robbed the forest of the majestic chestnuts. Sunshine watched with a warm and protective gaze as she unpinned clothing and tossed each garment into the basket at her feet.

She lifted the basket and carried it to the porch. Setting it down, she looked out over their small homestead. In the distance, the broad river ran. She had made sure her husband built their house far enough from the river so she wouldn't be pulling children from the water the way she pulled sheets out of the ringer washer on her back porch. She was a country woman who never learned to swim and who appreciated the water's beauty and danger equally.

The river was on her mind today. She didn't fully understand how far the water would come up. Shep had taken her downstream and shown her the predicted path, but it was more than she could take in. Sunshine didn't worry about the future. She concerned herself with immediate things, the important things—especially the two-legged kind. Everything else, she left to the discretion of the Almighty and the abilities of her husband. If the river took the gristmill, so be it, she thought. Shep had assured her he could get money for it and a job somewhere in Wytheville. He wasn't worried, so she wasn't worried. She knew Shep would take care of them.

A scuffle erupted near the swing and a caterwauling child interrupted her thoughts. "Lucas, quit kicking at your brother. Let him swing. I'm gonna whip your behind if I gotta call you one more time," Sunshine yelled across the yard. "Lucas! Ya hear me? Emaline, lift Teddy down. Looks like he's stuck."

The boys and their sister scattered in the yard.

Sunshine set the basket beside the kitchen door and walked to the side porch, where she pulled another load of wash from the drum and began feeding and pulling it through the wringer. When she saw storm clouds gathering in the west, she set the wet clothes aside and stepped into the yard to look at the sky. She licked her finger, sticking it in the air, watching the clouds to see which direction they were blowing. Then she retrieved a second basket of clothes.

"Emaline," she called to the tallest child. "Come over here and help me."

The girl, a miniature of her mother, left her siblings and ran. She grabbed a handful of clothespins from the muslin bag slung over the end of the clothesline and dropped them in her pockets. Mother and daughter worked silently, struggling at times to keep fluttering shirts and pants from taking flight in the stiff breeze. When a rumble of thunder carried through the yard, Emaline looked at her mother.

"It's goin' north, Emaline. You jus' keep pinnin'. It's goin' 'round us."

The wheel at the gristmill ran counter to the sun, a fact that had always bothered Shep McCleary. He would have preferred that everything in his life run at the same speed, the same direction, the same rhythm as nature. To him, this waterwheel seemed counterintuitive, a perversion of how things ought to be. But as goes much of life, what Shep thought should happen and what actually did happen sometimes ran in opposite directions.

He opened the sluice and watched from the shed of the gristmill as water cascaded through the millrace and rushed the wheel's paddles. Slowly the wheel began to turn under the weight of the water. The joints that held the millstones strained and creaked as the wheel began moving. Above his head, leather belts started to roll. Shep stood back and folded his arms across his chest as he watched the mill come alive. The water was like blood flowing, moving through the wood structure, generating life. He wanted to remember the sight and sound of it.

There was a special sentiment here, a desire to recall a part of life. The gristmill had been his father's business. His father, Malcolm McCleary, had run it for as long as Shep could remember. Shep grew up here helping his father, and when his father passed, the gristmill had gone to the son. He had married Sunshine the same year his father died. Even though he had lost his father, he still felt his presence here where Shep, as a boy, had worked alongside him—as Shep's boys worked with him. But that was all coming to an end.

Shep dumped a bag of dried corn into the hopper. He watched as it cracked and feathered between the millstones. Dust rose and drifted on the summer breeze. When the funnel was half empty, he lifted another bag and poured it in with the swooshing sound that had always meant a steady supply of cash for his family—and food for the hollow's residents.

He closed the sluice, and the wheel gradually came to a stop. Lucas, his eldest son, gathered the coarse meal into sacks and carried them to the dock, as Shep had done so many times. Shep looked at his watch.

"Lucas, line up those bags. They'll be here pretty soon to pick 'em up."

Shep had decided to keep the gristmill open as long as he had customers, but during the spring their numbers had dwindled until fewer than a handful were left. It was tough closing down a business he always thought he would see to the end—his end, not the end of the gristmill. He always imagined the gristmill would outlive him. Shep had planned to hand the business down to his own sons, as his father had done, hoping someday to hang a sign that read "McCleary and Sons." That would not happen now, not with what was coming.

The company had offered him a fair settlement, which he had improved when he happened to mention a lawyer he knew in Roanoke—who might need to look over the agreement. It didn't seem important to explain to the representatives of the power company that the lawyer was an acquaintance disbarred for a dozen years. Though Shep McCleary looked like a simple country miller, he was a shrewd businessman. He knew they needed him to go—and how much they wanted him to go without a fuss. When Shep saw the final number, he had trouble maintaining a poker face. He had never expected a windfall.

Sunshine, his wife of seventeen years, wouldn't know any of this—or even that he had been negotiating—until it was all over, and the money was deposited in the Bank of Christiansburg. He had made plans to build a house on the east ridge. Shep was a hollow boy who had grown up in the shadow of that mountain, but he had always dreamed of living at the top in a house with a view and days that weren't cheated out of sunlight. Now he would have the chance. It took the sting out of losing the gristmill. He would find other work. Every man needs a purpose for getting up in the morning.

He hadn't told any of his neighbors about the deal he'd struck. They'd find out sooner or later. And Sunshine would find out on her birthday. That thought made him smile.

# Late June

Ned hurried through his breakfast. "I'll be late tonight," he said.

Sky looked at him with the question that he anticipated.

"You go on an' eat. I don't spect I'll be back before dark. I gotta go up t'ward Floyd. Moving Mr. Fowlkes and his wife today."

Sky nodded and ate another spoonful of grits. She had never met Mr. Fowlkes, but she knew him as the man who gave Ned paper and pencils and peppermint. He was the man with the peppermint.

Ned pushed away from the table. He'd never been so busy, but despite the rush, his prices hadn't changed. He charged what he'd always charged. That seemed fair to Ned and most folks seemed to appreciate it.

"You can keep somethin' warm for me." He patted her shoulder as he headed to the door. "See ya later."

Ernie and Ruth Fowlkes were waiting on their porch when Ned drove up. He backed his truck into their yard, close enough to the front porch to make it easy to load.

"Good mornin', Ned," Ernie said, after Ned had exited his truck and started up the steps. Ernie was freshly shaven and dressed to travel.

"How're you, Mr. Fowlkes? Mizz Fowlkes?" Ned dipped his head toward the woman who was sitting in the swing. She wore a simple belted dress and a nice hat with a wide brim. On her lap she held a potted dipladenia that she had nurtured as thoroughly as she had nurtured her children.

Her pocketbook and a narrow box of candles and candlesticks were beside her. Ned could tell she had been crying, but neither man acknowledged her pain. There was work to be done.

"Appreciate you helpin' us, Ned," Ernie said.

"Glad to."

"Lemme show you what we got."

Ernie led Ned through the front door. All the household goods were packed. The giveaways were gone, and what furniture was left sat along empty walls like orphans wondering if they would be adopted or left behind.

"You don't need to fool with the piano, Ned. We're giving it to the church, and the Reverend's comin' over tomorrow with the Shockley boys to pick it up."

Ned nodded.

"We ain't got room for it anyway," Ernie said, almost as an afterthought. "Here's where you take everything." He handed him a slip of paper. "You go on up past Lowman's Ferry and get onto Route 3. That'll take you over toward Jasper's Gap. Once you get onto Craven's Road going over t'ward Floyd, you hang a left and go on up in there, past a water tower and a little gray house. It's the next one on the left. White house with green shutters."

"I b'lieve I know where it's at." Ned folded the paper and put it in his pocket. He knew nearly every road across the highlands. He knew where the macadam was worn down and which roads regularly washed out during heavy rains. He knew which ones were steep and narrow and where the dangerous hairpin turns were. He knew the roads with views and the ones that disappeared down dirt footpaths. He knew which mountain roads his truck could handle, and which washboard ones would shake the axle and gears. And he knew the roads he'd have to abandon altogether and haul furniture on a skid instead. This was all part of Ned's world, but a world that Sky had never known—and now, after all these years, he worried if her only chance to know it had disappeared decades ago.

Ernie and Ned stepped back out onto the front porch.

"We're goin' on ahead," Ernie said. "Ruth here wants to do a little cleaning up 'fore you get there. We'll be waitin' on ya." He slapped Ned on the shoulder. "We sure do appreciate this, Ned." He handed him a roll of bills.

"Thank you, Mr. Fowlkes."

"Oh, and Ned," he said, "here's this." Ernie reached into his pocket. "Thought you oughta have this." He handed Ned the small pitchfork upended in the hay bale. "Little souvenir for ya. Somethin' to remember."

"Why, thank you, Mr. Fowlkes. That's mighty thoughtful." Ned turned it over in his hand, examining it, thinking Sky would like to see this.

"I guess you can find you another counter to set it on. People's always needin' a good reliable man like you. You might try Hull Free up at the Esso station."

"Yes, sir." He wrapped the tiny souvenir in the wad of bills and slipped them in his pocket.

Ernie took a last look around.

"Well," he said, raising his eyebrows and looking at Ruth. Sitting in the swing, she seemed to be far away. "Guess we oughta be going. You ready, Ruth?" Ruth stood up and handed the box of candles to Ernie to carry. She hooked her pocketbook over her arm and cradled the dipladenia. Gently, Ernie put his hand on the small of her back. Together they stepped off the porch.

Ned saw Ernie's eyes glisten, so he got right to work as the couple made their way to their car.

Ned's boots made a hollow, empty sound as he walked through the house on the polished pine floors uncharacteristically dusty from all the packing. He looked at the fine woodwork, the windowpanes sagging like an old woman's face, the chests and shelves emptied of their contents, the bare walls with shadows where pictures had hung, and the stacks of boxes. It looked to Ned as though Ernie and Ruth Fowlkes had given away more than they were keeping. Ned was surprised at how little he would have to move. He assessed the job that faced him and started upstairs. He would clear that out first.

After Ned had unloaded the last of the furniture at the new place near Floyd, he helped Ernie set up the couple's bed.

"That oughta do it," Ernie said. "Appreciate your help, Ned."
Ned nodded. The men shook hands.

It was late afternoon when Ned headed toward home, toward Sky, but it was earlier than he had expected, so he altered his plans, turned onto a back road, and drove without a specific destination. He carried in his head the map of the entire hollow and the highlands that cradled it. His knowledge was as accurate a map as any expert cartographer could have drawn.

Ned stopped to fill up his truck at Hull Free's Esso station, and while the fresh-faced teenage boy pumped his gas, he slipped inside and bought himself a coke, some nabs, and a pack of Lucky Strikes.

"That be all?" Hull said.

"Yes, sir." Ned thought about Ernie's suggestion, but he wasn't in the mood to ask about work. Not yet at least.

As he left the filling station, he noticed a list of houses for sale posted next to the door. Ned stopped to look at them, all beyond the hollow. He memorized their locations.

Back in his truck, he tossed the cigarettes on the seat beside him, unwrapped the crackers, and propped up the bottle in a crack in the passenger seat. Then he drove. Ned's truck rumbled along the roads like a dog following familiar scents. He went to all the places where he had worked. Some houses were nothing more than shanties; others were solid, well cared for. Beyond the western ridge of the hollow, Ned saw farmland stretching out open and exposed. Ned shielded his eyes. He was more accustomed to the forest's covering than the wide-open fields.

Ned wasn't sentimental in the way that most homeowners were, certainly not in the way Ruth Fowlkes was. Ned was practical. A house was a house, a cabin a cabin, a home a home. That was not his dilemma at all. What he needed to accomplish was far more difficult than finding a house, and as he drove along the dusty road he wondered if it were possible at all.

The next morning Ned again left home early, this time headed for Christiansburg. He had planned to stop by the mercantile first. The summer air was intoxicating. It was no longer heavy with pollens that in spring had dusted everything with a thick coat of greenish yellow. It was all gone now, washed away by summer rains. The sky was solid blue. He could not see a single cloud.

Ned pulled into the empty gravel lot at the mercantile and killed the engine. The double doors, usually open and welcoming, were shut up tight. He stared at the building, abandoned, lifeless. A painful finality washed over him. Where would he get a new fan belt? Or oil for his truck?

Or peppermints?

He looked up at the mountains. The sun illumined every blade of grass, every leaf, every chimney across the hollow. Each bird that flew, each breeze that blew, every stream of sunlight that shone were in perfect harmony with Ned's heartbeat. No matter how hard he tried, he could not separate them. There was plenty of life left in the ancient hollow. Ned could feel its pulse, a strong life that should not end—yet it was nearing death. He had no anger, only a deep and profound sadness—and resignation. Sitting in front of the shuttered mercantile, Ned was alone. He was utterly alone.

Ned sat there for nearly an hour before he started his truck back up, shoved it into gear, and drove away.

⸺ ❧ ⸺

Sky was sitting on the porch steps that evening when Ned arrived back. As soon as she saw him, she stood up and went to the stove.

Ned parked his truck near the stand of white pines. He stepped out and lifted the hood. He needed to check the truck's radiator level; the engine had run a little hot during the trip home. He left the hood up while he puttered around the shed, waiting for the engine to cool down. He lined up his garden tools, lifted a can of kerosene to see how much remained, blew dust off two discarded truck batteries. He re-hung a coil of rope that had fallen off a peg. Probably the wind, he thought. Or maybe a raccoon.

After twenty minutes or so, he took a rag from a box near the batteries and returned to his truck. He pulled out the dipstick. The oil level was fine. He checked the radiator. It was a little low. He added some water before he closed the hood and went into the cabin.

Sky was humming. Ned rolled up his sleeves and washed his hands in a basin filled with water.

"Smells good," he said over his shoulder. He smiled at Sky before he sat down at the table where she had set out a glass of buttermilk and a loaf of salt-rising bread. His stomach growled. Brunswick stew, Ned thought. It was one of his favorites. She ladled stew into two bowls and sat down opposite Ned. He prayed and then they ate.

After supper, Ned took the jar from the shelf and added his day's earnings before retreating to the porch while Sky washed the dishes. He lit a cigarette. Fading sunlight flickered across the river. Soon Sky joined him and together they watched the night arrive.

# July

Miss Louisa sat alone in her front room, sipping a cup of sassafras tea. Although the morning was bright and sunny, her heavy velvet draperies were pulled closed. The room was hot and stuffy and smelled of Murphy's oil soap, rosewater, and onions. These were smells children noticed when they visited her, especially her granddaughters, but not Miss Louisa. They were too familiar, like every view, every step in her house, every corner, and every cabinet.

She had closed the draperies purposefully. She didn't like what was coming and the draperies felt like the only defense she had. Mounting any resistance, even a false one, gave her enough strength to absorb it all. She knew that she could not change what was coming. She had to face it, but nothing made it easy.

Miss Louisa—no one called her Mrs. Leaberry—was the hollow's oldest resident, eighty-nine come September, and she still lived alone. She liked it that way. Soon, however, she would move in with her eldest daughter, Agnes, and her family in Chilhowie. Even though she loved her daughter and her three beautiful granddaughters, she did not want to go. They would be good to her, she knew. They had always been good to her, as had her other children. Still, she cherished her independence. It would be hard to give that up, but she was also realistic. She had lived long enough to know that reality usually emerged the winner against dreams and hopes, especially foolish or stubborn ones. She would face reality head on and be happy about it. Age could make a person ornery, she knew, but she refused to be like that. She would choose a different mindset, even if she had to plaster it on her face with a smile that her heart did not wholly support. She would try. She was determined to try.

The sale was slated for a week from Saturday. She had done all she could to prepare for it. She had gathered a few items on her dining room table, items that she would take with her—not a whole lot. Agnes did not have much room. Her daughter had explained this, anticipating that her mother might want to bring everything, lock, stock, and barrel, into her small house, which sat on the side of a hill outside of Chilhowie. Everything else would have to go. The auctioneer had been kind and attentive, and Miss Louisa, who possessed a clear mind and an able body, had discussed with him the dispensation of her belongings with calm and reason. What else could she do?

"I understand things change," she had told Mr. Trinkle, the auctioneer, who had traveled from Lexington at her children's behest to survey the contents of her house. "My Daddy always told us to embrace change. You can't hold onto anything forever, Louisa, he'd say. You just cling to Jesus and the things that matter. It was mighty good advice, Mr. Trinkle. Mighty good advice."

"Yes, ma'am. It sure was," he had replied, pausing long enough to change the subject. "Mizz Louisa, you've got some fine pieces here. Some mighty fine pieces. Like that chest there. Walnut's getting scarcer and scarcer. Someday, I expect, you won't be able to get it at all. Once the dealers up toward Roanoke get wind of this, they'll be a-comin'."

"I'm sure you'll do your best. You come highly recommended."

"Thank you, Mizz Louisa. I appreciate your confidence." He then opened a notebook and began making a list.

Miss Louisa's house, built with money her husband had inherited from his grandfather, was Italianate and elegant, the most elegant house in the hollow. She refused to think about its fate; that was too heavy a thought to bear. Over the years, it had gotten a little rundown. She had not kept it up as she should have. She regretted this, but she had done the best she could as a widow of more than fifty years. She always did the best she could.

"What about this piece, Mizz Louisa?" the auctioneer had asked, pointing to a large hunt chest in the dining room. "I could get a right good price for this one."

"No, Mr. Trinkle. That goes to my niece in Hillsville. She'll come get it before the sale. She said she would, but if she doesn't, you'll make sure it doesn't get away. Please. It was my mother's. She asked for it because she remembers it from when she was a little girl. It was in her grandparents' dining room."

"I will do that, Mizz Louisa." The auctioneer had made a note and tied a small yellow tag on a knob.

Miss Louisa's lack of emotion had surprised the auctioneer. He had heard she had a good head for business. Now he believed it. This was, after all, a business transaction. He wished more of his clients were like her.

But today, a few days ahead of the sale, with the clock ticking, Miss Louisa was struggling. It had all become too real, too close, too sad. She had gone to her pastor for advice and ended up doing most of the pastoring herself. The man was losing his church. He had simply listened.

"Now, Reverend, this was gonna happen one time or another. I know that. Most times, though, it's when you've passed on. When you're lying in your grave, you have no say over what happens—and I suppose it really doesn't matter—but this way, I get some say. I'm looking at this in a positive way, and you should, too."

Her teacup rattled in her hands as Miss Louisa sat alone. "I get to choose. Yes, I do." She had gone through her house, one item at a time, one furnishing at a time. She hated the idea of her things being sold this way, but she had no choice. She would do what needed to be done, no matter how hard the duty. She had faced hard things before. This was just one more, perhaps the final one.

She looked around the darkened, stuffy room. Tied to every significant piece of furniture was a tag marked with a name. Tags read "Agnes" or "Robert III" or "John" or "Esther," or "Regina." In addition to the hunt chest, several other pieces were marked for her niece. Two larger pieces would go to the Presbyterian Church. She had offered the house outright to a local college, but they declined. Dissembling and moving a house— even one so architecturally interesting—was impossible, they said. And if not impossible, certainly too costly. Everything else—from her bread bowl to her garden tools—would go to auction. Agnes had taken a handful of things that were sentimental to her, but she didn't take much.

"No point waitin'," she had told Mr. Trinkle bravely. "No point in gettin' sentimental about it. The best things in life aren't things. That was my momma's favorite sayin'—and she was right as rain. All this means nothing without the people you love. I learned that a whole lotta years ago—when my Mr. Leaberry was called home."

Spread across her dining room table were the few items she was most sentimental about. There was a small bone china box, green and white. On the bottom, she had written in grease pencil "Virginia," the name of her eldest granddaughter. The box had been a gift to Louisa from her own grandmother. She hoped Virginia would treasure it as she had.

A thin flat box tied up with kitchen string was labeled "baptismal dress." It was marked for Robert III, her eldest son. She had written out for him the history of the lacy white dress—that it had been her husband's— Robert Leaberry, Jr.—when he was baptized into the Presbyterian Church, and his father's— Robert Sr.—before that. Both of her own boys had worn it when she and Mr. Leaberry had presented their infants for baptism.

On the far end of the table, twelve flint arrowheads were lined up seriatim, one for each of her grandchildren. She and her brother had found them as children—dozens of them—relics of the hollow's earliest residents. Many had disappeared over the years. Only these were left, enough for the grandchildren. Beside them was a stack of envelopes; she would label each with a child's name.

One item remained unmarked because she could not decide which of her children should have it—her husband's Bible, the one given him when he graduated from the Institute. Perhaps she would keep that for a little while longer. Perhaps she would take it with her to Chilhowie. The Bible wouldn't take up much space.

From across the room, her tall clock ticked. Dangling off its face, attached to a tasseled brass key, a tag was marked: "to Agnes house." The clock was to go in the back room she would be taking. It would barely fit, Agnes had told her, but Miss Louisa had insisted. She knew its perpetual rhythm would help her adjust. It had always reminded her of her late husband. He had been gone fifty-four years this November, but she still missed him. She remembered so clearly the two of them sitting together in the shadow of the clock as it clicked off time. The sound, the rhythm, the memory tied her to him.

"That was Mr. Leaberry's clock," she had told Agnes, referring to her late husband as she always had. "Mr. Leaberry bought this himself. It was the only piece of furniture he ever insisted on, and it is the only one I insist on bringing. It was your daddy's clock. He would want me to keep it."

Agnes had sighed and agreed. "All right, Mother. We'll make sure it comes. We'll find a place for it somewhere."

Notwithstanding her outward courage, Miss Louisa had misgivings. She had seen the dismay in her daughter's eyes when she realized that her mother had no other place to go. Miss Louisa had balked at moving to Wytheville, into a suitable home for the elderly. The proprietor had been gracious and inviting, but Miss Louisa would have none of it. She had flatly refused.

"I would rather die, Agnes. I really would," she had said with uncharacteristic tears in her eyes. After all, Miss Louisa had reasoned, family should take care of family. She had not had to say it outright to her daughter because she had repeated it most of her life. It was her mantra: family took care of family. She had cared for her own father during his years of decline, and it became an unspoken expectation that she should be afforded the same consideration. Agnes had volunteered, perhaps with reservations, after her brothers had made it clear that their wives would not welcome their mother-in-law's moving in, even at her advanced age. It was the daughters' duty, they had said.

The one saving grace was Miss Louisa's attitude. She refused to complain. She refused to become a burden—instead, she had decided to do everything in her power to make sure Agnes would be glad she came.

As the sun rose higher in the sky outside, the room heated up. Miss Louisa fanned her face. Finally, she stood up and went to each window, uncurtaining them one by one. She lifted the heavy sashes, which slid up and thudded into the high jamb. The paraffin that she had rubbed on the sash cords every spring and fall kept the windows moving smoothly. Instantly, a breeze freshened the room. She breathed deeply. Her verbena was fuming. She would have Estes dig up some for her, and she would insist he take some to Parthenia.

"What will happen to Estes?" she said out loud to the empty room.

"My goodness. I almost forgot Estes." She looked around the room. "Parthenia always did love my cane rocker." She took a sip of her tea before she reached for another tag and wrote: 'for Parthenia Adams.' Estes was coming in the afternoon to help her box a few more things, so she decided she would let him choose something for himself. He might want some of Robert's tools he'd been using all these years.

⸎

Ruth Fowlkes rolled over in bed. The room felt unfamiliar and strange. She had awakened for thirty years beside the same man, with the same morning sunshine, the same silver maple outside her window, full and flush in summer, bare and bonelike in winter. But this morning the only familiarity was the sunshine, and it came in the windows at a strange angle, a western slant. Around the room's perimeter, stacks of boxes, corrugated troves of the possessions she had accumulated, sat waiting to be unpacked.

Under Ruth's careful direction, the furniture in the room had been arranged satisfactorily. The new house was smaller but adequate, and in some ways it was nicer. Certainly newer. The walls had been painted a pale yellow and the woodwork, a nice white, colors she had chosen after Ernie's suggestion that they have Mr. Siever come in and paint the entire house ahead of their move.

"It'll give the house a nice freshenin'," he had told her over breakfast after they had agreed to buy the house. "And it'll keep you from havin' to wash down all the walls. I'll call him. You jus' go on down to the mercantile and pick you out the colors. Anything 'cept pink, Ruthie. If you don't mind. Pink ain't my favorite color." She looked with satisfaction around the freshly painted room. Even with boxes strewn about, the room felt happy and welcoming. Ruth hadn't expected this. She hadn't expected to feel any joy at all, but she did. And she welcomed it. She would hang the children's pictures on the wall away from the window, so they wouldn't fade.

Lying beside her, Ernie snored gently. She would let him sleep. He had earned this good rest. Lately, he had been especially generous, agreeing to her every request as she had packed and planned. Ruth smiled, listening to his soft palate vibrate. She was used to this sound but not the sound of the

250

traffic along the road. She thought she heard a truck pull into the driveway and then out again, but she dismissed it. She would have to adjust to the new sounds.

It felt odd to be so close to Christiansburg after decades in her house in the hollow. Tucked under the mountain, her old house had felt secure at the end of their gravel drive, protected by a stand of white pines that she and Ernie had planted as a windbreak the first year they had lived there. The house had never been fancy or elegant, but it was large and ample like a grandmother's lap. It had been a good place to raise children.

Their first daughter had been born there the next year, and then four more children came in rapid succession. The pine trees grew, the house filled up with children and all the commotion that comes with a large family. They lived happily. Then one by one the children left, leaving behind memories for Ruth to savor. She would forever long for those sweet days, but Ruth was not one to dwell on the past. In the same way, she refused to think of the water, how it would consume her front porch, her parlor, the fireplace, and kitchen, and eventually the roof.

Whenever such thoughts arose, Ruth got to work.

She slipped out of the bed, pulled on her chenille robe, and tiptoed to her new kitchen. It, too, was strewn with unopened boxes. She thought she would whip up a little quick bread for breakfast. *Might as well celebrate as cry,* she thought.

The kitchen was bigger than the one she'd left, and it had shiny new appliances—another extravagance Ernie had surprised her with. She rummaged around in a few boxes until she found her baking pans and a mixing bowl. She found a tin of flour, a box of cinnamon, and the dozen eggs they had carried in the car, along with the candles and her dipladenia, her jewelry box, and an oil lamp that had been her aunt's. They had given away all the chickens, so they wouldn't have fresh eggs until Ernie could put up a new chicken house. She would need to find a new market.

For Ruth, cooking was therapeutic. She mixed the bread and slid it into the oven. She fiddled with the dials on the stove until she felt it heat. Ernie had hooked up the Delco plant that came with the house, and it was working fine. She started a pot of coffee on the stove and water for grits before she dug through another box to find her silverware.

While the bread baked, she took a handful of flowers from a box full of cut blooms sitting on the bottom stair step. Pulling a drinking glass out of a box, she filled it with water and arranged the flowers. She set them on the table, and then stepped out to the porch to see this new view Ernie had been so excited about. She hadn't bothered to find her slippers and felt the cool porch under her bare feet. The floor was gritty. After breakfast, she would sweep it. She had to admit the view was fine. The new house looked east. In the hollow she had always looked up at the ridges. Now she looked out across them as the sun, climbing across the ridge, defined the mountain's undulations. She liked it, this new view, but she wished the house were a little bigger, especially for when the children came home. *Perhaps this is for the best.* She thought about her children. They had their own families now. *Idn't this how it's supposed to be? You're born into a family that holds you till you're grown. Then you find a person to spend the rest of your life with and you got you a new family. Your first family begins to fade.* Ruth thought of her own parents, her own siblings, how her family with Ernie had become satellites of her mother and father's family. This understanding had become clearest when her parents passed. Now it was she and Ernie who were stepping to the background. The family they had created was fading. The thought might have made her sad, but Ruth understood that this was the right order of things, and for this she was grateful.

"At least they have their own," she whispered to the morning. She smiled, thinking of her five children and her twelve grandchildren—every one of them a towhead with blue eyes. *I am blessed.*

As Ruth turned to go back into the house, she spotted a flat-top trunk pushed against the railing at the end of the porch. *That's strange,* she thought, *that's not ours.* Just then, she heard Ernie come down the steps.

"Ernie, come out here."

"Whatcha need?" he said, stepping over the box of flowers and out to the porch. "Where'd you get the flowers?"

"Out back. There's a pretty little garden. It's jus' full. Out behind those ol' boxwoods. Pretty as can be."

"Jus' like you," he said. He leaned over and gave her a frisky little peck on the cheek.

"You musta slept good," she said.

"Sure did. So, was I right about the view?" He gestured toward the vista.

"It's nice, Ernie. It really is." Ruth kicked her foot in the direction of the trunk. "You know what this is? Do you know who it belongs to?"

Ernie shrugged. "No idea at all. Ned musta left it here by mistake. You open it?"

"No, I don't think much of opening somebody else's trunk."

"Well, we gotta know who to return it to, Ruth"

"I am not openin' somebody else's trunk."

They stared at the trunk. Its leather straps were mostly intact, but one lock and handle were missing, and one wooden slat on top was cracked.

"Surely somebody's missing it, Ernie. Can you ask Ned about it?"

"Don't know when I'll be seeing him again."

"Cain't you find out? Somebody's bound to know. I'd like to get it off my front porch."

"Be a whole lot easier to open the trunk."

"No, Ernie. I'm not goin' to go pokin' in somebody else's trunk."

"All right. I'll ask around."

He held the door open for his wife. "Something smells mighty good, Ruth."

A hot breeze blew through the empty gristmill where Shep McCleary had come alone to have one last look. He had heard the floodgates would close sometime in the next few weeks. Taking the iron pole he had used to stir the grains, he pried loose the sign above the door: McCleary's Gristmill. He laid it in the bed of his truck with several bags of cornmeal he had scraped out of the meal bin after the final run. Sunshine would be glad to have them before she had to start buying from the store up on Route 100. He realized how convenient it had been for her to have him bring home whatever she needed. Standing on the deck, he pondered how much their life was changing. He smiled as he recalled Sunshine's reaction when he'd told her all that had transpired and what he had planned for their family. She had not believed him at first, but when he showed her the check, she had hugged his neck and sobbed happy tears.

The mill floor was littered with grains that winds had not already blown into the cracks or out into the yard. The waterwheel was stopped, baking in the summer sun. He had closed the sluice, diverted the water away—why, though, he was not sure. It wasn't necessary. Why not let it roll on, roll until it could no longer turn? Or roll until it could go eternally as a wheel without a purpose. Shep knew some of his neighbors felt this way, but Shep needed to see it stopped, to see the end. He picked up a short stack of burlap sacks and tossed them in the back of his truck, securing them underneath the sign. Sunshine could certainly put them to some good use. He watched the belts rock gently above him on the hot breeze. He looked over everything carefully. He wanted to remember.

Shep wished he owned a camera. Maybe somebody at the *Roanoke Times* would come by for some last pictures. *I ought to suggest it*, he thought. He could ask the hardware in town if he could use their telephone to make the long-distance call. Might be nice to have a picture. Somebody ought to.

Before climbing into his truck, he took one last look. The waterwheel was still. The decks were bare. The bins sat open and empty. Waiting.

As everyone in the hollow was waiting.

# Early August

August opened with a flawless blue sky and moist air that blew lazily under a hot sun. It was a perfect day in the hollow, the kind where every leaf, every tree, every stone shimmered in brilliant benevolent light. More than ordinary, the day had the quality of a fine painting.

Ned stood on the porch. While he waited on Sky, he smoked one of his last cigarettes. Without the mercantile, the closest place to buy them was the Esso station, and their supply had dwindled over the past few weeks. Too much demand. Ned had never been one to hoard, but on his last trip he had bought a few extra packs.

Sky came out the cabin door. She was grinning. In her arms was a makeshift picnic basket—a cardboard box left in the back of Ned's truck after a job. It was filled with food.

"You ready?" Ned said, taking the last puffs before tossing the butt on the steps and grinding it out with the toe of his boot.

"You go?" she said, a phrase Ned understood to mean, 'Are you really going this time?'

Ned smiled. "I said I would."

"Collier, come?"

"Yep." Ned whistled for the hound and went to look for him.

Sky sat down on the steps, holding the box on her knees. When Ned returned with Collier, he added a piece of oilcloth to her box, along with two bottles of coke he'd been saving. He grabbed a knife off a nail high on the porch wall. "Gotta be able to open your co-cola."

Sky smiled up at him with an expression of happiness that touched him deeply.

He bent down and took the box. "I'll carry that," he said, taking it from her and helping her stand up. Over the summer her legs had swelled some, and she often seemed out of breath.

Ned snapped his fingers. "Forgot somethin'," he said, teasingly. Balancing the box on his hip, he pulled two peppermint sticks out of his pocket and slipped them into the box. Sky squealed.

"Let's git goin'," he said. "You lead."

She pointed up toward the ridge. "Up."

Ned nodded. They set off together, Collier running ahead. The sun followed them.

Sky's face was a mixture of delight and disbelief. Ned had never gone with her to this high, out-of-the-way meadow before. While she had always had time for leisure, he had never had the luxury of exploring the remotest areas of the hollow.

With Collier lumbering along, they made their way through the hollow toward the western ridge, the farthest point from Jasper's Gap, until they reached a meadow fenced on two sides by thick stands of hemlocks and hardwoods and mountain laurel. The laurel blossoms had faded long ago, but their scent lingered.

Sky knew the way, the way one knows the road home. This was her favorite spot, the wide meadow, flush with grasses and flowers—blue cornflowers, wild white roses, Queen Anne's lace, black-eyed Susans. The expanse was breathtaking, and its beauty took Ned by surprise. He had a vague remembrance of finding this as a child, but that was a lifetime ago.

Sky led Ned along a narrow deer path to the center of the meadow where an outcropping of limestone, the result of some ancient vaulting of the earth, offered them a makeshift table of flat boulders. Ned set the box on one broad rock and unfolded the oilcloth. Sky climbed up on the tallest rock and spread open her arms. A warm breeze rustled her hair and stroked her skin. She was as excited as a child would have been. Sky was a child in so many ways, but over the years Ned had seen her age, seen her steps slow, seen her labor and sometimes struggle to catch her breath. In vague and troubling ways, this called up his remembrance of the Dunkard's last days. It worried Ned. But today, all that worry was left deep in the hollow. Sky was a child again.

A cry of unconstrained joy, like the call of a meadowlark or the cooing of a mourning dove, came from Sky and sailed out across the meadow. A flock of pheasants flew up, swooped through the sky, and flew off. Ned had forgotten how plentiful the birds were. He had forgotten their chirps and squeals, the brush of their wings through the air, and how they animated the sky.

Sky turned around and looked at him, as if she were seeing him for the first time.

"You see birds! Pretty birds! See?"

"Yes. I do." Ned looked skyward. *The birds!* Ned thought he heard a voice, but it must have been the wind.

"They fly! See! They fly! Pretty! They fly!" She waved her arms. "I fly with them!"

Ned marveled. It was as long spoken as his sister had ever been. In the bright sunlight, he shaded his brow, and watched her. He knew her secret wish.

"I fly!"

After a while, Sky climbed off the rocks and sat down beside Ned. She gestured for a drink. With his knife, Ned popped the tops off the two coke bottles, handed one to Sky, and slid the box of food between them. He watched his sister. Her eyes hardly left the sky. After they ate, Ned stretched out against a rock and rested while Sky walked in the meadow. She belonged to this land, to this hollow. She belonged here. Nowhere else.

It was late afternoon when they left the high meadow, allowing enough time to reach the cabin before dark. Ned carried the box. The empty bottles clinked one against the other. Sky's face was pink from the sun, and she was as happy as her brother had ever seen her.

For Ned, though, there was finality to this trip that made his heart ache.

❧

Ruth was standing in the kitchen when Ernie came through the back door. Two little towheaded boys raced by him into the dining room, rattling

Ruth's china, and slamming the front door, but his wife just stood there, seeming not to notice at all. Something was odd.

Ernie yelled after his grandsons: "You boys stop running through the house." Ernie grabbed a hand towel and wiped his forehead. "Something on your mind, Ruth?"

His wife held out a folded piece of paper. Her hand was trembling.

Ernie tossed the towel over a chair and noticed pictures scattered across the kitchen table. "What are those?"

Ruth didn't answer. She just looked at him and shook the paper.

"What's this?" Growing alarmed but not letting on, Ernie took the paper. "Somethin' wrong, Ruthie? You don't seem like yourself," he said as casually as he could.

"The trunk," she said, beginning to cry. "I looked in it."

"You looked in it? I thought you said you'd never do that."

Ruth could barely speak.

"Well, who's damn trunk is it? What's wrong, Ruth?"

"Read it," she said, and she cupped her hands over her mouth.

"What'n the world's goin' on here?" Ernie sat down at the kitchen table and unfolded the paper.

Ned leaned against a tree behind the shed, out of sight of the cabin, and wept. Collier sauntered over and nudged his leg, the same way a friend might have put a hand on his shoulder. It would have felt good to have a friend just now, but Ned was a solitary man. He had never had time for friendship. The need was embedded in his soul, nonetheless. Especially now.

As he bent down to rub the hound's head, he saw his own hands, gnarled and worn. He stared at them. He noticed, as if for the first time, how old he had grown. It was a quiet and sobering realization. His hands, rough and worn like the bark of the tree, marked time as surely as the tree marked time with its height and girth. When it had been a sapling, he had lashed pieces of broken glass and hung them from its branches to catch the light, each small shard trapping a piece of the sun and jettisoning it through the forest, a javelin of light carrying with it a baby girl child's rapt attention. For hours his makeshift mobile had entertained his sister, closed up in the dog run for safekeeping while he worked. The dog run had never failed him. Neither had his hands.

As he leaned against the tree, Ned reviewed his life and concluded that for all its trouble and difficulty, it had been a good life. Against all odds, the brother and sister had thrived, had made a life in the Dunkard's cabin beside the river. It was a simple life but a good life. Ned had purpose in work and taking care of Sky. Sky's purpose was to love and be loved by the hollow and by Ned. The brother had seen to that. He had always seen to that. Long ago, his mother had charged him with her care, and he had never shirked that duty. It would be like failing to breathe.

Ned had worked hard to take care of Sky. This was the only way he knew to live: to rise with the sun, take up his plow or gun or axe or shovel, or to start up his truck and go to work. It was all written there, laid out in his hands, the work of his hands.

Once again, the Holy Word, so ingrained in Ned, wandered through his brain: *Hast not thou made a hedge about him, and about his house, and about all that he hath on every side? Thou hast blessed the work of his hands, and his substance is increased in the land.* Ned folded his hands together and thought. He knew only work and caretaking. He could navigate nothing more.

Ned pushed away from the tree and stood, resolute. He wiped his face with his faded handkerchief, returned it to his pocket, and stared out across the river. From this vantage he could not see across to the other side. He would have to wait until the sun reached the ridge before it would illuminate the far bank.

⚬⚬⚬

That night, after Sky had fallen asleep, Ned went down to the river. Clarity came to him as the darkness loomed. It had come to him the way a friend delivers sad news. Underneath a full moon, Ned carried a dead-blow hammer and five good strong pieces of kindling toward the river. He hammered them into the earth, the first right along the water's edge, and the others at five-foot intervals straight up the bank. The last stake, he pounded into the edge of their hardscrabble yard. They went in easily, piercing the earth.

He walked back through the yard toward the cabin. The sound of crickets animated the darkness. Moonlight shimmered on the river and cast shadows throughout the hollow. Before he reached the cabin, Ned turned around to observe his work. He examined it with a detached, determined sentiment—and with an aching but resolute heart.

# Late August

It was a beautiful morning, yet Ned could hardly breathe as he stood on his porch and looked out across the river. It was just after dawn, and over the water hung a mist, a thick and swirling fog as thick as smoke. Soon the sun, breaking the ridge, would burn it off. Ned's mind was troubled but steadfast. For weeks he had watched the stakes. Gradually, almost imperceptibly, the river was rising.

He stepped off the porch and lifted his head toward the heavens for some inkling of reassurance that he indeed had been given the responsibility for Sky. Never before had he questioned it—never until the burden had grown so overwhelming, never until what was coming had squeezed him into this place, never until he had faced such a troubling future. A pain deep in his chest, as certain as a knife, ached, and although it slowed him, it did not stop him. It must not stop him.

Walking down through the yard, he was relieved to still count two markers, a strange stay that ran counter to the sure knowledge of their future. Ned understood the wish for a reprieve, but he no longer had any faith in its appearance.

That night, as thousands of nights before, Ned read long passages of the Bible to Sky, who lived so well in the moment. Their future was a burden the brother carried alone, as he had always carried their burdens alone. While he read, a steady rain started and drummed on the cabin's roof with an ominous cadence.

The next morning Sky awoke before Ned. Unlike yesterday, the sun was obscured. Intermittent rain had continued through the night, and the river was once again socked in with a soupy fog, common for August. Water dripped from saturated boughs that bent under the weight of the morning. The forest, cool and quiet, waited as if the hollow insisted on sleeping a little longer.

When Sky saw the dismal weather, she wrapped herself in a blanket to ward off the cool dampness and sat down by the window. She watched the sun struggle to illumine the sky and succeed only on the most basic level. Off and on, curtains of rain passed like the broad strokes of a wet broom. These passing showers scored the movement of time. From the far side of the cabin, Ned snored rhythmically. The morning's only other sounds were the pitch and brush of water dripping from the roof and an occasional whishing as wind blew rain out of the trees.

Once the sun rose high enough above the ridge to create a muted brightness, Sky slipped out onto the porch, stood at the top of the steps where she listened to the river run. In the veiled morning, she did not notice Ned's markers. Her eyes peered deep into the forest, willing her spirit to go where her body could not go—not until the weather granted her comfortable passage.

When she heard Ned stir, she went back into the cabin to prepare breakfast.

# September

All that was left in the hollow were lively winds that rustled through the trees, abundant animals—and Ned and Sky. Everyone else had gone, resettled ahead of what was coming.

For Ned, the future had grown heavier with each passing day and blacker with each passing night. This burden weighed on him heavier than anything he had ever carried. He was haunted—and driven—by the night the tree fell and pinned him. He kept it all to himself.

Ned had tried. He had done everything he could do. He had searched high and low. He had persuaded, tempted, encouraged. But he had not found a viable plan, a way forward.

For Ned, the flash-locked river struck a bleak absurdity. The water still fed the greening landscape and nourished the trees whose roots ran deep along the banks, whose leaves were mirrored in the slick surface of the water. He had watched the water's rise, suffering the anxiety to which Sky was oblivious. For Sky, nothing had changed. The forest was as alive and inviting as it had ever been. She spent hours walking. It produced a delight and joy in her as essential as blood.

Early one morning, Ned woke with a start. His throat tightened around a strange sense of foreboding. Something in the heavens had shifted. Time had stopped for a moment, but now, once again, it was marching to a furious and final crescendo.

When Ned left the cabin that morning, he noticed that the last of his markers had disappeared below the surface of the river.

This is what Ned had been waiting for.

# October

The night air was still, and the trees of the forest stood silent, resigned. Only the river waters flowed, lapping, lapping, lapping. Sky slept, lost in a pleasurable slumber. She dreamt of the day in the high meadow with Ned, a day of utter and complete joy, as most days of her life had been. Occasionally, she turned, smiled, and murmured. A guttural snort occasionally escaped her lips.

Ned was tired but slept only fitfully. Every time he drifted off to sleep, the image of the last marker interrupted. When he had last looked, the water had risen to the edge of the garden. With the last marker gone, so was his hope. He lay on his bed, listening to the sound of the river. It had always been a part of his life—but to his sister, the river and the hollow were life itself. They flowed through her spirit as surely as blood flowed through her veins.

If Sky had been puzzled by the markers that had disappeared one by one or by the river creeping toward the cabin, she asked no questions. For this, Ned was thankful. The river had come up this high before after heavy rains; a part of it was normal, natural, in the order of how it had always been. But Ned understood this rise was not natural at all. Sky would not understand.

Finally, Ned rose quietly and stepped out to the porch. As he looked out over the water, he wished to be wrong. Maybe by some miracle the water had receded. Maybe the last marker had become visible again. Perhaps the dam would crumble. Perhaps. In the moonlight, clearly, it had not. Hope, so irrepressible, spoke small taunting words to him.

Ned knew the truth. He thought of praying for a miracle—for everything that had transpired to be only a mirage that would disappear like the mist that hovered over the river. His mother had believed in mirages. Why couldn't he? Why couldn't he put his stock in miracles? God had parted the waters of the Red Sea, but who would hold back the waters of the river for Sky?

Ned sat down on the cabin's stoop. He was tired. The blade in his chest turned. He had never known such agony. It was an amalgam of pain, hopelessness, and despair lessened only by the knowledge that he had tried. He had tried with all his might, but some things were impossible to change. Sky would never leave the hollow. She was part of it, and it was part of her, as if she were rooted to the ground like an ancient blackjack oak, as if the hollow were an essential organ and to remove it from her—or her from it—was certain death. This was her world. There were no others for her. Finally, and reluctantly, Sky's devoted caretaker had made the only choice given him, and if he, in doing so, had sacrificed eternity, it was for Sky whom he loved.

A nervous wind rattled the trees, and Ned looked up as a sudden rustle of leaves broke the silence. Then the night fell silent again. Hushed were the crickets. Hushed were the bullfrogs. Hushed was the buzz of the night bugs. All surrendered to the sound of the quickening waters. In the air hung a strange, almost audible, stillness.

Ned left the porch. He walked along the river, back and forth, beneath the light of a waning moon, beneath the half-closed eye of heaven. His boots sank into the mud, but he did not notice. Thin ribbony semaphores of clouds trailed high above him as the night wore on. In the atmosphere, tension grew, the same way an audience waits before a great drama is to begin, one with a sudden and cataclysmic finale.

Gradually, a bank of thick clouds drew across the sky and extinguished the moon, drowning Ned and the earth in blackness. He stopped and stood motionless in the unconditional darkness. He listened to the waters and to the pounding from deep within his chest. Time pressed on. Oh, how Ned wished he could turn it back—time—to change its direction, to alter its path. But time and progress were unrelenting. And as nature waited—so did his duty.

In the darkness, Ned turned toward the cabin. He needed no light. He knew the way.

On the porch, he struck a match to light his lantern. As smoke curled up and out of the saffron light, Ned grasped the cold metal and held it until it warmed in his palm, every nerve ending in his fingers firing from synapse to skin to metal. In the shadowy light, his skilled hands supplanted his eyes, as he lifted the loaded barrel.

The weak flame in the lantern flickered and died on a quick breath of night as Ned stepped through the cabin door. His heartbeat thundered through his temples. His own breathing was quick and shallow. His palms were clammy, his jaw, clenched tight. Again, he wanted to turn back to search again for a better solution, but there was none.

None.

He stood in the center of the cabin, pausing to let his eyes adjust. He listened for the familiar rattle of Sky's labored breathing—but all he heard was quiet. He strained to listen, but there was only silence.

Silence.

In the darkness, he listened again, steeling his resolve, summoning the courage to execute this final duty to his beloved sister, to fulfill her dearest wish to stay in her hollow. With all the courage he could marshal and compelled by the deepest of loves, he stepped toward Sky's bed and raised his rifle.

Nothing in the cabin moved. Ned's hands shook. Tears clouded his eyes. For a moment, he was overcome with the finality of his task.

Sky was faraway, deep in sleep, her breathing shallow, ragged, nearly inaudible.

He gripped his rifle. His arms trembled. His finger caressed the trigger.

Then he heard a voice: "Ned. Ned."

Like the Abraham of the Bible, he stopped. He lowered the barrel. Did he really hear? Or was this his own mind directing? His own cowardice? He listened. Waited.

And then with a sudden gasp and one long exhalation, Sky's breathing ceased.

Ned stood motionless, struggling to understand. He was tempted to step forward to shake her, to revive her, but he was frozen in place. Was he relieved of this onerous duty? Had Sky been taken before he was compelled to act? Was this the mercy he sought?

Holding the rifle, he waited. Nothing changed. Sky lay still. Still. Still as death—still in death. Finally, carrying unbelief, he stepped forward and touched his sister's cheek.

Sky was gone.

Tears formed in Ned's eyes. A collision of emotions assaulted him—grief, pain, relief, and a strange, incomprehensible joy that Sky would never have to leave her beloved hollow. He fell to his knees beside the bed, bowed his head, and sobbed as he voiced a prayer of thanksgiving for this—he knew—was the mercy of God.

Still holding his rifle, he stepped out to the porch, and in an action symbolizing his unexpected reprieve aimed his rifle toward the river, the River of Death. One sudden concussion shattered the air and trailed across the river, skipping across the water, bouncing against the hills, and ricocheting, one side to the other, echoing, and recoiling overhead. The sound went on and on, like the tintinnabulation of a perfect bell, but finally, mercifully, it dissipated, and quiet returned to the hollow. An immense quiet. A supernatural quiet. Against it, Ned once more heard the unrelenting sound of the water lapping, but that was all.

⸎

In the late afternoon of the following day, as light illumined the ridge above him and soaked down through the hollow, Ned climbed into his truck and drove it to the edge of the rising river. He was tired. His clothes were soiled. His shovel, thrown in the back of the truck, was covered with black dirt, the kind that had nurtured, the kind that had sustained life in the hollow, the kind that now swaddled his beloved sister.

The knife in Ned's heart was gone, replaced with the numbness of absolute pain, and a strange and wholly unexpected sensation of peace. Mercy. This, he believed, must be the most generous forgiveness in the universe. He had steeled himself for guilt. Instead, he had found mercy.

Leaving the truck door open and the engine running, he climbed out of the cab and slowly shambled back to Collier's run. He unlatched the door, broke his long pole in half over his knee and with the two pieces, he propped open the run. He stood alone in the slanting light for a few minutes as he watched Collier stir and stand.

"Collier," he said, calling the hound. "Come." The hound shook himself and ambled toward Ned. "You take care of yourself, ol' fella." He crouched down to rub his dog's neck. Then he smacked the hound's rump. "Go on, now. Git."

Ned stood up, watched the hound dog lumber toward the forest, turn once, and then disappear into the thick underbrush. He seemed to go with a mixture of reluctance and joy—so much as a dog can be joyous.

Ned returned to the cabin, mounted the steps, and took up the broom to sweep the porch, every crumb, every clod of dirt, every cobweb, every beetle removed with the firm swish of the broom. He straightened the leather cover on the rain barrel, stroking its worn, weathered grain. Then he went inside.

From the windowsill, he lifted his jar of rolled bills, emptied them into his palm. He counted them and re-rolled them into a tight wad. He lit a match before he tossed the roll, a scrap of cardboard and the burning match into the belly of the stove. He closed the door, placed his palm on the top to feel the warmth. He set the two empty chairs straight under the table, brushed a few crumbs from its surface with his hand, and without sitting, lifted and opened his Bible to read aloud a verse. His voice was quiet, otherworldly.

"And David said to Solomon his son, Be strong and of good courage, and do it: fear not, nor be dismayed: for the Lord God, even my God, will be with thee; he will not fail thee, nor forsake thee, until thou hast finished all the work for the service of the house of the Lord."

Ned tore out the page, folded it, and slipped it into the pocket of his shirt over his heart. He turned to the fifteenth chapter of John and underlined the thirteenth verse. With tears obscuring his sight, he crossed out the last word and wrote in its place "sister." He closed the book and set it squarely in the center of the table. "Amen," he said. His voice cracked.

Ned surveyed the room. He thought of his mother and remembered the night she had delivered Sky into his arms. He could see his mother's silhouette clearly. He could hear the panic in her voice. He could feel the wet child thrust into his young arms. He remembered how cold the wind had swirled and how warm the baby had felt. How ill prepared he had been. How naïve. How innocent.

Ned whispered a prayer before approaching Sky's empty bed. He pulled up the blanket. He tucked it taut and smoothed out the creases. He stepped onto the porch and sat down on the top step where he bowed his head. He wondered if his mother were watching. He wondered if she would understand. He wondered what the Dunkard would say; this thought he dismissed. It did not matter anymore. It did not matter at all.

After a few minutes, Ned lifted himself off the steps and walked back down to his truck. He could not feel his hands or his feet or his heartbeat. He focused on the river with the courage of necessity and the understanding that his work was complete. Light sparkled on the water's face, capturing splinters of sun, and holding them like the sweat on a workingman's brow. He moved along slowly. A solitary figure.

Unburdened.

The untied laces of Ned's boots floated in the lapping water as he looked out over the hollow to the sharp sunlit ridgeline, to the deep, scarlet forest, to the trees flush with life. The hollow was exquisite—one last exquisite autumn. He heard animals scurry and watched birds fly. The birds! They would escape, inconvenienced but unscathed.

Ned's truck door creaked as he pulled it shut. The expanse of water before him looked calm but ran deep and strong. He shielded his eyes from the hot afternoon sun that glinted off the water. Up and down the river, birds flew from one treetop to another, branch to branch. Caddisflies hovered in luminous swarms above the water, and an occasional fish jumped to snare one, breaking the waters' calm, and sending small circular wakes out across it. He killed the engine. Ned let the truck roll forward.

After a while, water crawled up onto to the matte black hood of the truck, lapping gently, and in a strange way, calmly. He watched the water glaze the faded paint as if the water could make it new again. But just as quickly, the sun would burn away the water as it ebbed forward and fell back.

He turned and looked back at the two graves, side-by-side. Ned had never felt so alone. He had never been so alone. Beside him lay his rifle.

He had planned to pull the brake and roll into the rising river, but Ned did not. Soon he felt water at his feet. He sat in his truck, his hands gripping the steering wheel, thinking of Sky. He thought of the runnels where she had played as a child. The river—it was one giant runnel today. On his mind was a pressing sense of completion and a strange and validated peace, a peace that seemed out of place, a peace he could hardly comprehend, yet a peace that soaked through him. He had done his job. He had finished the race. All his striving, all his work, was done.

Once again, a scripture wandered into his brain. This time, though, it came in the Dunkard's voice: "I have finished the work which thou gavest me to do." Ned looked up expecting to see the face of the man of his childhood. Instead, he gazed into a vacant blue sky. It beckoned to him in a new way, with a fresh understanding of what the Dunkard had taught him. A promise fulfilled. It was the same sky, the same longing he had seen in the Dunkard in his last days—he had been young, shielded by youth but not unaware, while his mother sat beside the old man's bed, wiping his brow, shooing away flies.

As evening came and the sun reflected off the river, Ned climbed out of his truck and walked into the forest, in one hand the Dunkard's dog-eared Bible and in his pocket, the tiny pitchfork and hay bale.

Throughout the evening that followed and the weeks that came after, the water rose steadily, slowly consuming everything. Collier came back once, lingered, and loped away again, disappearing into the forest, following wonted footsteps. By all other measures, though, it had been an ordinary day.

The moon rose. The sun rose. The moon rose.

In time, the truck was gone, the cabin was gone, the hollow was gone, submerged beneath the dark waters—and with it all that had been.

# Epilogue
# Summer, 1969

Chandeliers sprinkle light across the coffered ceiling and the grass-cloth walls and the faces of guests who spill through broad arched doorways trimmed in thick Georgian moulding. The room is alive with the babble of dignitaries and socialites and aficionados. They mill about and coagulate into groups like dancers in small elite troupes, posing on Persian carpets laid on Italian marble. They sample fancy hors d'oeuvres from silver trays passed by young women dressed in crisp black and white. They sip beverages that bubble in narrow glasses, holding them with bangled or cufflinked hands as they chatter like squirrels.

Banks of French doors at one side of the vast room open out over a lake where the sun dazzles on the water. A sophisticated breeze blows through. Laughter, words, and the swish of fine fabrics ride the traveling air. The chandeliers tinkle on the breeze.

Throughout the room on curving walls, dozens of delicate drawings hang. Each is encased in a small, gilded frame or shadow box lined with black velvet. Images of leaves, stones, birds, of squirrels, of deer, of trees—each hauntingly beautiful.

Each is perfect.

"The curator has done a wonderful job," one guest opines.

"Yes, it is a lovely presentation," agrees another with a throaty but elegant voice. "I am so intrigued."

"It makes one terribly curious about the artist, doesn't it?"

"I do wonder who she was?"

"Or he," chimes an angular man with a swath of thick dark hair, a cleft chin, and the look of artistic haughtiness. He scoffs. "Why would you presume the artist to be a woman?"

"Sir, it was a woman." A large officious matron wearing pearls and a flowing green caftan steps toward him. "A nameless woman."

The man scoffs again. "Nameless? No one knew her? I can't imagine that."

"Well, sir! I'll beg your pardon, but that is the truth. No one knew she existed." The woman with the pearls waves to the curator. "Mr. Risotti! Mr. Risotti! Come over here, please."

A refined man in a black tuxedo turns and strides in her direction. He is smiling.

"Hello, my dear," Mr. Risotti says. He leans down to kiss her plump, powdered cheek.

"Would you tell us again—how you acquired these?" She shoots a smug look toward the man with the cleft chin.

"It was a gift. Part of a large bequest," he says. Mr. Risotti unfolds his arms and gestures with a wide sweeping motion. "Enough to fund this gallery. It came out of the blue." The eyes of the gathered follow his hands, and then settle again on his face, eager to hear more. "It came from a couple named Fowlkes. Ernie and Ruth Fowlkes. They lived near Floyd. I understand he ran a mercantile years ago. Nice people, the Fowlkes. I never had the pleasure, but that's what I've been told. He died a few years ago, and she followed shortly thereafter. They left the collection to the college because their children weren't interested in keeping it, and they thought it should stay here in the area. When I talked to their son, he told me he didn't know exactly how his parents acquired the drawings. He had no idea who the artist was. All he knew is that his parents had kept them in an old trunk."

The man with the cleft chin raises a brow. "That doesn't prove the artist was a woman."

"Ah, you're quite right, sir." Mr. Risotti winks at the woman with pearls. "But this does." He opens his jacket and slips out a yellowed letter from his breast pocket. With a bit of drama, he unfolds the letter and clears his throat.

Dear Mr. Fowlkes,

I been saving for a good long while and seeing as you and
Mrs. Fowlkes got you a big family and because you was
always one to show me kindness, keeping me up with my
jobs and all, I wanted you to have this. Or I reckon you'd
know somebody who might have a need. I got no need no
more. You do as you see fit with the money. I thought you
might like to have all these pictures too. My sister made
them. You never knowed her cause she was painful shy. I
never did bring her up to your store. But the good Lord
gave her the gift to draw. I always thought they was pretty
good. I'm thinking you might could give them out to
people who lived in the hollow—might remind somebody
how the hollow used to be. Before the water came.

Ned

"Who is Ned?" The question comes in a small chorus as Mr. Risotti
refolds the letter.

"No one knows, I'm afraid. A few old timers remember him vaguely—
an old hermit—but no one knew much about him. As they tell it, no one
ever knew he had a sister."

"It's such a shame no one remembers," muses the woman with pearls.
"But isn't that the way it always is—all that's lost when someone dies." She
shakes her head. "My, my. What a perfect eye she had. I would have loved
to walk with her."

"Perhaps you can, my dear," says Mr. Risotti. He offers his arm to the
woman with pearls. She smiles and lays her bejeweled hand on his sleeve.
"Let us walk through our new gallery—and let our forgotten artist show
us what she saw."

"Our forgotten artist. I like that Mr. Risotti. Our forgotten artist."

"Forgotten in name only, my dear. Only in name."

As they traverse the gallery, wind blows through the French windows and rattles the chandeliers. Across the lake, under a perfect blue sky, clouds gather, white caps rise—and over the vast waters a blue heron glides.

# Author's Note

I have often thought that if one of Scotland's deep lochs were somehow translocated to the Virginia Highlands, it would look like Claytor Lake, a deep and elongated body of water created along the ancient path of the New River. Perhaps its creation was an ancestral pull, a need to re-create what was left behind by the pioneering Scots Irish who populated the region. Or perhaps it was simply the American spirit of progress. Either way, a hydroelectric dam built on the New River in 1939 created Claytor Lake, forever changing the landscape.

In this ancient stretch of mountains and valleys where untamed rivers—the Roanoke, the Holston, the Clinch, and the New—once flowed freely, this story lives. The New River is thought to be the second oldest river in the world, behind only the Nile. Its headwaters begin deep in the Carolinas' Smoky Mountains and flow north—the only American river to do so. It snakes through valleys and hollows and gaps in Virginia until it becomes the Gauley and joins the Kanawha in West Virginia, where next it meets the Ohio and eventually merges with the great Mississippi to flow southward again into the Gulf of Mexico.

In the mid-1700s, the Virginia highlands—and the New River Valley that traverses it—marked a passageway west for those seeking adventure and freedom. Some stopped and settled in the New River Valley. For many Scots Irish Presbyterians and for Native Americans of the Cherokee and Catawba tribes, the highlands were rich and nourishing lands. Joining them were members of Pennsylvania's Ephrata Brethren, known locally as the Dunkards.

Having fled Germany seeking religious freedom, the Dunkards—their name a perversion of "Tunker" or "Dunker" meaning "dipper"—established a community originally called Mahaniam, meaning two camps. They were, as described herein, a peculiar people. Their neighbors—the more social Scots Irish Presbyterians—also settled in the rugged mountains and valleys. They too sought a kind of religious freedom since Presbyterians and Baptists did not enjoy the endorsement of the state government, a status lent only to Anglican Episcopalians. In this regard, the Dunkards and Presbyterians had a common foe. Not until 1786 did the Commonwealth of Virginia pass the Statue for Religious Freedom.

History teaches us that the Dunkards eventually abandoned Mahaniam. Life on the frontier was challenging. Some historians contend that the Dunkards, unwilling to kill, were unable to defend themselves against Indian attacks. For others, life was too difficult. Some Dunkards returned to Pennsylvania; others moved into the Carolinas. A few of the hardiest souls, however, stayed, adapted, and assimilated with their Protestant neighbors.

For centuries, the New River ran unencumbered. But in the 1930s, in perhaps an inevitable effort to bring electrification to the region, Appalachian Power Company tapped the river's power, building a hydroelectric dam south of Radford, Virginia.

For individuals living in the area known today as Dunkard's Bottom, and herein as the fictional Dunkard's Hollow, progress came at a price. When the dam was finished, the New River's water flooded the narrow hollows and broad meadows of the mountainous landscape—the land where Mahaniam had existed, where farms and homesteads were abandoned. The 1939 opening of the dam created a 4,500-acre lake with 100 miles of deeply forested shoreline.

For the purposes of this story, I have compressed time, telescoping the short-lived Dunkard settlement of the 1700s, the region's culture during the mid-1800s, and the period of rapid change during the late 1930s. Such collapsing of time has within it a measure of authenticity because progress came slowly to the region—and because the traditions and philosophies established long ago continue to infuse the region known more broadly as Appalachia.

And no two traditions are deeper than the region's commitments to place and to family. While the damming of the river took the land, it did not steal the highlanders' love of the land or their devotion to their neighbors and kin. Devotion to family is reflected in Ned's selfless caretaking of his sister, Sky, an autistic savant. Only a few years after the fictional Sky died in 1939, Donald Triplett became the first individual identified as "autistic." He was born in 1933 in a small town in Mississippi. Like Sky, Triplett had remarkable talents, his for music and math, displaying characteristics of a savant. The town where he lived embraced Donald Triplett, and their generosity gave him the freedom, the mercy, and the support to live 89 good years.

While autism was not recognized as a disorder until the twentieth century, there is little doubt that the condition existed throughout history. Many have speculated that individuals such as Leonardo Da Vinci, Albert Einstein, and Benjamin Franklin exhibited traits of autism. It is a fascinating subject only now being unlocked through the exploration of neuroscience and brain studies. One can only imagine how, a century ago, families and those who cared for individuals who were clearly *different* might have adapted to the peculiarities that autism exhibits.

The fiercely independent people who first settled in these Virginia highlands never lost these bedrock commitments to land and family. Their devotion was—and is—a spirit of entrepreneurship far removed but far more enduring than the modern definition.

As a child, I water-skied near the dam, regularly spraying water at an old stone chimney. Anchored like a limestone buoy, it stood some forty feet from the shoreline. I often wondered what had happened to the people who must have huddled in front of the hearth to stay warm during the cold mountain winters and who lived simple, unrecorded lives along the banks of the New River. That question became the genesis of this story. In 1989, the chimney was removed from the lake and set on land as a memorial to those who once lived there, whose lives were upended for progress.

The characters in this book are fictional, but it is my hope that this story is a fitting tribute to those people whose devotion to the land and sacrificial commitment to family remains deep and abiding—all qualities of Southwestern Virginians. While much of modern society has lost such virtues, the tried-and-true wisdom of the people of this beautiful part of Virginia is worth remembering. The Dunkard's faith, a love of the land,

and Ned's unfailing commitment to Sky are homages to the people of Southwestern Virginia and their enduring ethos.

# Acknowledgements

Writing a book takes enormous time, energy, and determination. It also requires affirmation, and for that I am forever grateful to my husband, Mark. He has never wavered from offering that all-important encouragement—as well as giving me time to write, endless patience with my obsession, and great feedback.

I also am grateful to my friend, fellow writer, and editor Jean Young Kilby and to my graphic designer Stephanie Pierce. In lending me their abundant talents, I can write with complete assurance that they will always make my books the best they can be.

And I am thankful for my beta readers, Linda Peay Dale, Mary Mullen, and Sarah Pierce. Their encouragement often kept me going.

Finally, I cannot fail to thank all the book clubs that have hosted me and the readers of my first two books who have asked me, "When is your next book coming out?" This is music to an author's ears.

Gratefully,
Martha Graham
*September 2023*

# Books by M.K.B. Graham

## CAIRNAERIE

In this sweeping historical fiction, *Cairnaerie* unfolds across the landscape of Civil War Virginia and the 1920s eugenics movement that follows. Geneva Snow commits the unforgivable Southern sin. No longer the apple of her father's eye, she is a pariah, defying her society's most sacrosanct rule. The consequences are severe. She is hidden away but remains determined to have her way. After years of solitude, a wiser Geneva is desperate to leave a legacy worthy of the father she loved and lost. She engages an unwitting young history professor to help her secretly attend the wedding of her granddaughter—a girl dangerously unaware of her lineage. But when a postman's malevolence and a colleague's revenge converge, Geneva's long-kept secret is exposed. For a second time, she faces a calamity of her own making. Only this time, there is no place to hide.

## FLEURINGALA

Abandoned by her no-count mother in a rundown shack on the outskirts of Lauderville, Virginia, seven-year-old Ruby Glory is alone. Her only friend and sole companion is her faithful dog, Arly. Then along comes Tack, the teenage son of Lauderville's prominent and well-heeled Pittman family. Despite a sincere desire to help Ruby, Tack learns quickly that no good deed goes unpunished. His involvement with the child of a woman of ill-repute sends his family and the citizens of Lauderville into a frenzy of rumors and gossip, presenting Tack with a dilemma. Will the uproar spell the end for the mismatched friends—or set in motion adventures that neither Tack nor Ruby could ever have imagined?

*Available from all online booksellers*

www.ingramcontent.com/pod-product-compliance
Lightning Source LLC
Chambersburg PA
CBHW031213020726
47499CB00002B/563